THE RECKONING

THE LION'S DEN BOOK 6

EOIN DEMPSEY

This book is for my niece Saoirse.

1

The 10.17 train from Paris to Le Havre, Monday, August 15, 1938

The fields and glens of Normandy flashed by the train window like a beautiful mural. Maureen Ritter was silent as she rested her forehead against the glass, gazing out. She saw the reflection of her green eyes. Her hair was darker than it had been a few years ago, more brown than blond.

Deep in thought, she jumped slightly when the sliding door behind her opened.

The short and stocky ticket inspector made cheerful small talk while punching her ticket and that of her twenty-year-old brother, Michael, and his wife, Monika, the only other two people in the compartment. After the man returned their tickets, Maureen shoved hers into her handbag, then took out the newspaper she'd bought at Gare du Nord station in Paris and scanned the headlines.

The whole front page was dedicated to the situation developing in Czechoslovakia, the latest country the Führer had set his sights on to subsume into his glorious thousand-year Reich. She lowered the broadsheet to her lap and resumed staring out the window.

Her father, Seamus Ritter, was right; Paris was too dangerous for them now. After everything that had happened, it was best that they moved back to America. The cash he'd given her was strapped around her waist in a money belt, the list of New York contacts in her handbag.

Yet something inside her regretted fleeing France before the fight was over.

The wounds from the torture the Nazis had inflicted upon her in that château south of Paris had healed, physically at least. She still saw Ullrich's cold eyes in her dreams. Her torturer's willingness to inflict any amount of pain on her to get what he wanted haunted not only her body but her soul. She had begged him to think of his mother, sisters, his future daughters, but his dedication to his cause had overridden every shred of human compassion.

She had killed him after she'd been rescued. There was no redemption for men like that. Just as with rabid dogs, death was the only way to control them and stop them from spreading their foul disease.

She hadn't hesitated when the time came to pull the trigger and kill Ullrich and the traitor who had betrayed them, her so-called friend, Hans. It wasn't revenge or even justice. It was an act of war and something to show the Nazis in Paris that they couldn't act with impunity. It was about sending a message that the jungle the city had become was just as dangerous for the agents of Hitler as for those who opposed him. What was a war without foot soldiers?

The newspapers and politicians still spoke of the possibility of war as if it were some abstract idea and could still be avoided. But Maureen knew now that it was impossible to prevent something that had already begun, something that had been set in motion the day the ill-fated decision was made to install Hitler as German Chancellor back in '33.

The Sudetenland in Czechoslovakia, and the false narrative of liberating its German-speaking citizens by bringing them back into the open prison that the Reich was becoming, was the latest Nazi lie. Another excuse to expand the borders of the state Hitler had subverted to his will. The Allies were clamoring to oppose Hitler's plans in some minor way. Still, it was difficult to envision the public in France or Britain uniting to support a country in central Europe of which they knew little or nothing. Maureen was sure the Führer would get his way again.

Meanwhile, her father continued to fatten his wallet by selling bullets and airplanes to the Nazi armed forces. The money in the belt around her waist was from the sale of weapons, just like those that had rained death down on the citizens of Guernica in '37. People like her father and his cousin, Helga, enabled such destruction by providing the Nazis the most sophisticated weaponry the world had ever known.

The contradictions in her father's life gnawed at Maureen. She didn't know what to think. His original factory still employed Jewish workers despite the ever more dangerous political environment, and she was almost positive he was providing secret information to the American embassy. If he was against the Nazis, why didn't he just sell his interests in those infernal factories and leave Germany? She knew her great uncle had inserted a clause in his will that her father couldn't sell his half of Ritter Metalworks until 1942, but surely some way existed that he could sell and go home.

Instead, her father was still in Berlin with her youngest siblings, Conor, 13, and Fiona, who would be 17 in December, even though his half-Jewish second wife, Lisa, and her daughter, Hannah, were now in exile in France.

Her father said his hands were tied both by his younger

daughter and his loyalty to his Jewish workers, who relied on him for protection. Maureen knew he was still trying to organize his employees to leave, and offering money to help them facilitate that. Maureen's little sister, Fiona, had fallen down the Nazi rabbit hole. Her room was adorned with portraits of her beloved Führer. The proudest moment of her life had been performing for the dictator during the Olympics back in '36. She was a problem, a beloved problem, and Seamus Ritter wasn't prepared to leave her behind in Germany. Her boyfriend, Harald, was training to join the SS, and Fiona's heart was still with him, even if it seemed to Maureen that his was elsewhere.

Not so long ago, she'd been angry at her father for bringing them to Germany from America, but at 22, Maureen was mature enough to know that the offer he had received from his late uncle to take up a senior position in his metalworks factory back in '32 had been too good to resist. Who could have foreseen all that had happened in the six years since then? Who could have known that the upstart Adolf Hitler would become the most important leader in the entire world?

The train slowed as it entered the station at Harfleur. The platform was packed, and few people alighted. It seemed everyone was on their way to the port town of Le Havre on the English Channel.

"I wonder how many of our fellow passengers are Jews," Michael murmured to his wife.

Maureen's brother was muscular and fit. Not as much as he had been in '36 when he ran in the Olympics, but still fitter than most would ever be. The adoration he harbored for his wife was visible in his eyes. Monika was beautiful. Her auburn hair fell beyond her shoulders, and her pale, flawless skin shone in the sunlight.

"Or trade unionists," she agreed. Her father was head of a

trade union until the Nazis imprisoned him, and he'd never returned. Now Michael and his family were all she had.

"Or Roma," Maureen said. Her mind harked back to the Roma family she and her brother had extricated from the Nazi camp in Berlin. That was the night she killed the Nazi policeman who'd shot Michael and tried to force himself on Monika. She felt no remorse for that act of self-defense.

Who was she now, with so much blood on her hands? Had the Nazis changed her too?

And who would she be if she were to abandon what she saw as her mission? Gerhard was alone in Paris now, the young man who'd been tortured with her and had shared in the retribution. Sure, he had dozens of others to talk to about resisting the Nazis, but when the time came for action, was there anyone he could trust? He would be slow to believe in anyone after Hans had been revealed as a Nazi spy, especially if Maureen were to run out on him to save her own skin.

She remembered her education—not the time she spent in school or even in university in Berlin—but the meetings with the subversives, a group of free thinkers who met in secret. There she'd learned the true horror of the Nazi regime and how there might be hope for something better. The coup that she, Gerhard, and her stepmother had hatched with the famous actress, Petra Wagner, had failed when the Gestapo executed Gerhard's father, the Luftwaffe general Horst Engel. But did that mean Maureen's struggle was over? Or that Gerhard no longer needed her?

The train began moving once more. Michael looked across at Maureen and addressed her directly. "This is the right thing to do."

"Leaving Gerhard behind with no one to trust?"

"Paris is too dangerous, and with what's coming...."

"War? Hopefully it won't come to that," interrupted Monika,

though her face showed that she didn't believe the words coming from her mouth.

"I've been thinking about what father said," Maureen said as they pulled into the station at Le Havre. Michael didn't answer. He just stood up and reached for their luggage.

"You're having second thoughts?" Monika asked, moving to sit beside Maureen.

"Something just doesn't feel right."

"We can't go back to Berlin," Michael said, pulling down cases. "If it's our sister and her Nazi allegiances you're worried about, there's nothing we can do."

"It's more than that," said Maureen. She seemed stuck to her seat. Her limbs felt like they weighed a hundred tons and wouldn't let her move.

"Father's right," her brother said. "It's just too dangerous in Paris now. The Nazis might not know what your real name is or what you look like, but what if they infiltrate another meeting? We have a life waiting for us in America, and enough money to set ourselves up. We have the apartment in Manhattan that Father has bought us. I'm going to get a job and start running again."

"It's true, Maureen," Monika said. "It's time to leave the chaos over here behind. Look at what we've been forced to do these past few years. We've been lucky so far, but next time the Nazis drag you into some vile cellar we might not be able to find you in time."

Maureen looked into her brother's and sister-in-law's concerned eyes and knew they were right. She owed them her life. So, she owed them to take care of herself. A few moments later, she found herself on the platform among the swath of emigrants making their way to the steamer in the harbor. Michael carried his and Monika's suitcase, and Maureen had her own. It was all she had to bring from her time in Europe—a few of her best outfits, some letters, photographs, and her favorite books. There was so much she'd had to leave behind.

The three of them walked in silence.

The mood among the crowd of people getting off the train was markedly different from theirs. A Jewish couple with five children ambled in front of them. The youngest, a little girl about four years old, asked her father in German if they were in America yet. He replied with a laugh that they would be soon and promised her that wonders awaited in the New World. These were the lucky ones. The ones who'd obtained the visas the rest craved. These were the ones who could afford to pay the enormous taxes to escape the Reich and were left with just enough to afford passage to America. But soon they would be safe from the hideous laws the Nazis passed down seemingly at whim. And Maureen knew she would be, too, the moment she stepped off the dock and onto that boat.

The smell of the sea air and the sound of seagulls filled her senses as they crossed the street outside the station. The steamer to New York wasn't scheduled to leave for several hours. They found a café and sat outside in the shade. They ordered fish so fresh it must have been swimming in the ocean that very morning.

"What about Father?" Michael asked as they sipped their coffee. "When do you think he'll come?"

"He'll come to find Lisa and Hannah soon, and bring them with him to America," Monika said with certainty.

"I hope so, but what about his business?" Maureen said.

"I know. He's still working on getting the Jewish workers out of the country." Her brother nodded in agreement with his wife. "But after that...."

"That's not what I mean. As much as he insists that he's only running those factories because he is some self-appointed savior of the Jews, I think he enjoys his new role as master of the universe."

Neither her brother nor Monika spoke.

"I mean, who wouldn't?" said Maureen, with a dash of anger. "Think about where we were when we left America—the four of us sharing a room in Aunt Maeve's house. We didn't see him for two years when he rode the rails looking for work. Now he lives in a mansion. Has more money than he ever dreamed. Commands the respect of hundreds. What would you do in his shoes?"

"You seriously think money will stop him leaving Berlin?" Monika asked in a small voice.

"No, you're wrong." Michael's annoyance showed. "The money's not important to him. He's a better man than that. It's about Fiona. He can't let her stew in Berlin and fall further into Nazism. He'd never forgive himself. Remember, he tried to send her away to boarding school in Switzerland? How long did that last—five or six months? If he leaves now, Fiona could be lost forever. So, what would I do in his shoes? I really don't know, but maybe emigration doesn't seem like the answer. At least, not yet."

Maureen brought her café-au-lait to her lips. "I'm not trying to vilify him. I remember what he did for me just a few weeks ago—what you all did. But Fiona's old enough to make her own decisions and she won't leave the Reich."

"And Lisa's in Paris," said Monika. "He has to leave to bring her and Hannah with him to America."

They spoke about Seamus Ritter for a few more minutes, but there were no answers, just a myriad of questions, each one taking them deeper into the storm his life had become.

Then Michael tried to change the subject, to talk about America as if it were the answer to all their problems.

Maureen understood her brother's perspective. America offered him a fresh start—an apartment in Manhattan and a job in one of their father's friends' companies. He could start running again. Perhaps it wasn't too late to qualify for the next Olympics.

As for Monika, she had nothing in life but Michael. The Nazis had taken everything from her, even her ability to live in Berlin, the city of her birth. Maureen understood. The two of them had so much to gain from leaving, but to her, it felt like running away, abandoning not just the cause but Lisa and Hannah, Conor and Fiona, and her father as well.

Lunch ended, and it was only a few minutes' walk through the quaint town to the harbor it was named after. The sun was warm on their faces, but the breeze from the ocean made it much more pleasant than the stultifying heat of the city.

Monika was smiling as they moved through the crowd. The massive form of the SS Sud-Atlantique dominated the harbor, its gangway lowered over the swirling waters below.

"This is it," Michael said as they got in line to walk onto the ship. Monika led the way, and Michael nudged Maureen from behind, urging her forward. "Maybe we'll be back in Europe soon. Under happier circumstances."

Halfway up the gangway, Maureen found she couldn't move. She couldn't do this. It wasn't time yet. She stopped and turned to her brother.

"I can't leave."

"What?" His expression dropped. Any excitement on his face disappeared. "We're nearly on board. Don't change your mind now...."

The sensations inside her body burned like fire. She felt like a traitor either way. "I'm sorry," she said. "I'm not ready."

All three were standing, blocking the gangway, holding up the many travelers attempting to board.

"It's too dangerous in Paris."

"It's a huge city. I'll be careful, and it won't be forever."

She dropped her suitcase and hugged him and a shocked

Monika. A middle-aged man behind them began to grumble that they were holding up the line.

Michael cut him off. "The ship's not going anywhere without you. Give us a moment!" He embraced his sister. "Are you sure about this?" She nodded, and he hugged her again.

"Write me as soon as you arrive," she said. "Good luck!" She reached into her handbag for the book of contacts their father had given her. "Take this. And look after Monika."

Michael nodded, a grave look on his face now. "I will."

She wished they had more time to say goodbye, but the passengers were getting restless behind them, fearful of losing their last chance of escape.

"Go," she said with one last hug. "Make the life you deserve for yourselves in America. I'll be right behind you."

Her eyes were wet as she weaved through the line of people behind her toward dry land. Half an hour later, she stood alone as the gangplank was drawn back and the steamer embarked. Her brother and his wife stood at the railings, waving as the ship left. Maureen stood on the dock and watched the steamer shrink to a speck on the blue horizon and finally disappear.

Paris, Sunday, August 21

Maureen had grown to love this ancient city, so magnificent in some places and rundown in others. Its buildings and monuments told the history of a thousand years. Its nickname of "Gay Paree" had perhaps never been more fitting. The people who had money spent it with abandon as if they feared they might soon be unable to. On the fashionable shopping streets, elegant ladies stepped out of their limousines and sauntered in to peruse jewels, furs, and other luxury goods from every part of the world. Male dressmakers reviewed the ladies' figures and offered advice on enhancing their charms. The previous summer, the King and Queen of England had paid a state visit to the city. The Queen had changed her costume three times daily, and everything she wore had been photographed and scrutinized. In her wake, an English trend had arisen. The ladies all asked to be clad à l'anglaise, to which the dressmakers replied in the affirmative with glee. Anything to prise open the pocketbooks of those affluent ladies with nothing better to spend their money on.

At night, the shiny limousines lined up in front of mansions where the richest of the rich gathered to natter. In the chic restaurants and nightclubs, champagne flowed like water. Young ladies danced on the stages of the clubs, their skins painted every exotic color. The locals were always eager to remind anyone who'd listen that such lowly entertainments were for the tourists, that sophisticated Parisians did not care for them, and maybe it was so, but the men Maureen observed emerging from the shows seemed as French as any others she'd seen.

Surrounding the luxurious city of pleasure were suburbs, where the workers crowded into five-story tenements. Despite the chic nature of the city into which the workers commuted every morning, the masses of poor had it as hard here as anywhere else. Tough times were threatening again. The multitudes were at the mercy of economic forces over which they had no control. They saw the wealthy as slave drivers with whips, while the rich viewed the proletariat as uncouth, uneducated wild beasts in cages who deserved their place in society. The working class was kept in check with laws and institutions, which, to them, now seemed on the point of dissolving. They lived in poverty and insecurity, and their discontent was distilled into a hatred of their masters, whose way of life was revealed in shop windows, newspapers, and on cinema screens.

The City of Lights seemed like a simmering class war about to boil over.

Paris had been besieged and taken several times throughout history and had been the scene of revolutions and civil wars. It had always managed to survive. Perhaps it would again, but at what cost? How many of the poor would die defending France? And would the rich still throw their support behind Hitler once war erupted? They viewed him as the lesser of two great evils on the continent and perhaps the only person who could keep the Russian hordes in check.

Unlike the rich, the poor identified with Marx's teachings and reveled in the idea of unionizing and wresting back some of the power the rich had cradled for centuries. Maureen wondered how they would react to the reality of living under a Communist system that had destroyed Russia. Stalin used the excuse of progress for the workers to murder countless numbers of them. It seemed although democracy was a flawed system, it was superior to all the others ever devised.

Maureen lived alone now, in an apartment within walking distance of Place de la Bastille that previously she'd shared with her brother and his wife. The lease, paid by her father, was up in a few months, and perhaps that would be enough time to achieve the things that had kept her here and turned her limbs to stone when she tried to board that ship in Le Havre.

She wondered how her father would respond to her coded letter informing him of her decision to stay in Europe. She'd spoken of missing Paris, but hadn't mentioned that leaving felt like deserting everyone, including him. In some ways, she thought he needed her the most. Her affluent, armament-king father was living a dangerous double life, one that could destroy him body and soul. He was trapped in his wealthy mansion in Berlin with an enemy under his roof. Fiona was the worst kind of foe—the rare type that you loved more than yourself. Because of her family's love, she exerted true power and could never be defeated.

Maureen knew she also held her father's heart in her hand because of the danger she might be in. She was unsure of the scope of Nazi operations in the city. It seemed from her experience that only a dozen or so men were stationed in the château where she'd been tortured, that formed part of the German consulate. Her father had warned her about the SS presence in the city and that National Socialist spies were infiltrating society to prepare for an invasion, but were they really such a threat in a city of millions? Even so, it seemed to her the sensible thing was to stay away from mass anti-Nazi meetings, the kinds of places where German agents could search out people of interest with little difficulty.

The sun was high in the sky as she strolled along Boulevard Saint Germain toward the Latin Quarter and the only family she had left in the city. She moved with her eyes on the sidewalk, her hat pulled down over her face and sunglasses on. She greeted the doorman at the Hotel d'Angleterre in her improving French.

"Hello, Armand. How is your son?"

"Over the worst of it, mademoiselle."

"I'm sure he'll be back running around with his friends again soon," she said with a smile and continued inside.

Her stepmother greeted her with delight as she entered the hotel room, where Lisa and Hannah had been keeping a low profile these past few weeks. Seamus was reluctant to bring them back to a Germany that was getting more and more dangerous for those of Jewish blood. As well as that, Lisa had been a minor player in the plot to overthrow Hitler and was still unsure if her part in the failed coup was known.

The pretty woman embraced Maureen and led her to the large balcony where she had been sitting at a wrought-iron table enjoying some coffee. She offered Maureen a pain-auchocolat fresh from the boulangerie down the street, which melted in her mouth.

"Did you hear back from your father yet?" After recovering from the initial shock of Maureen's decision not to leave, her stepmother seemed pleased to still have her around.

"I'm not sure he'll have received my letter yet. It took me a few days to send it. Thank you for letting me be the one to tell him. I know you write him every day."

"Searching for the right words?" Lisa said.

Maureen replied with a careful smile. She took a sip of her café-au-lait and sat back. Her words had been in a secret code.

"How much longer are you planning to stay?" her step-mother asked.

"I'm not sure. I have some meetings with Gerhard and others—" She kept her voice down in front of eight-year-old Hannah, who had remained in the sitting room reading a book while the adults spoke.

"This again!" Lisa whispered back. "Maureen, tell me you're at least being discreet. Your father would have a heart attack if he knew you were going to get involved in the resistance again."

Maureen took a few seconds to answer. "I'm not planning on doing anything reckless. I know the risks better than anyone. What meetings I have will be in intimate settings behind closed doors with people I trust."

"You trusted Hans."

"Don't remind me."

The broad balcony afforded a view of the street below. A delivery truck pulled up outside the hotel, and Maureen stared down at it for a moment. Once she was convinced Nazi agents weren't about to thunder up the stairs, she turned back to Lisa.

"I just want to see what develops over the next few weeks, as much with Fiona and my father in Berlin than anywhere else."

"You're not thinking of returning to Germany?"

"No. I'm more afraid of the police in Berlin than the underground Nazis in Paris, though I'd rather not tussle with either. The truth is I don't know what I'm going to do to help, and I'm not even sure why I couldn't bring myself to leave France. But something in my gut told me it wasn't time yet. What about you? Is it safe for you to return to Berlin yet?"

Lisa shook her head and reached for a fresh croissant sitting on the fine white china on the tray between them. She broke off the end but began speaking before eating it.

"I don't know if Petra was the only one who knew of my connection to the attempted coup. The Gestapo hasn't come looking for me at home, and Seamus hasn't seen anyone watching the house, and no one has come asking questions. Perhaps they threw poor Petra out that window before she had a chance to talk."

"Or she threw herself out, knowing what was in store for her. If she jumped from her balcony to save you, then you should be able to return anytime."

Lisa looked in surprise at her stepdaughter. "It doesn't strike you that Petra, who betrayed me in the past, might do so again?"

"After her efforts in trying to orchestrate the coup with General Engel? I don't see it. People change. I did."

Lisa shrugged. "I've had those thoughts many times, but not being sure makes it too much of a risk. And Germany is so difficult to live in these days, the Jew-hatred is depressing." She bit into another of the small delicious croissants. "So, I'm stuck here in this gorgeous hotel room in this wonderful city, waiting for my husband to see sense and join me."

Maureen got the impression Lisa wasn't enjoying the croissant, despite her bravado, and she reached over and took her stepmother's hand.

2

Berlin, Monday, August 22

Seamus Ritter grimaced at the portraits of the Führer plastered over much of the factory his uncle had left him. Several workers who'd pinned the posters to the wall greeted him with a respectful tip of their caps as he approached. He made small talk for a few seconds before checking the calibration of the machines. Everything was in order, and he moved on to the next section. He remembered when he knew nothing of this business. He'd first arrived back in the land of his youth less than six years ago, lost and out of his depth at his uncle's metalworks. That time seemed long ago. Memories of America bled into his mind on rare occasions now, and he often wondered if he'd even recognize home now, wherever that was.

"How's the wife?" Gunther Benz, the Nazi-installed head of the Trustee Council, asked. The Trustee Council was the equivalent of a union in a country that now forbade them. Its functions were strictly to glorify the Führer and reward those most loyal to him within every organization in Germany.

"She's fine," Seamus replied, feeling only distaste at the sound of his wife's name in that mouth.

"I heard she was away."

"Taking in the sights around Europe. Who knows what's around the corner?"

"Whatever happens, the Wehrmacht and the Luftwaffe will be the finest supplied military forces in the world."

Seamus nodded and went to inspect the next set of machines.

The remaining Jewish workers greeted him no differently than any other employees, but their segregated section was bare. No portraits of the Führer stared down from the walls. Seamus spoke to no one else before heading back upstairs to the offices that overlooked the factory floor. He entered Gert Bernheim's office and closed the door behind him.

Gert set down the ledger he'd been examining and sat forward. He looked pale, almost sickly. "What can I do for you, Seamus?"

"You can tell me what's going on. Every day I read about Jews safely leaving Germany, but too many of my Jewish workers are still here."

"Alfred Blanke was in here a few minutes ago."

"So?" Seamus said. Blanke was Jewish and had worked in the factory for fifteen years.

"He was due to leave Germany next week but his exit visa was cancelled."

"Cancelled? Why?"

"Because he was deemed to be privy to sensitive information in here. I suppose the Gestapo are paranoid about "enemies of the state" emigrating with knowledge of the armaments trade."

Seamus felt cold. "Did he appeal?"

"To whom? Who's going to listen to a Jew these days?

"What does this mean? Has anyone else experienced the same thing?"

"Not yet, but I fear we'll all suffer the same fate. Why would they stop him leaving and not the rest of us?"

Gert shuffled some papers and set them down. Seamus broke the silence after a second or two.

"Where does this leave the Jewish staff?"

"Stuck in Germany."

"Can we lay them off? Perhaps if they weren't working here anymore...."

"The Gestapo is nothing if not meticulous. They'd see through that ruse in seconds."

Seamus didn't know what to say. "I'll talk to someone. We'll get the workers out one way or the other."

"The Nazis certainly aren't letting up. You heard about the new law the government passed last week?" Gert asked.

Seamus collapsed into the chair opposite him. Trying to stay current with the latest racist laws and proclamations was exhausting. "I read something about it. It's hard to keep up."

"All Jews are now required to give ourselves names that will separate us from the rest of the German population. All Jews with German names, such as myself, will have the name Israel added to our official documents, while the women will add Sara. Our passports will be stamped with a red "J," so no one will mistake us for German."

Seamus felt like a great weight was crushing him from above. His wife had a Jewish mother, but at least she was safe outside the country. The Nazis hadn't come after those they called Mischlings or mongrels yet, but who knew when their whim would send them into a frenzy about anyone with even a spattering of Jewish blood? "I don't know how I'd begin to run this place without you, but it's time for you to leave, Gert."

"Yes, I've known that for a long time. It's funny, but I've always considered myself a German before being a Jew. I don't know anywhere but Berlin. I've lived here all my life, but the Nazis have changed everything. Up is down, water is no longer wet. They lie so much that people give up fighting to believe the truth."

"What about that visa application of yours? Any news?"

"Nothing. The Americans move slower than molasses when it comes to immigration. Every single Jewish worker has applied to the US embassy. Not one has received that precious piece of paper. And now the exit visas are in doubt. What use is permission to enter the United States if we can't leave Germany?"

Seamus took out a pack of cigarettes and laid them on the table, and soon they were both smoking.

"What about Palestine?" he asked.

"The British have curtailed the number of visas for Palestine," Gert said. "I know a few who went there—my brother included, but it's no easier than America now."

"Poland?"

"Too close, and look how they're treating the Jews at the border. They don't want us either. We could sneak in, but to do what? I couldn't get a job without a visa."

"Poland is probably next on Hitler's wish list," agreed Seamus.

"Yes, the Nazis have been talking about "living space" in the east since the start. That's Poland."

"What about Switzerland, where your older son is studying?"

"Getting in is no easier there," said Gert, stubbing out his cigarette in the ashtray. "I'm so thankful Ben is safe down in Bern. He can stay there even after he graduates. We don't have to worry about him."

Bernheim took out the secret ledger he and Seamus kept without having to be asked. It was a record of monies put aside by the Jewish workers that Seamus hid for them. It was a way of circumventing the Reich Flight Tax, now set at 90% of all a Jewish family's assets once they registered to move abroad. Many wealthy Jewish families had paid the exorbitant tax to start fresh, but Seamus's workers couldn't afford to lose 90% of the little they had. Their wages were fixed by the government. The system was set up to enrich the business owners and keep the employees in line. Seamus remembered the promises the Nazis made about empowering the working class, but the Nazis lied so often that it was more noteworthy when they didn't.

"Not a lot of money in here," he said.

"It's hard to save when you need all your money to eat. Apart from the couple of families who left for Palestine before the visa crackdown, we still have 22 Jewish workers working for us."

"And you."

"I often forget myself."

"How are you managing?"

"I've put away all I can. And I'll sell my house once I secure a visa."

"Won't the Nazis take note of the sale?" Seamus asked.

"Ten percent of the value is better than nothing."

"Don't worry, I'll make sure you have enough."

"No need to bother, if there's no visas."

Seamus felt a surge of frustration. The more money his workers saved to leave, the more the Nazis threatened to take from them. Any money he gave to them would also be taken unless he could smuggle it out of the country, and that was getting next to impossible. How could they leave without visas? Other countries weren't interested in welcoming impoverished Jewish immigrants. And now the Gestapo was banning Seamus's employees from getting exit visas. It seemed there was nothing he could do. He stood up and returned to his office. His working day was almost over, and his wife wouldn't be waiting for him when he arrived home.

Seamus left the factory as the night shift came in. Like his peers, he was under pressure to operate his manufacturing facilities twenty-four hours a day. The machines never stopped running now. The government's demand for armaments was such that it didn't seem possible to produce enough. The Nazis were gluttonous for weapons, and supplying them was tantamount to printing money these days.

His cousin, Helga, now one of the most successful businesswomen in a country that didn't promote women to be anything other than mothers, teachers, or nurses, ran the other factory they owned together. No divided loyalties there. All the workers were Aryan. Many were committed Nazis. Those that weren't kept their mouths shut for fear of what might happen if they offered even the gentlest of criticisms. It was the same everywhere in Germany. All dissent had been stamped out. The only public political discourse was the kind favored by the screaming masses at Hitler's rallies. Anything else could land a person in one of the dreaded concentration camps, or KZs, as they were known among the populace.

Seamus got into his new Mercedes and drove home to the exclusive suburb of Charlottenburg, west of the Brandenburg Gate and the massive Tiergarten park that dominated the city's center. His mansion felt empty these days, with Lisa and Hannah in Paris and Michael, Maureen, and Michael's wife, Monika, gone to America. Knowing they were all safe was comforting. At least they were removed from the Nazi madness that seemed to be swamping all of Europe. When he and the other children would join Lisa and Hannah in Paris and then America was a question he asked himself every morning when he woke up alone or slept in an empty bed at night. He missed his wife as he would the air that he breathed. Thirteen-year-old Conor would be glad to come with him, he was sure. But how could he leave Fiona behind?

In the hall, he put down his briefcase and picked up a letter addressed to him from the table by the front door. It was addressed in capitals, but he recognized Maureen's handwriting. The postmark was from Paris. She must have left it with Lisa to post. He put it in his pocket, not wanting to open it if Fiona was around.

Conor was reading in the living room as he entered and didn't look up from his book. He remembered when his son, the youngest of the four his first wife had given him before she succumbed to tuberculosis, would run to the door to greet him. It seemed like yesterday.

"What are you reading?" Seamus asked.

Conor held up the front cover to show him. The book was in English and wasn't Nazi-prescribed. Seamus took heart from that.

"Where did you get a copy of The Hobbit? I thought it was banned here."

"Percy Baxter, the son of the English diplomat down the block gave it to me."

"Just be careful. Don't bring it into school."

Conor rolled his eyes as if he'd never do something so stupid. "I know."

"Where's your sister?"

"Do you even have to ask?"

Seamus shook his head. The frustration that marked his days bubbled inside him. The thought of Fiona marching up and down with the other Hitler fanatics almost forced tears into his eyes.

"She's obsessed," Conor added, as if his father didn't know.

"What about you?" Seamus asked. It was a question he asked on a regular basis, just to check in.

"I like being part of the gang, but I think the fanatics are weird. I'd rather we did the camping and the exercises without the rest of the other stuff, but I guess everything's political these days."

"Unfortunately," Seamus replied.

He sat down across from Conor to open the letter. It had already been opened by the censors who read almost all the mail from abroad, and he had to rip off the tape they'd used to re-seal it.

PARIS, TUESDAY, AUGUST 16

SEAMUS,

I DECIDED NOT TO GO ON MY LITTLE TRIP. I'M SURE YOU'LL HEAR FROM THE OTHERS SOON. I'LL BE CAREFUL HERE IN THE BIG CITY—YOU HAVE MY WORD.

I LOOK FORWARD TO SEEING YOU AGAIN.

LOVE,

AUNT REBA

He closed his eyes and crumpled the letter in his fist.

Conor called out to him, asking what it said, was there a problem?

It took him a few seconds to regain his composure enough to respond. "Just a work issue. Nothing important."

The front door banged, and Fiona appeared in a League of German Girls uniform adorned with

swastikas. She was every inch her mother, and somehow that made it seem even worse for her to be dressed in such a uniform. Seamus had tried to make her see that Jews were human beings by sending her to the Bernheims' house to spend time with them. She'd paid them back by throwing a brick through their window with a mob of Hitler Youth. His intelligent, robust, and beautiful daughter was the ultimate puzzle in his life, and she was slipping away like a wet bar of soap through his grasp.

"Hello, Father."

"Hello, Fiona." He realized he still had the letter in his hand and stuffed it into his pocket.

"How was the Hitler adoration club?" Conor said from his armchair.

"I'd really rather you didn't call it that! And have some respect for our Führer."

Her brother laughed and returned to the novel she could report him for reading.

"I can't stay long," Fiona said. "I have another meeting soon."

"Another one?" Seamus said and pushed his fingers back through his hair. "What could this possibly be about?"

"I'm a group leader now. I have responsibilities," she said in a caustic tone.

Seamus shook his head as Fiona stormed into the kitchen. She cooked with ferocious energy, chopping the vegetables as if they were enemies of the state. It was part of the National Socialist ideal, and she was happy to do it. It was the woman's job to cook and clean, and she did both, even when her father protested that she should be catching up on school-work or reading. He went into her when the chicken was in the pot.

"We don't have many spices or sauces," she said.

"They're hard to get now," her father said. "The Führer's policy of German self-sufficiency translates to empty market shelves and goods that we used to take for granted being consigned to memory."

Fiona knew all this, but a part of him wanted to punish her, even in just this small way. He wanted her to admit out loud that Hitler's path might not be the best and that other alternatives might exist.

His daughter didn't say a word. He turned to leave when he heard her voice again.

"I've been thinking for a while now, and I've made a decision—I'm not going back to school."

He whirled around in disbelief. "What? You're quitting your education?"

"What's the point? I know enough. I can cook and clean, and one day soon, I'll start a family."

"With Harald, is that your plan? Throw your life down the toilet for him?" Seamus couldn't stop himself from shouting. Fiona tried to speak, but he cut her off. "Didn't he tell you he's not ready to settle down? And isn't he in SS training at the moment?"

"We're still in touch."

"Are you even a couple? Does he have the same feelings you do?" Seamus said, and regretted it in milliseconds.

Fiona's face dropped. "I know that one day soon he'll need a wife to produce sons for the Führer, and we have spoken about my role in that."

"Like a job interview?" Seamus said, incredulous. He brought both hands to his face, frustration, anger, and guilt swirling around inside him. He calmed himself before he spoke his next words. "You deserve better than to be someone's child bearer." He reached forward to put his arms on her shoulder and realized he hadn't physically touched her in weeks. She drifted backward. He didn't follow. "You're a smart, beautiful, strong young woman."

"I'm aware of what I want."

"To serve Hitler and the Nazis? You're not even German. You're American. Half Irish."

"The League has never treated me like an outsider. They brought me in from day one and treated me like one of their own. I found the family there I never knew I was missing."

"We're your family, Fiona."

"I know that, but what about when you leave the Reich? When will I see you again? I have to create a life for myself here, in the paradise Herr Hitler is building for us."

"War's coming, my love. Why do you think the Nazis want all those bullets and airplanes so badly? They're not for show. They intend to use them. And soon."

"Perhaps. But who's to say war's not something Europe needs? A strong Aryan state is vital to keep the peace and to fend off the Bolsheviks. Because, believe me, Father, they're coming. The Führer is our Bulwark against the collapse of civilization as we know it. And those airplanes and bullets will save far more lives than they'll ever take."

The pot on the stove was boiling, and Fiona turned to take off the lid and turn down the heat. Seamus was frozen to the spot, just as he always was when he and his daughter had these conversations. Her leaders in the League of German Girls had taught her well. They warned all their young recruits, including those in the Hitler Youth, that their parents would try to dissuade them from the cause. They armed their recruits with words that the sons and daughters of Germany now spat at their parents like bullets.

"What if we all returned to America? Would you stay here alone? Because of a political leader? One man?"

She looked disgusted by the insinuation that Hitler was just a man. "Adolf Hitler is so much more than that. He's the savior of the Reich, and perhaps of the world. His ideas will improve the human race and the lives of every German."

"And what of the Jews? And the Roma, and the Socialists, Communists, and Social Democrats? Where is their utopia? The Nazi crash down their doors in the middle of the night and spirit them away to concentration camps."

"To reeducate them."

"Not the Jews. The Nazis despise them because of their blood." He stopped short at bringing up what she and her friends had done at Gert Bernheim's house. He knew that would be the end of the conversation.

"The Jews should find another place to live, like Lisa and Hannah have done." She caught her father's expression and hurried on with a slightly guilty look, "I don't agree with every single thing the National Socialists preach, but what politician do you agree with entirely?"

"I thought Hitler was greater than a politician. I figured he was some kind of celestial being himself. Infallible," said Seamus through gritted teeth.

His daughter ignored the comment. "Of course, I'm glad Lisa is happy in Paris. I hear many full Jews are settling in Palestine, and America."

"They're not able to get visas anymore...."

"Dinner's ready," Fiona cut him off, carrying the food into the dining room, refusing her father's offer of assistance.

The three of them ate in near silence. Fiona was gone in less than five minutes, insisting the men leave the dishes she'd clean up once she returned home.

Conor took advantage of his sister's domestic goddess act and retreated to his room. *If I don't get her away, she's lost forever*, Seamus thought as he washed the dishes alone.

"If she's not already," he said out loud.

His voice echoed through the empty kitchen, which was once so full of life.

Fiona shut the door behind her. Increasingly, she felt like a stranger in her own home. Conor was a good brother and didn't bother her, but he was naïve like their father. They clung to their corrupt liberal American belief system no matter how much she tried to expose them to the truth of the National Socialist cause. It was frustrating beyond measure. Why couldn't they see what she and many others around the country did?

Living with them was difficult, but perhaps she wouldn't have to much longer. It was better Michael and Monika were gone, and Maureen as well. The new Germany didn't suit them either. They would be happier in New York. Her brother never capitalized on the glory of running for the Führer in the Olympics, and she blamed her father's influence for that.

Yet, she was so confused. Father was a vital cog in the machine feeding the armed forces, which would restore Germany to its place among the most powerful nations on earth. Why couldn't he be prouder of his role, like Cousin Helga, his business partner? Helga was a true patriot and a prime example of what even a woman could achieve in the new Germany. It was sad that she was unmarried and it was too late for her to have children, but at least she contributed to the cause in many other ways. Business and commercial success wasn't for most women, but a handful of girls in her troop wanted to emulate Helga. Tonight would be a unique experience for them.

She jumped on her bike and pedaled down the driveway past her father's new car. Maureen and Michael were both driving at her age. Yet, her father had only given her a couple of cursory lessons. Another way she suffered for the cause. One day she would have her reward, just like every other good German.

It was a twenty-minute ride to the meeting hall, and Fiona parked her bike with dozens of others outside the venue. No need to lock it—crime rates had plummeted since the Nazis came to power. Why steal when you could have a job and be a productive member of a great society? A crowd of her friends had already gathered outside the hall and greeted her with smiles and Hitler salutes. She clicked her feet together and gave her best "Heil Hitler" before embracing her friends.

"This is so exciting!" her friend Inge, who had also graduated to become a troop leader, said.

"You must be proud," her other old friend, Amalia, said. "I can't believe you managed to set this up. Your father's cousin is an inspiration, just as he is."

Fiona beamed at her, relieved none of them could know about the conversation she had just had with her father. They walked into the hall. Dozens of benches were arranged on either side of an aisle, facing the stage, and soon, all those on the left were filled with the boys of the Hitler Youth, while the girls of the League sat on the right.

It was a surprise to Fiona to see the boys. It was heartening to know they were prepared to listen to a woman.

She sat in the front row, which had been specially reserved for her troop, wedged between Amalia and Inge. The air of excitement among the girls was palpable. A Hitler Youth leader Fiona didn't know climbed onto the stage and stood at the lectern.

She was surprised to see a Youth leader leading the meeting, rather than one of the League, but then she realized that if the Youth was present, you couldn't have the forum run by a woman.

The Hitler Youth leader, a young man about twenty, quieted the crowd's murmurs with a raised hand.

The discipline here is exemplary, Fiona thought to herself.

Inge poked her in the ribs and whispered in her ear. "It's so great about Harald, isn't it? I spoke to Georg outside." Inge's cousin, Georg, was Harald's best friend.

Fiona hadn't received a letter from Harald in a few weeks but smiled anyway. "Yeah, it's wonderful," she whispered back. "But about what exactly?"

"That he'll be home in a few weeks. His SS training is almost up. Didn't he tell you?"

"Of course he did." Fiona's heart turned over. His letter must have gotten lost in the mail. It happened all the time. It was okay, she assured herself. Just knowing that the man she was going to marry was coming home was enough. It didn't matter that he hadn't been the one to tell her.

The young man on the stage spoke for a few minutes while the latecomers took their seats. Fiona tried to listen but found it challenging. Her excitement about Harald was electrifying her just too much.

"Next this evening," he said, "we have a special guest, a patriot helping arm our military against our many enemies. A person who helps keep us all safe in ways you might not ever think of—Helga Ritter."

The young man gave a Hitler salute and exited the stage as Helga walked on from the right, wearing her familiar black business suit with a tight skirt stretching below her knees. Like everyone else in the crowd, she had a swastika armband over her bicep, but she differentiated herself with the Nazi pin she wore on her lapel. It was solid gold. What a way to honor the Führer and National Socialism! Fiona was sure the Hitler Youth Leaders standing in a row just below the stage, facing the audience, were all jealous.

Cousin Helga offered a nervous smile as she took the lectern. She was a shy woman, not one for speeches or loud proclamations.

Fiona made an effort to focus, to clear her mind of Harald and the letter he must have sent to tell her the momentous news of his return. She made eye contact with Helga and gave her a little wave of encouragement.

Helga took a deep breath. "Thank you for having me here tonight. It's truly an honor to address the finest generation of young Germans this country has ever produced. I know in your hands, the Reich will be safe from all threats, both foreign and domestic." A round of applause followed. Fiona followed along until her hands hurt. The Hitler Youth did like to clap for themselves.

"I stand before you today, as a humble servant of the Reich," Helga continued. "The country was a very different place when I was your age. We were at war against the other great powers of Europe, Britain and France in the West and Russia in the east, among others of course. That conflict should have cemented Germany's place as the preeminent power in Europe, but thanks to the cowardly politicians who stabbed our brave armed forces in the back, we lost that war and have been paying for it ever since."

"It was the Jews," came a voice from the Hitler Youth. "Don't forget about the Jews!"

Helga nodded slightly and continued. "My generation was lost among the disastrous experiments with democracy in the 20's. Some of you might not remember the days of hyperinflation when ordinary citizens would have to push a wheelbarrow full of money to market to buy food for their families. The British and the French forced us into submission, punishing our great nation for the war they caused, and that we should have won. But no longer. Just when we needed him the most, Adolf Hitler came to rescue us. Not from ourselves, for we always had greatness inherent in us, but from the foreign powers that were so afraid of that greatness. The allies knew that if we were ever allowed back on our feet that we would once again live up to our true potential as a nation—"

"A nation of Aryans!" one of the Hitler Youth boys shouted. A thunder of applause followed, and Helga waited with a smile for it to die down before she carried on.

"...that if we could fulfill our true potential, we would become the greatest country in the world once more. They were terrified of that, so they tried to keep us down with repara-

tions—huge debts they saddled us with to destroy our economy. And they almost succeeded. The previous generation of
sniveling, cowardly politicians weren't brave enough to stand
up to the foreigners, or the threat of the Bolshevik hordes..."

"Don't forget the Jews!"

"...I used to go to bed at night begging whatever powers
there might be in the universe to send us a savior—someone
brave enough, brilliant enough to reject the bullying tactics of
the allies and lead our country back to greatness. And my
prayers were answered." She turned to the portrait of Hitler
hanging on the wall behind the lectern and saluted. Everyone
in the audience followed suit, and in seconds hundreds of
screams of "Heil Hitler," pierced the air. Fiona felt the giddy
thrill of being part of something, of belonging, as she stood
with them. What a time to be alive!

Helga waited until the shouting abated again before
continuing.

"Adolf Hitler is exactly who this country was crying out for,
exactly when we needed him. His unerring genius has already
seen us go from a third-rate power to a nation our enemies fear
once more. All over Europe the preeminent families I meet
express their support for our Führer and wish they had
someone like him for their own nations. My life is utterly
changed since he rose to power. Back in '32 I was working for
my father in a minor role at his metalworks factory. Now, I'm
one of the most successful businesswomen in Germany."

A brief round of applause followed. Fiona was glowing. So
proud.

"Women shouldn't be in business," came a loud voice from
the throng of Hitler Youth. Fiona turned her head to see who'd
called out, but it was impossible to tell. None of the leaders at
the front did a thing to object.

Helga hesitated a moment and then continued. "And I go to
bed at night content that I'm protecting this great nation. Ritter

Metalworks now produces bullets, shells and airplanes for the Reich. We work with the most cutting-edge technology in the world to produce planes like the new Dornier Do 217 bombers which can drop bombs on land and sea, and provide the ultimate deterrent to those who mean to do us harm. We work with the representatives of the Luftwaffe and the Wehrmacht to ensure that they have everything they need to keep us safe. The Führer is devoted to our cause and is determined that every German will enjoy the peace and prosperity we all so deserve."

"Women have no place in business," came the voice again, but there was also a smattering of applause from the girls' side.

Helga, looking nervous again, resumed her speech. "Some might ask why we're producing so many weapons of war when all the Führer wants is peace? The harsh truth is that our enemies don't want the same thing. The Bolsheviks in the east are determined to destroy our way of life, enslave our people and drag us back to the last century. The French and the British are jealous of our success and bitter that we're no longer under their yoke. Mark my words, if war does come, it won't be because of our Führer. He's doing all he can every day to avoid it."

This time a raucous round of applause followed, and many gave the Hitler salute again.

"I stand here," Helga said. "As one more humble servant of the Führer—a grateful recipient of his wisdom and a once again proud German."

Helga stood back a moment. Fiona was on her feet, along with many of the other girls. She noticed none of the boys were, however. One League of German Girls troop leader asked Helga if she'd take questions. She agreed with a happy nod.

Dozens of hands went up. The troop leader pointed to a hand, and a young girl with blonde pigtails stood up. "What would you say to girls who think a woman's place is in the home?"

Helga stepped to the lectern once more.

"I think there are many different ways to serve the Führer. We all need to find our own path, but to keep the end goal of honoring his wishes paramount in our minds at all times. If we do that, he will steer us right, whether that be by having seven sons or by starting a successful business."

The girl seemed happy with the answer and sat down as a Hitler Youth boy stood up to ask the next question. He was tall with broad shoulders and smiled as he began to speak. "Do you honestly believe that you'd be in your position if you didn't inherit it? And why did you think it was appropriate to go against the Führer's express wishes for women in our society. Kitchen, church and children. That's what he says."

Several boys shouted in agreement. Again, their leaders did nothing.

Helga's face went white. "As I said, there are many different ways to serve the Führer—"

"Even a dried-up old hag like you?" the boy said, and most of the cohort of Hitler Youth laughed. "I think you're a disgrace, and a bad example to the girls on the other side of the room."

A few League of German Girls leaders stood up to protest, but their male counterparts shouted at them to sit down, and they did.

"I can't believe the leaders of this meeting have tried to hold you up as an example when you're exactly the opposite," the young man said. "I just hope none of the girls here tonight get any stupid ideas. You should be talking to them about cooking and raising children, not about a business you have no idea about!"

The Hitler Youth erupted in cheers. The girls stayed silent, including Fiona, who was dying of shame and embarrassment.

The boys started chanting "Children, Kitchen, Church!" the rallying cry of the National Socialists to describe women's role in society. The leaders at the front joined in, too, conducting the boys like an orchestra.

With a shocked expression, Helga inched back from the lectern and then scuttled off stage as the boys continued their chant.

The League of German Girls leaders had seen enough and ordered the girls out of the auditorium in orderly rows. Fiona and her friends were last. The boys' chants continued even after the girls filed outside. And for the first time in as long as she could remember, Fiona felt excluded, and her heart bled for Cousin Helga. Perhaps the boys were right, but why do this to a loyal National Socialist? Didn't they care about their fellow Germans? Women were part of the Reich too.

3

Paris, Friday, September 2

Maureen ran her finger around the rim of her wine glass. The café where she was sitting outside on Boulevard Henry IV was packed. The light of day was fading, and the setting sun painted the city a beautiful orange-gold. She was questioning her decision to stay in Paris. What kind of a life was this when she was afraid whenever she left her apartment? Glancing around her at the packed tables, a cold fear slithered down her spine. She tried to dismiss it as paranoia.

"I must be crazy," she said under her breath.

Gerhard appeared and sat down opposite her, smiling, after kissing her on each cheek. "I can't say I was surprised to get your note," he said.

She'd waited almost two weeks to contact him, and then it was a note slipped under his door. She drew comfort from the fact that the Nazis still hadn't come for him and that he seemed to be living with impunity in the city.

"I know what you're thinking," she said.

"What am I thinking?"

"That I'm crazy, and I should have gone to America to live a safe, comfortable life."

The waiter came. Gerhard ordered a beer and pulled a pack of cigarettes from his pocket. "No, in fact, I might be the only person who understands why you didn't leave. I wouldn't have either."

An ugly scar extended across his left cheek—a permanent reminder of the torture the Nazis had inflicted on them. She was lucky. Her only visible scars from the château were on her arms—the others were in places other people couldn't see. "I have unfinished business here," she said.

"I know," he answered. "I could have left too. I didn't have an apartment to go to in New York City, but I could go anywhere. I chose to stay."

He lit the cigarette and sat back.

"You think about what happened in the château much?" she asked.

He took a drag. "I try not to, but I don't have much choice at night, you know?"

"I do."

"I try to think about how Hans and Ullrich will never do that to anyone again. I draw some comfort from that."

"When I think about all the other Nazis lined up to take their places, all those kids in the Hitler Youth, and those crowds at the rallies, I feel—"

"Drink some of your wine," he said. "It helps."

She did as he suggested. "I haven't gone out much since I came back."

"I'm not hiding," said Gerhard. "The Nazis never knew our real names. Ullrich and Hans are dead. They'll check the anti-Nazi meetings for a while, maybe someone remembers what we look like, but I haven't been to any in weeks, I've just been working behind the scenes. The police aren't interested. The story about our friends in the café in Pithiviers faded in two days. Everyone knew who those men were. The Germans have more pressing matters to take care of, like preparing for their invasion. They'll give up looking for us before you know it. If they haven't already."

Maureen drank some more wine. "I admire your confidence," she said.

"You know it's true."

"So, you're back as before?"

"Pretty much. The situation in Paris hasn't changed, even if we might have."

"What did I miss these last few weeks?"

"Not a lot. The socialists are still quarreling with the social democrats about what pamphlets they want to print up and smuggle into Germany." Gerhard looked around to make sure no one was listening in. A middle-aged man with a thin beard was talking loudly to a much younger woman at the next table. The table on their other side was briefly empty. "The supply chain is through Strasbourg now. The Nazis got wise to the road into Saarbrucken."

"Pamphlets," Maureen said, flicking a piece of dirt off the end of her finger. "We're not going to beat the Nazis with pamphlets."

"I agree with you, but real change in Germany is only going to come from the people, and without anything to contrast with the constant propaganda the people are subject to, they'll continue accepting the Nazis' lies."

"You sincerely think that one crumpled up pamphlet is going to change someone's mind who's been subject to Goebbels' propaganda on the radio and the newspapers for five years? Would it change your mind?"

"It's an uphill struggle, but does that mean they should give up?"

Maureen slumped back in her chair as the young woman

beside them erupted laughing at something her middle-aged suitor had said. "Hitler seems to have set his sights on Czechoslovakia next. Perhaps the Allies will stand up to him this time and snuff out this madness in Germany."

"The Allies aren't ready for war. You know that as well as I do. They'll do whatever they can to preserve the peace and Hitler will win once more."

"You don't know that."

"Don't I?"

Gerhard finished his beer and lit up a cigarette. Other than Lisa, he was the only person in the city she could completely trust. Her brother might have left on the boat to America, but she'd gained another in Paris.

"Have you been in touch with your brothers since your father's death?" she asked.

"No," Gerhard said, tapping the ash off his cigarette. "My father was my last link to them. I'm sure they'd blame me for what happened. They're committed Nazis. They'd kill me with their bare hands if they got the chance. I can't say I'd blame them. I'm the reason my father is dead."

"He made the choice to rise against Hitler himself. General Engel was a German patriot who put the Reich before the Nazi Party."

"I am proud of who he was. It's ridiculous because I hadn't seen him in so long, but I miss him," said Gerhard.

The coup Maureen and Gerhard had tried to orchestrate with his father, the Luftwaffe general, and the actress Petra Wagner had felt like their chance to make a genuine difference to the peace and prosperity of the world. But it had failed, and Gerhard's father and Petra were both dead now.

"We're each other's family now," she said.

Gerhard regained his composure and smiled. "So, you didn't get on that boat. You want back in? I could use someone I can trust—someone who's not afraid to get their hands dirty when it's called for."

Maureen glanced again at the older man and his young girlfriend. Two young male students had just taken the table on their other side and were ordering wine. "What we did in Pithiviers—that's not going to be a regular event. I'm not—"

"Nor me. We did what had to be done. Nothing more. I'm not some avenging angel, but if it's a choice between my life or some Nazi's—well, that's no choice at all."

"I agree."

∾

Berlin, Wednesday, October 5

Seamus started his car and pulled out of the factory parking lot. Hours earlier, a man called Herr Strumpf had called his office, wanting to discuss an order of knives and forks, goods the factory no longer dealt in. But Seamus understood the code well enough, and now he drove toward Wedding, a working-class area of the city north of the Tiergarten. It was one of the areas Bill Hayden liked to meet in most often, along with Kreuzberg. Those neighborhoods had more than their fair share of dingy hotels, the ones in which the Nazis didn't plant listening devices. The better the hotel room, the more likely someone was listening in. Ofener Strasse was perfect—dark and dirty.

It was a fine evening. Conor would be out playing football with his friends in the Hitler Youth while Fiona was probably at some meeting. She had been true to her word and had refused to return to school. She seemed to be counting down until Harald returned from SS training to marry him and start having children.

Meanwhile, she had become Helga's assistant, doing filing and typing. She refused to talk to Seamus about it, although there was nothing unusual about Fiona not speaking to him. He saw her in the factory he ran when she worked there, but she spent more time in the new airplane factory Helga oversaw. Sometimes whole days would go by when Seamus barely saw her at all.

As he drove across the city, he was relieved to note that it had returned to its usual self after the celebrations and parades that had sprung up to greet the taking of the Sudetenland in Czechoslovakia, a region of some three million people inhabited by a majority ethnic German population. Another triumphant parade for the Nazis. Seamus wondered how many more there'd be before the decade was out, for no serious person who'd been paying attention these past five years believed Hitler's promise that it would be his last territorial claim in Europe.

In Wedding, the acidic smell of trash hung in the air. He parked in an alley and walked on, checking around to ensure no one had tailed him. A homeless man with a sign identifying him as a veteran of the Great War held up a plate with a few pfennigs in it. The Nazis' militaristic outlook didn't stretch to looking after the hundreds of homeless veterans sleeping on the streets of Berlin every night. It was yet another example of National Socialist hypocrisy in action. Seamus threw some coins onto the plate.

The hotel looked as if it had been around since Bismarck was a boy, and the interior suggested it hadn't been cleaned since then, either. The jaded desk clerk didn't even look up as Seamus strolled past. Confidence was key. No one would ever stop you if you looked like you knew where you were going.

He jogged up the threadbare staircase to the second floor. Hayden had mentioned the number 212 on the phone, so that was the door he made for. He knocked once, then twice. The door opened, and Hayden shook his hand.

"You made sure you weren't followed?"

"Of course."

The US diplomat led him to the table and chairs he'd already set up by the window, which overlooked a brick wall. "I apologize for the view," he said with mock seriousness.

"You're going to have to send a strongly worded letter to the state department," said Seamus, glancing around the room's interior. The sheets on the bed were grey and looked like they might come apart if you tried to get between them. Worst of all was the red stain that adorned the pillow. "I wonder what happened there?"

"I think it's best that remains a mystery," murmured Hayden. He had the bottle of whiskey he always brought with him and didn't bother to ask Seamus if he wanted a glass; he just handed him one instead.

"At least I'm getting something for my service to the republic," Seamus said as he sat down and sipped at the whiskey, which seemed to be of good quality.

"It's not much more than I get. You have anything for me?" Hayden's official title was that of a diplomat, but his role for the US government was anything but diplomatic. Seamus had been feeding him as much information as possible about the buildup of the Reich's armed forces since '36. Their meetings had been less frequent lately due to the worsening security situation in the city. The Gestapo's grip on German society was more potent by the day.

Seamus reached into his jacket pocket for an envelope and handed it to his old war buddy. "The Nazis are stepping up bomber production. The testing on the citizens of Spain was a success."

"Anything else?"

"It doesn't seem there's any end to the Nazis' appetite for

armaments. The orders keep coming. My workers can hardly keep up with the demand. We've had to hire more and we're running 24 hours a day. We can't train the new employees quickly enough."

"Easy money, eh?"

Seamus winced. The jab stung, and Hayden raised his hand to apologize before pouring more whiskey into Seamus's glass.

Seamus drained the bitter liquid, his good mood broken. "I wonder if they used any of my bullets in the excursion in the Sudetenland."

"If they didn't use yours, it would have been someone else's. Don't beat yourself up about it. You should be proud of the role you're playing."

"Thank you for saying that, but the whole thing makes my blood run cold."

"Mine too."

Hayden shook his head. "The Nazi plan leading up to taking the Sudetenland in Czechoslovakia was textbook, despite a few speed bumps. I'll say one thing for Hitler—he can think on his feet. First thing he did was to establish the *legal* reason for moving his troops in. The Nazis transplanted their operatives into the Sudetenland in secret and started the ball rolling in their favorite way—by plundering Jewish stores. The Czech government's first mistake was to declare martial law. Then the Nazis issued their ultimatum, demanding the withdrawal of Czech troops and police from the Sudetenland. No one was shocked when the government ignored that garbage. Then the agitation began. Stormtroopers attempted to seize barracks and public buildings, using hand grenades, machine guns, and even tanks brought in from the Fatherland, I hear. The fighting was a lot more bitter than the newspapers reported. Some say two hundred men were killed on each side. But the Czech government didn't give in. The putsch failed and the agitators fled back to Germany, where the Nazis hailed them as heroes and martyrs, and denounced the Czechs as terrorists and murderers. Then, once he had his excuse, the glorious Führer announced he was going to make his move, and began massing troops—to protect the poor Germans there from those murderous Czechs."

"You think it was a bluff?" Seamus asked.

"Probably, but who knows? Maybe not even the Führer himself. I don't think he'll be shy when it comes to unleashing the might of the German military when the time comes, but perhaps he didn't think they were ready."

"Either way, Chamberlain was ready to fold at the conference he called to sort it all out. What does the US government make of that debacle in Munich?" asked Seamus.

In a last-minute attempt to avoid war, the British Prime Minister, Neville Chamberlain, had proposed a conference to settle the dispute over the Sudetenland. The French, German, British and Italian leadership convened in Munich on September 29. The Czechs were not invited to participate in the negotiations over their own country. The other powers capitulated to Hitler's demands, and the Sudetenland was lost. Before leaving, Chamberlain and Hitler signed an agreement stating that this would end the Führer's foreign aggression. Few expected him to keep it.

"Yeah, that whole charade was embarrassing," Hayden continued. "I don't see FDR lying down like that. At least, I hope not. 'Peace in our time.' What a load of baloney! Anyone who's read a newspaper in the last ten years knows that Hitler was gambling."

"And he won. Again."

"Yes, he did. Watch now as Hitler breaks the agreement in the next few months. He'll occupy the rest of Czechoslovakia by the summer. I guarantee it."

"He wants the Skoda works in Mlada Boleslav, I'd bet my last dollar on it. It's one of the biggest in Europe. I can only imagine how many planes and tanks he'll be able to churn out once he takes it."

"You know the owner?"

"No. They've been hostile to any approaches from within Germany in the past."

"I wonder why," Bill mused. "What about Roland Eidinger? Has he any contacts in Skoda?"

Seamus hadn't spoken to his friend Roland in a few weeks. Eidinger ran one of the biggest shipping companies in Germany but was no fan of Hitler.

"I can ask. I think Roland's getting sick of dealing with the Nazis. He's been talking about leaving the Reich for a while."

"What about Lisa, and the kids?"

"Lisa's still in Paris with Hannah. I haven't seen her in six weeks."

"I appreciate you playing it safe, but I don't reckon the powers that be know she had anything to do with the plot between the general and the actress. I don't think the Gestapo threw her out the window. They would have taken her to Prinz-Albrecht Strasse. I think she saw that coming and gave herself an easier death–exactly what I would have done."

"I understand your point and I probably agree, but would you risk it? Besides, the Jew-hatred was getting to her. As you know she's classified as a *Mischling*,"

"A *mongrel*. The Nazis are disgusting."

"Who knows if the laws are going to get even tougher for anyone with Jewish blood like her?"

"I don't blame her for that. So, you're stuck here with Conor and Fiona. At least the others are safe."

"Michael and Monika are, yeah. Maureen didn't get on the steamer back to America."

Hayden burst out laughing. "I'm sorry, Seamus, but it's laugh or cry, isn't it?"

"So's my whole life."

"That kid," he said, staring into the amber liquid at the bottom of his glass. "She's going to save the world, isn't she?"

"If she doesn't, it won't be for lack of trying."

"I think that deserves a toast," Hayden said and held up his glass. "Here's to Maureen—the bravest person I know."

Seamus didn't know how to react but clinked glasses with his friend.

"How are things in the embassy after Munich?"

"Tense. The ambassador's at his wit's end. He's had it with the Nazis. It's not the easiest posting. If Hitler breaks his word on the agreement he made with Chamberlain, the whole idea of diplomatic relations between the allied powers and the Reich is going the way of the dodo. I wouldn't be surprised if they pull the whole lot of us."

"Then what use would I be?"

"You're joking, aren't you?" Bill said. "If I withdraw, you're the eyes and ears on the ground in Berlin for the state department. And working with the Nazis to build their war machine? Your importance couldn't be overstated. You will be vital to the security of our country, Seamus. I'm sorry about the situation with your family, but I also know you're a patriot. Hitler and his buddies are about as dangerous as anyone we've ever faced."

Hayden must have seen the look on his friend's face because he reached over to clink glasses again.

"Anyway, it might not come to that. Maybe Hitler will keep his word, and we'll all be able to sleep at night again."

"Yeah, maybe," Seamus said.

Conor and Fiona were both in bed when he arrived home. The house was deathly silent. He ascended the stairs to sleep alone. The thought that his family's future might depend on Hitler keeping his word kept him awake for hours.

4

Paris, Thursday, November 3

Maureen was sitting on the balcony of the apartment, drinking coffee and reading *A Farewell to Arms* by Ernest Hemingway. Thoughts of her father filled her mind as she placed the paperback on her lap. He never spoke about his time in the Great War. It was a side of him that remained a mystery to her. A knock on the door echoed through the apartment. It seemed like an empty vessel now that Michael and Monika were gone. Though she was expecting Gerhard, she took a moment to peer through the peephole. It was him, but he had brought a stranger with him. Suspicious of everyone now, Maureen hesitated to open the door, but then decided that she trusted her friend. She clicked back the lock to let him and the other man in.

Gerhard greeted her with a kiss on each cheek. "Maureen, I'd like to introduce you to Herschel Grynszpan," he said in German.

Herschel didn't look more than 17 and offered a meek handshake. He was dark-skinned with slicked-back black hair and dark eyes to match. He looked nervous, and it seemed like he had to force his gaze from the floor to meet hers.

She led them through the apartment and onto the small balcony overlooking the narrow cobblestoned street of Rue de Lappe, where she pulled up some more chairs and fetched a bottle of wine.

The young man refused the Cabernet she offered, putting his hand over his glass. She shrugged and poured some for herself and Gerhard instead.

"I met Herschel at an anti-fascist meeting a few nights ago," Gerhard began.

"You're going to meetings again?"

"Just hanging around in the wings. Don't worry, my friend. But Herschel caught my attention with the story he told." He touched the boy's shoulder. "Herschel? Will you tell Maureen what you told me?"

Herschel blushed and raised his head, making eye contact with Maureen, then dropped his eyes again. He began speaking in a thick German-Yiddish accent, softly at first but with increasing passion.

"I was asking for money to help my family," he said. "I was born in Hanover. My parents are Polish Jews. I was never recognized as a German citizen due to the laws of the land, and we retained our Polish citizenship. We were known as Eastern Jews, looked down on by the German Jews. I tried to emigrate to Palestine but, after getting a Polish passport, made it to France instead—illegally. My Polish passport expired in January and in March the Polish government passed a law depriving any Poles living abroad for five or more years of their citizenship."

Maureen had heard several stories of these so-called "stateless people" in her time in Paris. The Polish government had a lot to answer for.

"I live with my uncle and aunt, but they're struggling to support themselves let alone me."

"Don't you have a job?" Maureen asked.

"I'm afraid to look for one in case they deport me to Germany, even though I miss my family so much. My heart aches for them."

"Tell her what happened," Gerhard prompted.

"The Gestapo came for all the Polish Jews last week, my family among them. The papers said 12,000 were picked up and brought to the border to be deported."

"But the Polish government revoked their citizenship," Maureen said.

"Wait," Gerhard said, and put a hand on her forearm.

"My parents, my little brother and sister and thousands of others were packed off to the border, but the Polish police wouldn't admit them, and the Gestapo certainly wasn't about to let them come back. It turned into a standoff."

Herschel's voice shook, and tears welled in his brown eyes.

"I received a letter from my father, sent with the help of the Polish Red Cross—the only people who seemed to care anything about the thousands of people at the border with no food or water. My family was only allowed to bring one suitcase, and are sleeping in a shanty town." Herschel was crying now. Gerhard put a hand on his shoulder. "I went to the meeting to try and raise money to send to them. I got a few francs, but most people there were more concerned about the coming invasion. I don't know if I got through to them at all."

Herschel's tears dried, and his fists became like two steel balls. His knuckles turned white, and he let out a horrible whining sound, like a dog in pain.

"It's okay, my friend," Gerhard said, patting his shoulder. "We will help you."

Taken aback, Maureen looked at Gerhard. "It's a terrible

story, but Gerhard, how can we help? I can give money, of course, but not nearly enough to make a difference...."

"I want to speak to you about that. Herschel, if you could leave us alone for a moment?"

"Please," the young man said directly to Maureen. "Their situation is growing more desperate by the hour." His face was red, and his eyes were on fire. He seemed like he was about to jump up and shake her by the shoulders.

"I'll see what I can do," she replied. She had to stop Herschel from looking at her like he was trying to bore holes through her with his eyes.

"That's all we can ask for," Gerhard said. "Now Herschel..."

"You have to help!" the boy cried. "They could be dead in a few days. Some people are talking about trying to escape back to Germany! Can you believe that? A Jew trying to return to Hitler's Reich? They're desperate!"

"I think she understands, Herschel," Gerhard said. "And all we can ask—"

"I'd kill every Nazi in Paris tonight if I could," Herschel said. "Blood for blood!" His words came like bullets from a machine gun.

"Calm down," Maureen said. "You think you'll serve your family if you're behind bars? We all have those feelings some-times. The Nazis are trying to make us do stupid things so they can justify their crimes. We need to be better than them."

"You're wrong," Herschel said between gritted teeth. "The only way to deal with a mad dog is to take it out into the yard and shoot it."

Maureen shivered, remembering shooting Hans and the other Nazi. "We must try to stay within the law."

"No!" Herschel shouted and stood up, knocking the bottle over. Wine cascaded all over the wood floor.

Gerhard jumped to his feet, and Maureen took the opportunity to escape to the kitchen to fetch a cloth to clean up the spilled wine.

Herschel followed her, looking nervous again and full of apologies. "I'm sorry about the wine. I'll replace it. Shall I go now? You can wait here while I go to buy some."

Maureen held up her hand to slow him. "Forget the wine and keep your money. Just wait here until I call you."

She went back out on the balcony and closed the doors behind her.

Gerhard kneeled down on the floor beside her to help her soak up the wine.

"I feel bad for the kid," he whispered. "I know he's crazy and angry, but it's only because of what the Nazis have done to his family—"

"Keep an eye on him. He seems like a volcano about to blow. He could bring the police down on us all."

"So, could your father help, do you think?"

"With what? Saving his family?" Maureen sat back on her haunches, staring at Gerhard in shock. "What have you been promising that boy? You can't tout my father as the man to save every Jew in Germany. If the Gestapo got wind of that notion, he'd be in a concentration camp within hours."

"I swear, I've said nothing about your father. I haven't promised the boy anything, but he was about to go off and start shooting people. I had to tell him something to get him to come here, so I just said that you're a good person, you have secret contacts, you might be able to help him, that's all."

He was still kneeling, a cloth in his hand, his eyes on her face.

"I'll speak to my father."

"Thank you." He took her hand and pressed it. "But speed is of the essence here."

"I'll call him tonight. It's not going to be easy, but I'll try and get the message across."

The Jewish boy's knocking on the balcony door cut their conversation short. They got up, and Maureen opened the door.

"I need to go now," he said.

Maureen nodded. "Please say nothing about this meeting. I hope I'll be able to do something to ease your family's suffering."

"Speak to whomever you need to, but please, help my family. My parents are good people. My brother and sister are so young. You've got to do something."

The boy's unjustified belief in her was daunting. She felt her entire body tense up.

Herschel reached into his jacket pocket for a small piece of paper and handed it to her.

"All the details you'll need are written on there. But hurry. They could be dead in a matter of days."

It was an impossible task. "I'll do what I can."

"Time to go," Gerhard said, putting his arm around the boy's shoulders.

As they left, Gerhard hung back and said to Maureen. "I'm sorry, you were all I could think of. I just thought if you heard his story from his own mouth...."

"Goodbye, Gerhard."

Cold loneliness descended upon Maureen as the door closed. Herschel's black eyes stayed with her.

I have to do something about this.

She'd put off calling her father since she'd turned back from the steamer in Le Havre. Long-distance calls were expensive, and it was hard to communicate your thoughts when you had to pretend to be someone you weren't. You had to assume someone was listening in.

She put on her jacket and shut the door behind her. *That kid will kill someone if we don't help his family, which will be bad for everyone.*

A gentle rain was falling as she emerged onto the street. She jogged to the hotel and waved to the desk clerk she'd spoken to a few times. A line of public phones sat to the side of the front desk. Each was in use, and she had to wait three agonizing minutes before one became available. Her hand was sweaty as she picked up the receiver. She gave the operator the number for her father's desk at work. It rang three times before he picked up.

"It's me," she said before he had a chance to say anything.

He sputtered a few times. "Why did you stay?"

"I tried to go. Truly. I just couldn't."

Several seconds of silence followed. Maureen knew her father had to be the one to speak next. "Some things never change," he said with a rueful laugh.

"Have you heard about the situation at the Polish border?" she said.

"I read something about it."

Maureen closed her eyes. How to say this and not incriminate either of them? "Our old friends Zindel and Rivka Grynszpan are there." Her father remained silent, so she continued. "They have something for you. Can you go and see them and pick it up?"

"I'm not sure I can," her father said.

"It's ever so important. I'd be eternally grateful if you could just find the time to visit. They're in Zbaszyn. Have you heard of it? Write it down."

"I see it on the map."

"Time is of the essence. They could be gone soon."

"I don't know."

"Please look into it. Make sure our old friends are okay."

"Are you? Do you need to see me?"

"All is well here," she said. "I should let you get back to work. A faithful servant of the Reich such as yourself never rests."

"It's good to hear your voice."

They said goodbye, and she hung up the phone.

An intense longing to see her father and the rest of her family swelled her heart. It had been years since she'd pined for them like this, not since her mother died. Perhaps she should have gone back to America with Michael instead of staying in Paris alone. Missing Berlin wouldn't do her any good —she was wanted there, and returning could mean her head on the executioner's block. The police didn't take kindly to one of their own being killed. It didn't matter that the officer was trying to rape her sister-in-law when Maureen intervened. Not one bit. Perhaps she could return, but, much like her step-mother, she'd erred on the side of caution. One of the other policemen who'd been at the camp imprisoning the Roma people during the Olympic Games could recognize her. She and Monika had sat with them for hours the night they'd broken Willi and his family out before that monster tried to assault her. Maureen was just thankful the Gestapo had never harassed her father and accepted his story that she and Michael had moved abroad.

A tear slid down her cheek. The rain on the street had thickened, but she stepped out into it anyway. Thomas, the boyfriend she'd left behind when she fled Berlin, appeared in her mind. He had another girl now. She'd lost everything because of the Nazis. Her family. Her first love. Her education. She tensed her fists, thinking of the mass rallies in Germany and the Nazi flags, the people she'd seen "euthanized" outside that hospital in Babelsberg, and the people she'd been forced to kill. And she saw Ullrich, her Nazi torturer, and his dead eyes. The same anger that rippled through Herschel had a hold of her now. She fought to rid herself of it, but it lingered below the surface like a crocodile in the river of her consciousness. Always there. Waiting.

5

Thursday, November 3

Seamus looked at the map of Germany and the surrounding countries on the wall behind his desk. Zbaszyn was a border town almost directly east of Berlin, not much more than a two hours' drive. The coverage of the expulsion of the Polish Jews wasn't a big story in the newspapers. Most were still basking in the glory of the Führer's great victory at the Munich conference, but Seamus saw it and knew what was going on. The Nazis, after the Polish law deprived citizens living abroad of their citizenship, saw an opportunity to rid Germany of more Jews. Little had been seen or heard from the thousands sent to the border since they'd left.

This was the first time he'd heard from Maureen in weeks, and it was just a few coded words.

He knew his daughter. She was operating on some kind of instinct. Something inside her was telling her not to return to the safety of America. Was she so determined to stop the Nazis' inevitable march across Europe alone?

He had written the two names Maureen called out to him

on the phone—Zindel and Rivka Grynszpan on a notepad. Who were they to her?

"Am I really going to get embroiled in one of Maureen's schemes again?" he said out loud. Her plot to break Willi Behrens out of the camp in Marzahn during the Olympics had almost cost Michael his life. And now she was in exile for fear of the Berlin police herself.

He crumpled the page and threw it into the wastepaper basket.

A knock on his door proved a welcome distraction, and Fiona's face appeared at the glass. He smiled as he saw his daughter, and she almost reciprocated.

"Hello, Father," she said. "Helga's in her office. She's here for the meeting with Oberst Langer and Oberst Kaymer."

Seamus thanked her, but privately wondered what his cousin was thinking. The clients were Luftwaffe men, both fliers in the last war. He knew these men. They had little interest in having a woman in the room unless she was serving tea. Helga knew as much, but still insisted upon attending. He never asked her not to join a meeting but sometimes alluded that it might be better for her to do other things. Women were looked down on in German society, but the Nazis took it to extremes. Still, he wasn't about to say anything to stop her. This company was as much hers as his. He just hoped his daughters wouldn't be treated the same way if they pursued a career in business. For some reason, his cousin wanted to attend this meeting. Perhaps it was because of the passion she had for producing warplanes.

Ten minutes later, the two men entered Seamus's office in full uniform, offering bone-crushing handshakes. Langer was in his fifties, with a pot belly and a twirling grey mustache. His colleague was a few years younger and several pounds lighter. Kaymer was tall and exposed his bald scalp when he took off his hat. Seamus did his best to separate the men he met in his office from the Nazis they represented. These were soldiers, not politicians, or so he tried to convince himself.

"Hello Ritter," Oberst Langer said as they walked inside.

"How's business?" Oberst Kaymer said.

"Robust," Seamus replied. "One might ask what the government intends to do with all these bullets, shells and airplanes."

"Ours isn't to reason why, ours is but to do and die," Kaymer said.

"You enjoy Tennyson?" Seamus asked.

"Would it surprise you if I said I did?" the Oberst answered.

"Not a little bit."

Fiona appeared at the door. Seamus knew better than embarrass her by trying to introduce her to the clients. "Tell Frau Ritter the gentlemen are here," he said to her instead.

The military men looked at each other and then at Seamus.

"Want a drink?" he said and walked over to the table he kept for liquor. Both men accepted, and a few seconds later, all three were sipping fine whiskey. Helga arrived, and the jovial atmosphere was broken. The two Luftwaffe men shifted in their seats, but didn't bother to get out of them to shake her hand.

"Afternoon, gentlemen," Helga said. "I trust you're here to discuss plans for the production of the Messerschmitt Bf 109." Seamus had already pulled up a seat for her, and she sat down with a folder in her hand to go through pricing and specifications. The two military men looked at Seamus again as if to ask why she had to bring business up so quickly.

Seamus knew his cousin didn't drink, so he couldn't offer her a whiskey.

"Jumped right in, didn't you?" Langer said and turned away from her.

Helga continued. "The speed and reliability of the Bf 109 will make it the backbone of the Luftwaffe for years to come. Test pilots have called it a revelation—"

"Ever been in a plane yourself, Frau Ritter?" Langer asked.

"I was on a test flight—" she said with a smile that melted as the officer interrupted her again.

"Oh, you were on a test flight? Anyone shooting at you during it?"

"Of course not," she replied in a flat voice.

"Hard for you to know what it feels like for a pilot in combat, then, isn't it?"

"I don't think that's pertinent," Seamus said. "How's your wife, Oberst Kaymer?"

"Pregnant again," he replied, "Fat as a sow and squealing twice as much!"

The two military men burst out laughing. Helga looked cold and alone and clutched the folder to her chest.

"I don't think I could stand women if they didn't look the way they do," Langer said. "I'm away most of the time with work. My wife understands I have needs she can't always satisfy."

"Perhaps we could move onto business now," Seamus said.

"Already?" Langer said. "I'm not even finished my first drink."

"We haven't even gotten through one bottle yet!" Kaymer said. "Last time we were out on the town together you sang a different tune, Seamus."

"My cousin is one of Germany's foremost experts on production of the Bf 109. I just thought since we had her with us—"

"Yes, just what we need, a woman who's never flown organizing our military," Langer said.

"I think I have another meeting," Helga said and stood up.

Seamus held up his hand, his face hot. His cousin paced to the door. Langer and Kaymer didn't say a word, and she shut the door behind her.

Two hours later, Seamus walked the two Luftwaffe officers to the door and waited as they climbed into a taxi.

"Leave your cousin in her office with her papers next time, eh?" Langer said as he shut the door to the car. Seamus turned and walked back inside the factory. Helga was gone, and his daughter with her. He sat down at his desk once more. The guilt he felt about Helga's humiliation and his lack of support for her was soon replaced in his mind by Maureen's request. He swiveled around in his chair and cursed as he felt his eyes drawn to the map and Zbaszyn like magnets.

"I can't," he said, "I have a business to run." Then he cursed again as he got out of his seat to fish out the crumpled note.

6

Thursday, November 3

Darkness had fallen in earnest as Fiona left the League of German Girls meeting held in her school. Her friends Amalia and Inge caught up with her at the door, and they walked out into the crisp night air together.

The conversation among the troop leaders had been about pivoting back to the message that a woman's place was in the home. Too many of the girls were still talking about the ill-thought-out speech Helga had made in the summer. It had raised too many questions about young girls starting their own businesses or even going to university. After all, how many of the girls' fathers would allow them to follow in their footsteps? Most loyal German men would never dream of permitting their daughter to take over their businesses, let alone encourage them to do so. It was contrary to the Führer's teaching and could thus be seen as a shallow form of dissent or even treason. That wasn't the message the leadership was trying to communicate at all.

Fiona cringed as she recalled the uncomfortable meeting.

She felt guilty over the scene Helga's speech created, although her League leaders had kindly taken full responsibility for allowing it to happen. Her superiors acknowledged that they should have known better. Fiona had merely been the one who'd suggested her father's cousin speak, which was an honest mistake for an eager young girl to make.

The leaders had praised the boys of the Hitler Youth for pointing out that young girls should not be aspiring to a role in business. It was far more important to create a good home and provide sons to protect the Reich. The role of women had always been clear through the centuries of civilized human existence. Why should so-called "modern thinking" alter the foundations upon which the human race was built? Helga was to be pitied, not envied, and she certainly should not have been held up as a role model. She was a woman in her forties with no husband and no children. Her only saving grace was that she produced weapons for the military.

"Are you all right?" Amalia said. "It can't have been easy to hear that."

"Everyone makes mistakes," Inge said and took Fiona by the hand. "You were hypnotized by Helga's wealth—the troop leaders said it themselves. I don't think they'll hold it against you. It won't interfere with any possible promotions you might receive."

"I hope not," Fiona said.

A voice from behind them interrupted her thoughts.

Harald, in full grey SS service uniform, walked across the schoolyard. The outside lights gleamed off his blond hair. He was every inch the perfect Aryan man and more gorgeous than ever. The intense physical training he'd undergone had only served to bulk him up even further. Fiona spun around in shock, trying not to scream with delight.

"Hello girls. Good meeting?" he asked.

"Yes, we were discussing marriage and babies," began Amalia, looking starstruck.

"Amalia and I were just leaving," Inge grinned, taking her friend's arm and pulling her toward the school gates.

Fiona was left alone with the man she knew would someday be a father to her children.

She blushed and stammered. "I didn't expect to—"

"I got home from training this morning. I wanted to see you, but you weren't at home. Conor said you were here."

"You look so handsome in that uniform."

"I'm prouder to be SS than anything I've ever known. We are Hitler's elite. The best that the finest race on earth has to offer."

Fiona realized she hadn't touched him yet and reached up to give him a kiss. Not knowing where to put her lips, she planted an awkward peck on his smooth, sculpted cheek. He accepted it with a smile and took her hand. Electricity flowed through her body.

"Shall we walk?"

"I'd love to," she replied.

They strolled out of the school grounds and onto the street. Amalia and Inge had already disappeared.

"Tell me about your training," she said, loving the feel of his hand in hers.

"It was an incredible exploration of the limits of mind and body. I feel hard as granite, not just physically but mentally too. The focus of our training was "blood and soil.""

"Explain to me?"

Harald smirked. "As a girl, you wouldn't understand these things, but it's about loyalty, courage, and self-sacrifice. Our loyalty is exclusively to the Führer. We express it in the vow every SS man takes, "I vow to you, Adolf Hitler, as Fuhrer and Chancellor of the German Reich, loyalty and bravery. I vow to you and the leaders you set before me absolute allegiance unto death. So help me, God.""

"You believe in God?"

"I believe in Adolf Hitler. He is how I picture God to be. Our trainers ingrained in us day and night the absolute importance of loyalty, and that lack of it is the only unforgivable crime for an SS soldier."

They were passing a large park, deserted, save for a few locals out walking their dogs. Fiona felt completely safe as Harald led her inside and down a long path toward some woodland. She was so blessed that he wanted to be alone with her. He was one of Hitler's elite. Not everyone was allowed to join the SS, only the most racially pure. The tarmacadam path was lit every fifty paces by overhead lamps that cast a golden aura on them as they walked.

"I wanted to talk to you about your father," Harald said.

"Really? Why?" Fiona was surprised and disappointed. Her father was the last thing she wanted to talk about. Their future together, yes, babies, yes, but not her father. Unless Harald was planning to ask him for permission to marry her. Her heart lifted. "Are you worried he doesn't like you? He will when he gets to know you."

Harald shrugged. "I don't care about that. You've mentioned before that he was considering moving back to the United States, leaving that big house. Is that something he's ever discussed with you?"

"Of course not," she lied. "He loves Germany. How is *your* father?"

She'd heard Herr Schmidt had fallen on hard times, but not from Harald.

"He's fine. Proud of me," he said dismissively. "If your father doesn't intend to leave that mansion, do you think he'd allow us to live there with him? I'm trying for a posting in Berlin."

The exultation Fiona felt was like nothing she'd ever experienced. "Are you asking to marry me?"

"Not yet," he said. "I need to finish my training and get a ring, you know. Tell my parents. There's so much to organize."

"Oh, Harald!" She threw her arms around him. They kissed, and he pushed her against a tree, running his hands all over her. His mouth was hard against hers, and when she tried to pull away, he grasped her hair and forced his hand down her shirt. The weight of his body was pressed against her, crushing her against the rough bark of the trunk.

"Not here, my love," she murmured. She didn't want the first time to be against a tree in a public park. "Somewhere else."

He started to undo his belt. He'd never done anything like this to her before. She tried to push him away, but he was too strong. His arms coiled around her. He took his mouth from her lips and kissed her neck, finally giving her a chance to say something.

"Please, Harald. This isn't the time or place. Anyone could see us."

"No one's around," he said. "Have you any idea what I went through these past few weeks? I deserve this."

Her breath quickened, and again she used all her strength to push him off.

"I've told you," he said, "we're to be married—"

"Then let's wait for that." Her face burned with the effort of holding back her tears.

"How can I? Have you any idea how many times I thought about this when I was alone in my bunk in the training barrack?"

"About this or about me?"

He didn't respond and moved in again, pinning her against the tree. A cry of pain escaped her.

"Okay, not here," he said. He grabbed her by the hand and

dragged her deeper into the woodland. "Is this private enough for you?"

Terror infested her body like a swarm of locusts. "I just don't want to do this right now!"

"Fräulein? Are you all right? What's going on?" came a voice from behind them.

"Now look what you've done." Harald shot her an ugly, hateful look, then he glared at the middle-aged man in a flat cap standing among the trees with his dachshund on a lead.

"This is none of your concern, old man," Harald said. "Keep moving."

The man ignored Harald's order. "Are you okay, Fräulein?"

Fiona looked at Harald—the boy she loved. He was still on a high from his training and had lost the run of himself. He never meant to hurt her. "I am," she said. "We were just—going home, weren't we?"

"This is nothing to do with you, old man," Harald interrupted. "Take your silly little dog and get out of here before you get hurt."

"I don't enjoy your tone, and it seems to me the lady isn't interested in what you're offering. Do you want to come with me, Fraulein?" He reached out a hand to Fiona, but Harald slapped it down.

"She's not going anywhere. Stay out of this."

The man, who was shorter than Harald by several inches, stepped up to him. "The girl's coming with me."

He reached for Fiona again, but the SS soldier pushed him back with a hand in his face. The man stumbled over a root, and Harald threw a punch which sent him to the ground. His dog howled. Fiona screamed as the man she wanted to marry descended on the fallen figure. Harald tried to pin him down with a knee on his chest, but the man pushed him off. Both were on their feet now, their fists in the air.

An ugly smile spread across Harald's face.

"Stop it. Please, Harald!" Fiona shouted, but a demon had taken control of him. He punched the man, bloodying his lip. The dog walker tried to fight back, but the young SS man was too strong and was soon on top of him again, pummeling the older man with his fists while the dog ran barking in circles.

Fiona tried to pull Harald off, and he reared up and threw an elbow at her, connecting with the side of her jaw, sending her crashing to the ground, her ears buzzing.

A golden retriever came running through the trees, pursued by a young couple who stood and stared in amazement at the scene before them. Harald was still hitting the man. The second man tried to pull Harald off.

"You want some too?" Harald roared and unleashed a punch to the second man's jaw. The young woman with the golden retriever began screaming, and this time Harald just glared and walked away, leaving the two men who'd challenged him bloody and beaten.

Fiona propped herself up against a tree stump. Her vision felt dim. The man on the ground, the one who'd saved Harald from doing something he would have regretted, was groaning. His dog was on his lap, trying to lick his face. The young woman was tending to her husband, saying his name over and over. It sounded to Fiona as if she was speaking underwater. She couldn't make out a word. But she knew what was next. They'd call the police, and no matter what she said about Harald not meaning what happened, the others, if they found out who he was, could charge him with assault.

She staggered to her feet and away through the trees. No one followed. She kept on until she found the gate of the park and walked the rest of the way home. Two miles, crying all the way. What had happened to the man she loved? Who was that brute who attacked those men in the park? She couldn't tell anyone what had happened. Not Inge or Amalia or any of her friends. She knew they would be shocked. But they didn't understand the pressure Harald was under. His father's business was dying, and all he wanted in the world was for Harald to be an SS soldier. Fiona couldn't imagine carrying that much weight on her shoulders. He'd gotten carried away in the park, but the two of them were inexperienced in the ways of love. Perhaps he didn't know any better. It wasn't like they taught romantic matters in school. No, Harald was confused, but at heart, a good Aryan boy who would make a fine father someday. The logical side of her knew that what had happened in the park was an anomaly and not the everyday actions of the boy she loved.

Her tears had dried by the time she reached her father's house. The mansion was enormous, cavernous, now that so many of her family were missing. Harald had talked about them living here one day, and she knew her father would come around to that idea in time.

Her father was in the living room as she came in. He put down the book he was reading and stared up at her with wide eyes. "Have you been crying? What's the matter?" He stood up and went to her, but she stepped back as he tried to hug her and mustered a smile.

"Yes, but they were tears of joy. Congratulate me. I'm getting married to Harald."

"What?" He didn't look as pleased as he should have been. Clearly, Harald was right about her father not liking him. But he would in time, once he got to know him. "He's back?"

"He came to meet me after the League meeting."

He saw the leaves and dirt on her uniform. "What happened?"

"We walked home through the park. I tripped."

Her father shook his head. "Tell me the truth. Are you sure you're okay?"

"Father, I'm going to be married. Have you nothing to say to that?"

Before he could answer, she left him standing and stomped up the stairs in a rage.

~

Friday, November 5

Fiona didn't want to talk to or even look at her father. She'd slept little the night before, raging against him in her mind. He had shown complete disinterest when she'd told him she was getting married. Would her mother have been glad for her if she were still alive? It was hard to form a complete picture of who that woman was in her mind; Fiona was only eight when she died. Seamus had said in the past that Fiona reminded him of her, but he rarely said things like that anymore. All he talked about was how wrong she was in everything she thought and did.

She longed to talk to someone about Harald, but the only other person at the breakfast table, apart from her father, was her thirteen-year-old brother, who didn't have a clue about anything, particularly the honor of marrying a man in the SS. Conor went to Hitler Youth, but only because all his friends did. He wasn't committed to the cause. He seldom went to rallies and didn't even have a portrait of the Führer in his room. He was just like their father—a reluctant German.

"Would you like a ride today, you two?" her father asked as he folded away his newspaper.

"Yes, please," said Conor, delighted.

"Fiona?"

"No, I think I'll cycle today."

"Are you sure? It's cold outside and it's looking like it might rain."

"No, thank you."

She found her satchel and slung it over her shoulder. Her father was right—it *was* cold outside, but riding through the freezing air was preferable to sitting in the car with him. Particularly after his reaction to her news about Harald last night.

Helga was at her desk when Fiona arrived.

"What happened to you? Did you hurt yourself?" She said and stood up. Helga reached up and touched the spot where Harald had hit her with his elbow. "I'm fine. Just clumsy. I slipped in the park last night."

"You were in the park at night?"

"It's okay, Harald was with me."

Fiona picked up a pile of papers on the desk. Out of kindness, she resisted the temptation to tell Helga about her forthcoming marriage. She'd probably be sad and jealous.

"Is this to be filed away?"

"Yes please."

The morning moved like a glacier down a Swiss mountainside, but lunchtime eventually arrived. Fiona was sitting at her tiny desk in Helga's office when Greta, one of the other remaining secretaries, poked her head around the door.

"Someone's downstairs looking for you," the young secretary said. "Handsome boy! In full uniform too. Lucky you! Looks like you won't be working here much longer."

Fiona's heart fluttered. "Do I look presentable?"

"Lovely," Greta said. "You have a mirror?"

"No, I—"

"Don't worry!" Greta disappeared and returned a few minutes later with a pocket mirror and a hairbrush and brushed a little foundation over the bruise on her jaw.

"Those SS types don't like women wearing makeup, but he won't notice this. Now you can just tidy yourself up."

Fiona smiled and took a few moments to fix her hair.

"Gorgeous!" her friend said. "Now, your guest is waiting."

Fiona's hands were clammy on the railings as she

descended the stairs to the factory floor and

she could hardly breathe as she stepped out into the parking lot outside the front door. Harald was standing alone. The bouquet of flowers in his hand was in stark contrast to the dull grey uniform. He smiled and held them out to her. She crossed her arms, feeling she had the right to express a little anger.

"Please accept these." He pushed the carnations at her, his smile fading.

Her arms remained locked across her chest. "As an apology?"

"Yes, yes, I came here to apologize."

"Good. Let's go for a walk." As they crossed the courtyard, she asked, "How did you know I was here?"

"I visited your father in the factory and he told me."

Fiona didn't want to ask what kind of reception her father had given him.

He began again as they reached the street. "I thought about you so much during training. You were all I wanted."

Another unexpected spurt of anger bubbled over inside her. "You wrote me two letters the entire time. I found out you were coming home through my friends."

"What did you want me to say, that I ran fifteen miles that day and puked my guts out? The important thing is that you were in my heart the whole time. You were the only thing that got me through it. The thought of coming home to you and giving you everything you ever wanted is what drove me on."

"Not your dedication to the Führer?"

"That goes without saying, but you occupy a different corner of my heart."

"What you did last night—"

Harald smiled and shook his head. "I'm sorry, but you're so beautiful. You can't blame me for not being able to control myself around you. And for what I did to those people in the park, I've been trained to eliminate any enemies, and to protect everything I hold dear. I suppose, in that moment of passion, I saw those men as a threat to you."

She refused to give in to him just yet. Her mouth twitched, but she said, "They were trying to protect me. From you."

He looked amazed. "I'd never hurt you. Surely you know that. You're the future mother of my children. One day we'll deliver a dozen sons for the Führer."

Her cheeks were warm, and she wanted to fall into his arms. "I should get back to Cousin Helga. I left the coffee pot brewing."

"Tell me you're not angry anymore." He held up the flowers again. She took them. It was hard not to smile as he looked at her. "You still love me?"

"Of course, but no more beating up people in the park."

"You have my word as an SS soldier." He kissed her hand.

Any remaining anger melted inside her. How could it not? He was everything that she'd been taught to want. He was strong and handsome, with a steadfast dedication to the Führer. What else could she ask for in life? What else did she deserve?

The rest of the day passed quickly. Her father came by at the end of the day.

"Nice flowers," he said and pointed to the bouquet Harald gave her, now in a vase in the corner.

"From Harald, my fiancé." She glared at him, daring him to say anything negative.

He inclined his head. "I'm sure my cousin approves of him."

"And you?"

"I'd like to meet him first. We've never had a proper conversation."

"Okay." Fiona was pleased with her father for the first time in what seemed like years. "I'd like that. You'll see what a fine young man he is."

"I hope so. There's something I'd like in return, however."

"What?"

"I need to take a trip tomorrow. I want you to come along with me."

"Why?"

"I need you."

"Is Conor coming as well?"

"No, he has an all-day camp with the Hitler Youth. But I am bringing a friend who might interest you."

"I hope you've told him I'm engaged."

He laughed. "Don't worry, it's only Clayton. This isn't a ploy to prise you away from the handsome Harald. The truth is, our journalist friend needs someone who can take photos, and I've no idea how to work a camera. He's working on a story about the crisis at the eastern border. And as you did that photography course with the League, I offered you."

She was flattered but doubtful. "What are you asking me to do?"

"Please, sweetheart. His photographer and his driver are both away and he needs us to help him out. "

"So, what's this story about?"

"The situation at the border."

"Illegals trying to sneak into the Reich?"

"Exactly."

"Well, in that case...."

"Deal?" He held out his hand. She reached out and took it.

"Okay."

It was the first time she'd seen him smile in weeks.

"You want a ride?" he asked.

"I have my bike, remember?"

"I'll see you at home in that case."

He carried on into Cousin Helga's office and shut the door behind him.

7

Saturday, November 6

Clayton Thomas was on the stoop outside his apartment as Seamus and Fiona pulled up. Seamus had met him on the steamer coming over to Germany back in '32, and they'd remained friends ever since. Clayton was a reporter for the New York Times, and his press credentials would make it more likely they'd reach the camp. The young correspondent had promised not to press Fiona about her Nazis sympathies. He'd also sworn not to reveal that this entire trip was not his idea. The young journalist was happy to go along, but only after Seamus suggested it.

Clayton greeted Fiona like a niece and took his place in the back, refusing her dutiful offer to make way for him in the front.

"Thanks for picking me up." He reached into the satchel he was carrying, pulled out a camera, and handed it to Fiona.

"Your father told me you did some photography with your League of German Girls troop. You ever used one of these before?"

"Something similar."

"Great. We'll need all the pictures we can take."

"How's the journalism business?" Seamus asked.

"I don't know how to answer that. I can say my editor is delighted by all the ready-made information the government supplies us with. We barely have to come up with anything of our own. This border story hasn't been covered much though, so we thought it might be of interest."

"If there is an invasion of illegal aliens, people certainly need to know about it," agreed Fiona.

"Precisely," said Clayton, meeting Seamus's eyes in the rearview mirror.

The journey to Zbaszyn took a little more than two hours. Clayton was happy to pretend to write as Seamus chatted with his daughter.

The first topic on her mind was Harald and her excitement to be his wife.

Seamus was relieved that the boy hadn't told his parents yet. Harald and his wish for a dozen sons was the last thing he wanted for his daughter. Although at the same time, he hoped she wouldn't get her heart broken.

She looked so beautiful when she was happy, her coldness toward him melting. It was tempting just to agree with her about everything, that women shouldn't be working, that the SS boy was the height of German manhood, and that his devotion to Hitler was a sign of modern saintliness.

He dreaded restoring the icy hurt between them. Still, he had to do something. His daughter was almost gone. His first wife's second daughter. They passed a sign on a country road declaring that Jews weren't welcome in this area.

"What do you think your mother would make of all that?" he asked, gesturing toward the sign.

Fiona shrugged. "I don't think Mother knew any Jews growing up in Ireland, so I don't think she would have been interested."

"Still, she might have had an opinion."

"I think mother would make up her own mind about the revolution in Germany. That's the beauty of National Socialism —everyone is free to form their own judgments."

Seamus held his tongue. It was hard not to fight with her. But that wouldn't serve any purpose other than to alienate her more.

"Your mother was a kind person."

Fiona didn't answer.

Five miles outside Zbaszyn, they came to a roadblock. Several men in plain clothes with the familiar Nazi armbands across their biceps lined a barricade.

"Stop a few feet short," Clayton said. "I'll handle this."

The reporter climbed out and greeted the stony-faced Gestapo agents like they were old friends. Seamus heard the conversation.

"We need to get through to the camp at Zbaszyn," he said. "I'm with the New York Times. My assistants are with me. My photographer and my driver."

Seamus waved.

"This doesn't seem right—lying to the police," Fiona whispered, troubled.

"He's not lying. I'm driving, you're holding the camera."

One of the Gestapo men examined Clayton's papers for a few seconds before handing them back to him with a warning not to create any trouble.

Seamus started the engine, and they inched through the checkpoint, the Gestapo men staring in the windows.

"Clayton, I want to know exactly what this is about," said Fiona as the reporter climbed back into the car.

"The Red Cross have set up a refugee camp for Polish Jews

that the German government is trying to deport. The Poles won't let them in so there's a standoff at the border," Clayton said in a neutral voice.

"Is this safe?" Fiona said. "These people are being deported for a reason."

"No, no, only because they're Polish Jews," Clayton said. "Although they're not Polish any more, actually, because Poland has revoked their citizenship."

They drove for another five minutes before reaching the edge of the refugee camp set up on the outskirts of the small town of Zbaszyn. Seamus pulled over, and they climbed out. The sky was punctuated by plumes of black smoke from the camp. A sea of grey tents spread hundreds of yards in either direction. Entire families sat on upturned crates. Some people wore expensive clothes, while others were nearly in rags.

German soldiers stood chatting, smoking cigarettes, and laughing. Polish guards stood a few yards away on the other side of what seemed to have been designated a no man's land between the two countries.

Clayton asked Fiona to photograph a well-dressed family with five small children sitting on the grass outside their tent. Their one suitcase sat beside the tent, which was barely big enough for two people. A pot hung from a pole set above a fire, and the air was thick with the smell of the stew they were cooking.

"How long have you been here?" Clayton asked the father after showing his press credentials.

"Three days. We were in Frankfurt for eleven years. All my children were born there. Then, the Gestapo showed up at dawn and told us we had fifteen minutes to gather one suitcase of belongings, and we weren't allowed to bring anything valuable we owned. We were packed onto trucks and taken here but the Polish soldiers stopped us. The Gestapo dumped us in this field with no food or water."

Fiona kept taking photographs as Clayton instructed her, mainly of children playing, especially the ones in good clothes. She seemed unmoved by their plight, not horrified as Seamus had hoped she might be, but almost bored.

Seamus stood beside her and said, "I'm sure the vast majority of the children you see here were born and raised in Germany and have never known anywhere else."

She nodded. "I agree, I'm sorry for them, it's not their fault. It's their parents. I'm glad you brought me here, It's an education. I'm going to tell Harald and my friends in the League about this."

A rush of love for her surged through him. Her heart was still the same as it always had been. She just needed to understand the truth of who her masters really were.

She continued, "Maureen was always telling me that it was only the Nazis who didn't want the Jews around. But it's pretty clear the Polish authorities don't want them either. Nobody does."

He turned his head to hide his frustration.

"What's the matter, Father?"

Not knowing what to say, he walked off as if he'd spotted something interesting.

The camp was organized in a thin straight line, just a few tents deep, but widening as it reached the edge of town. Dozens of people were milling around, their clothes dirty, humiliation and loss all over their faces. He passed a young mother trying to feed her crying infant as tears streamed down her face. Several campfires spewed smoke into the air, though it was a warm afternoon for the time of year. Seamus dreaded to think how the people would keep warm at night in their tents.

He approached a young couple standing outside a tent and asked for Zindel and Rivka Grynszpan, hoping he was pronouncing it correctly. The young Jews shook their head, and Seamus walked on, asking again and again. They were nearing the town when an older man with a long gray beard directed them to a group of tents on the outskirts.

Seamus called out the names until a man in his fifties raised a thin arm. He was balding, with round spectacles sitting on the end of his nose. His wife was a large woman wearing a head scarf. She looked defeated, sitting on the ground, and barely raised her head as Zindel stood up to greet them.

"Who are you?" Zindel said.

"My daughter met your son Herschel in Paris. He asked that we come check up on you, see if you needed anything."

The man rubbed his forehead. "We need so much. Most of all to return home, but the Nazis will never allow that."

"Have you enough food and water?"

"Only for a few more days. The Nazis haven't given us any indication of when this will end and the Poles are no better. I dread to think what will happen when winter comes."

"Where do you purchase food? In town?"

"At the one grocer who'll serve us, and even then, only after the local citizens have picked all the best items."

"Do you have much money?" Seamus asked.

"Very little, enough for two more loaves of bread."

"Here," he said, reaching into his pocket and handing Zindel enough money to last several weeks. The Jewish man's eyes bulged.

"Why are you giving me this?"

"It's from your son, Herschel," lied Seamus. "Nothing to do with me."

"Where did he get—"

"I have no idea."

"How is he? He's such an emotional boy. How's he reacting to all this?"

Seamus had no idea how to answer the man's question. "He's taking it the best he can. It's difficult to hear about any injustice to your family, let alone something like this."

"I just hope he doesn't do something he'll regret. If you speak to him, can you tell him we're in good spirits and that this will all end soon?"

Seamus almost laughed at the lies he and Zindel were telling each other for the sake of a boy stranded in Paris, a thousand miles away.

"I'll tell Herschel exactly what you said. Hopefully this will all be resolved by the end of the week."

He shook the man's hand and bid his wife goodbye. She didn't get up and only mumbled a reply.

He zig-zagged through the mess of tents back to where he'd last seen Fiona and Clayton. The journalist was sitting on a rock talking to an older woman.

"This is Abigail," he said to Seamus.

The woman looked at least 80.

"Tell them what you just said to me," Clayton said as Fiona took several bored photos of the woman.

Abigail turned to them. Her eyes were startlingly liquid blue. "I've seen pogroms against the Jews before. My brother was beaten on the street back in 1884, but I've never seen anything remotely like this before. The hatred we grew up facing was confined to a few bullies and bigots. They were widespread, but it wasn't government policy. The kids these days are taught that we're thieves and rapists and need to be eradicated like vermin. I fear for every person here. Soon there'll be nowhere left to run."

Half an hour later, they were back in the car.

Seamus's entire gait was so stiff with frustration that he could barely put one foot in front of the other.

"I don't think that'll be the last time we'll see people forced from their houses into desperate straits," Clayton said.

"That old woman is right," Fiona said in a flat voice.

"Nobody wants the Jews. I don't understand why they don't just go and live in Palestine."

"They probably would, if they could get visas," said Clayton, seemingly trying hard to hide the contempt in his voice. "But the British won't allow it."

"Hitler should insist on them allowing it," said Fiona. "It's as if the world thinks the German government should be responsible for everyone else's Jewish problem. It's disgusting no other country is prepared to share the burden."

Neither man answered. Seamus started the car, and they set off back toward Berlin.

_____

8

Paris, Monday, November 7

Herschel Grynszpan woke with the dawn, pulled back the wafer-thin sheets on the mattress he slept on, and moved his feet to the icy floor. The anguish that had taken hold of him the last few days had doubled overnight, and he hadn't slept more than an hour or two. He clamped his eyes shut, envisioning taking Hitler by his throat and squeezing until the Führer's eyes popped out. Such thoughts were the only things that distracted him from his family's plight at the Polish border. He stood up in the bare room his uncle let him have in their tenement.

The card the American lady had sent him was on the dresser. He didn't need to reread it. He knew every pathetic word by heart. A deep stabbing pain felt like a flaming dagger in his chest and caused him to double over. It was too much to take. The meeting with the American woman and Gerhard, which had given him so much hope, had turned out to be useless. The woman's contacts in Germany had given some money to his family. So what? No one cared enough to rescue them.

The only way to do something productive was to bring the story to the attention of the Jews in America. Perhaps with their money and power, they could force the Polish government to open the border. He wasn't naïve enough to think the Nazis would allow them back into Germany, and even though Hanover was their home, he would be glad if they could live anywhere else.

The pain in his chest abated enough that he could stand up and walk across the room to the window. He looked down at the courtyard below. Several orthodox Jews sat out reading in the morning sun. He enjoyed living in this Jewish enclave and, apart from trying to rally support for his parents, had spoken to few other Parisians in the time he'd lived here. It was a pleasure to be among his fellow Jews, and he felt closer to God as a result. The only people he could trust in this city were all here.

Gerhard and Maureen had made some gesture toward doing the right thing, but now, with their consciences satisfied, they'd soon forget him and his family. If anything were to happen, he'd have to do it himself. Finally, he arrived at a plan. It wasn't going to be easy, but nothing worthwhile was. He took a blank postcard from the dresser and, addressing it to his parents, wrote, "God, please forgive me for what I'm about to do. I must protest so that the whole world hears me." Today would be marked in the history books as the day the Jews began to fight back against their Nazi oppressors.

Herschel dressed in his only decent suit and walked to the kitchen, where his aunt and uncle were eating breakfast.

They looked up, smiling when he entered. "That's a lovely suit." said his aunt.

"Thank you," Herschel answered. "I have a job interview. Soon I'll be working in a clothes shop. I know I've been a burden on you."

The relief on their faces soothed him. The lie was worth it. His uncle clapped him on the back as he sat down. "Good luck."

Herschel finished his breakfast in silence and let his aunt and uncle, who'd done so much for him, have this happy moment.

His uncle left for work soon after, and Herschel retreated to his room. The money he'd collected at the meeting was underneath the loose floorboard in the corner of his room. He stared at it for a few seconds before stuffing it into his jacket pocket. A pang of guilt stabbed him for not having sent it to his mother and father, but at least the woman's contact had given them some. He should possibly give it to his aunt and uncle for all the sacrifices they'd made for him, but all great deeds required great sacrifice.

He looked in the mirror. His mouth was twitching. Controlling his anger was impossible. All he could do now was to channel it, and use it to achieve something to alleviate his family's suffering. Perhaps future generations would remember his name when they recounted stories of Jewish heroes of the past.

The young man kneeled on the hardwood floor to pray for a few minutes. He opened his heart to God, allowing His voice to echo inside him. Herschel recited the words of the Shema, but God remained silent. It was a sign of his support for what Herschel was to do that day. With the clarity he needed, he stood up and left his uncle's apartment for the last time. Everything seemed different now. He greeted the other members of their little commune with a calm smile. Some seemed surprised at his demeanor. It was pleasing that this was how they'd remember him and not as the moody, angry young man who'd stomped around the hallways of the tenement building. He passed out of the courtyard and onto the street.

It was a fine, sunny late autumn morning in Paris. He regretted that he didn't know the city better. Exploring it had been the one pleasure he'd enjoyed these last few months. Without the wonder of this place, his life would have been unbearable. It had sustained him during the worst period of his young life, but its wonders weren't enough anymore.

It was all too easy to let cowardice rule what had to be done. He tried to control the voices within his mind urging him to return to the tenement, to sit down with the Rabbi and discuss his feelings. Closing his eyes, he shut out the emotions within him. *This is for the greater good—a cause bigger than me. This is for my family and is the only thing that will bring attention to their situation.* Herschel took a deep breath and kept walking.

The gun shop was on Rue de Faubourg Saint-Martin, a street he'd wandered along dozens of times. The man behind the counter looked him up and down but sold him the revolver nonetheless. Herschel placed the gun in one pocket, the box of cartridges in the other, and left without another word. The surge of power he felt was undeniable. Suddenly, he was a man to be reckoned with, and the tools to exact his revenge were at his disposal.

He walked south toward the river, through the Jardin de Tuileries, and over the Seine at the pedestrian bridge that led from the beautiful gardens. Doubtless, he would miss these places, but walking through the city felt like the proper way to say goodbye.

The German embassy was off the narrow street at Rue de Lille. The gate was open, and Herschel strolled through as if he worked there. "This is for all Jews," he said under his breath as he entered the opulent building. The floor was white marble. The walls were paneled in mahogany and a massive portrait of Adolf Hitler sat on the wall behind the colossal swastika flag. A young man behind a desk in the foyer dressed in a gray uniform adorned with the swastika looked up from his papers.

"I'm a Reich citizen," Herschel said in German.

The clerk looked bored. "What can I do for you?"

"I am a spy working on behalf of the National Socialist cause in Paris. I have in my possession an important document. I need to see his excellency the ambassador immediately."

The man behind the desk didn't seem any more excited at what Herschel had to say. "The ambassador just stepped out."

The young Jew did his best to control his breathing. The barrel of the pistol in his pocket was cool against his sweaty hand. "In that case I need to see the most senior official available. It's of utmost importance."

"I'll see who's available," the clerk said. He stood up and walked into an adjacent office, returning a few seconds later. "Herr vom Rath will see you. Follow me."

Herschel kept his eyes on the floor as he followed the clerk. His life was about to change forever, but so too would the lives of his family and all the Jews abandoned at the Polish border.

"Go right in," the desk clerk said.

A man in a grey suit with a receding hairline stood up to greet him.

"Now, what's this important document you have?" the man asked.

"You're a filthy Boche! Here's the document!"

Herschel pulled the pistol out. Every cell in his body was screaming with rage. The embassy official's face turned grey, and he held up his hands to try and stop what no one could. The gun exploded. Herschel fired five times, hitting the man in the abdomen. Vom Rath fell to the floor, clutching his belly. Herschel dropped the weapon and held up his hands as guards flooded the office.

The fuse was lit, and surely, soon, his family would be free.

9

Berlin, Wednesday, November 9

Everyone in the League meeting was talking about the great patriot Ernst vom Rath, who was callously shot by a Jew in Paris. Fiona's fellow troopers wept hot tears for a man they had never met and had never heard of two days before. But now he was the focus of every loyal Reich citizen. The instructors explained that Herr vom Rath was the best in all of them—a committed servant to Germany, a man who asked for little in return for safeguarding all Germans against the Jewish menace. The Führer was said to be distressed and sent his own personal surgeon to Paris to save the brave embassy worker's life. But the news came at the end of the meeting. It was what they'd all been dreading. Ernst vom Rath, the National Socialist hero, was dead. The teacher who announced it to the class of seventeen-year-old girls was crying as she relayed the news, and Fiona's fellow students were inconsolable. "This is a direct attack on everything that we hold dear," the instructor said. "This isn't just about one brave diplomat in Paris. This is about every loyal Reich citizen, and a sign of what will happen to each and every one of us if we don't stand up and fight for what we believe in." The troop leader, a slim blonde woman in her early twenties, dried her tears, and her voice changed. "Ernst vom Rath died for all of us!" she shouted. "And on this most sacred of all days—the anniversary of the Beer Hall Putsch when the Führer first came to national prominence back in '23."

November 9 was the most significant holiday on the Nazi calendar. Fiona's troop had been set to attend a rally that night, along with all the other Hitler Youth and League of German Girls in the area. Would it still go ahead? Perhaps it was best they postponed the celebrations out of respect for the new martyr. "But mark my words, girls," the teacher said. "A day of reckoning is coming for the Jews who carried out this horrific attack, and we must all stand together as one when it does. Without unity, the Jews and Bolshevists will destroy everything we hold dear."

The mood had changed in the classroom. No one was crying anymore. Fiona and the other students were sitting with their hands balled into fists, their faces hard as granite.

Seamus was in his office when the news from Paris came through on the radio. The broadcaster's mournful tone reminded him of what it might have been like if a monarch or a head of state died. He stood up from his desk and went to the window. The wireless was on down on the factory floor, as always. Several of the most ardent Nazis, including Gunther Benz, the head of the National Socialist-approved Trustee Council, were standing around with their hands on their heads. The Jewish workers on the other side of the building carried on as if nothing had happened. Benz, and his cohort, Artur Borst, began hurling insults across the factory floor. Pamela Bernstein, a young mother of two boys, began shouting back. Seamus slammed the door and ran down the stairs as the two Nazi sympathizers and a crowd of about ten others at their back stormed over to confront the pocket of Jews making steel helmets.

The tension between the Nazi employees and the Jews had been simmering for years, but this was the first direct confrontation. The two groups were standing inches apart, screaming red-faced insults at one another as Seamus arrived. He threw himself into the middle of the melee and held Benz and Borst back.

"You can't protect them anymore," Benz said. "The entire weight of National Socialist anger is about to come crashing down on their heads."

"This is one incident," Leonard Greenberg, a 25-year veteran of the factory, said. "What about Judith Starobin, who worked here for 12 years. Stormtroopers beat her up and killed her husband. Where's the justice for them?"

"This is only the beginning," Borst said. "The Jews will come for all of us!"

"Enough," Seamus shouted. But they weren't listening. "Go back to your stations!" he roared.

Gert Bernheim appeared at the top of the stairs, looking alarmed.

The shouting back and forth continued, and someone threw a heavy machine gun cartridge. In the next moment dozens of massive, heavy cartridges were raining down, forcing the Jewish workers to cower behind the machines, covering their heads with their hands as their Nazi colleagues laughed. The heavy shells rattled off the machines, falling into the mechanisms and doing untold damage.

"Stop this!" Seamus roared. "Those bullet cases are for your comrades! You're breaking the machines!"

Despite his appeal to the Nazis' patriotism, more shells rained down like hail, and several Jewish workers had blood running through their fingers as they held their scalps.

Bernheim arrived beside Seamus and shouted at the Jewish workers who hadn't already fled out the back door. "Get out of here! Go home!"

The Nazi sympathizers cheered as their colleagues turned and ran through the emergency exit behind them.

"Gert, you too. Benz, Borst, in my office!" Seamus ordered once the racket had ended. "And as for the rest of you—shut down the machines while the engineers check for damage."

The two Nazis representatives smiled to themselves and seemed happy to accompany Seamus.

He rippled with anger as he ascended the stairs to his office with the two grinning men behind him. He longed to fire them and the other Nazi workers at the forefront of the scrum on the floor.

Once in his office, Benz and Borst sat opposite Seamus with the smug grins of men who knew they were protected from on high. Their roles as heads of the Trustee Council for the factory meant they were untouchable. Only if the local Nazis deemed them untrustworthy or disloyal could they be dismissed, and that certainly wasn't the case. Seamus was sick of their sneering faces, and the sight of them almost turned his stomach, but he couldn't have this in the factory.

"What was that about?"

"The Jews have been sucking off our nation's teat for too long. People are sick and tired of cohabiting with vermin. It disgusts me that we have to share the same space as them."

"Feel free to resign anytime you want, Gunter. I'll accept it right now, if you please," Seamus said through gritted teeth.

"The murder of that poor diplomat in Paris was the last

straw," Borst said. "You need to cleanse this place of Jewish scum."

Seamus knew he had to choose his words carefully. Any misplaced sentiment or criticism of their beloved Führer could land him in a KZ. "Those people have been working alongside you and the other employees for years. I won't fire them because you don't approve of them. I've endeavored to find a way for you to share the space. I'm not asking you to spend summers together at the lake, just that you don't let your personal feelings get in the way of production. The scene on the floor today is going to cost me hours of production. I'll have to close the factory while it gets cleaned up and the machines are checked for damage. It will cost me money, and the military the bullets and shells they ordered. I won't stand for it."

"Then get rid of the Jews," Benz said. "Hire good, honest Germans and these problems will disappear."

"Or maybe I'll sell the factory, and you'll all be out of a job. How about that?"

The smile on Benz's face didn't falter. "Your cousin wouldn't let you sell."

"Try her. She could retire. She knows what you and the rest of the industry think of her as a woman in business. What I need from you is an assurance that this won't happen again."

"As long as the Jews remain here the workers will always be liable to rise up against the threat they pose," Benz said. "No assurance I give you will change that. We have our own Jewish problem here, and it's because of you."

It was clear this conversation wasn't going to solve anything. "Oh, get out," Seamus said to the two men and slumped back in his seat. He looked away as they left, not wanting to see their smug faces. Then he got to his feet and went to pour himself a whiskey.

A tap on the door followed, and Bernheim entered.

"I thought I told you to go home," said Seamus.

"Well, I came back. I had an idea. While the Jewish workers are still stuck here, let's just put them on at different times from the members of the trustee council."

"The workers still can't secure exit visas?"

"Not one. Myself included."

"Not a bad idea." Seamus offered the factory manager a crystal glass of whiskey. "I don't know how much longer we can maintain this," he said. "I feel like we're walking along a high wire, and gale force winds are blowing."

Gert gulped back his drink. "This situation is bad. The Nazis were looking for any excuse to ramp up their persecution of the Jews. I feel like something terrible was born in Paris."

Seamus poured them both another drink. The machines below were silent, nobody was working, but there were plenty of raised voices and occasional shouts of "Heil Hitler."

"I wonder what laws the Nazis are going to pass now," Gert said. "Sometimes I feel like a duck facing down the barrel of a heavy machine gun."

Gert arrived home just after six. His wife, Lil, greeted him at the door with a kiss. "Have you been drinking?"

"Yes."

"So have I."

Their grown son, Joel, was sitting at the dining room table. He stood up to hug his father. His breath smelled of the schnapps he'd been drinking at the table with his mother. Their other son, Ben, was in university in Switzerland, studying engineering.

"How was work?" Gert asked. His son had been bouncing between jobs. It was hard to be a Jew in the German work-force these days. His latest role was moving pallets in a factory.

"The manager sent us home early when the news of the Nazi diplomat in Paris came," his son answered.

Gert nodded and sat down before recounting what happened with the Jews and the Nazis in the factory earlier. Neither spoke when he finished the story. It didn't seem there was anything to say. Lil went to the kitchen and prepared dinner. Gert felt like he was being squeezed in a massive vise. The country he'd grown up in had become an open prison.

They turned on the radio as they ate dinner. Lil wanted to turn it off when Goebbels came on, but Gert insisted they listen. The minister for propaganda was speaking from Munich. He spoke of the German people's fury and how the demonstrations around the country should be allowed to go ahead. He stopped short of inciting the millions of Nazis listening to riot, but didn't tell them to stand down either. The speech was brief, and once it was over, the news reporters returned to eulogizing the diplomat in Paris once more.

"Perhaps this will all blow over in the next few days," Joel said.

Gert nodded. "I hope so."

They finished dinner in silence. After a few more drinks, Gert and Lil retired to bed. Gert was still awake when he heard his son's bedroom door closing an hour later.

The sound of shattering glass jerked him from his sleep. Lil sat up too. Gert reached for the lamp beside the bed and illuminated the bedroom. Another crash followed, and the sound of crowds of people on the street. It was almost one in the morning.

"It's happening again!" Lil screamed. It had been Fiona Ritter and her nasty little friends the last time.

"Stay here!" snapped Gert.

Someone was knocking on the front door. He got dressed and tiptoed down the stairs. Joel appeared on the landing.

"Get back in your room!" Gert hissed.

His son did as he was told.

The living room window was broken. A brick was lying in the middle of the rug with shards of glass all around it. The hammering on the door continued. Gert's hands were shaking so much that he had to place them in his pants pockets. Either he answered the door and spoke to whoever was knocking, or else they'd break it down like they'd smashed his window. His breath quickened as he began to descend. The sound of the crowd outside was audible against the thumping on the front door now. Lil was standing at the top of the stairs, crying, her son beside her. Gert kept walking. He opened the door. A crowd of about fifty was outside his house. They were holding Nazi flags, flaming torches, bricks, and clubs. This wasn't like when Seamus's daughter had come with her friends. These were their parents.

His neighbor, Herr Rostow, a quiet man he'd only spoken to a few times, stood at the door.

"Out of the house, Bernheim," Rostow said.

"What's this about? We've done nothing."

"This is about taking our country back. We're coming in. I'd advise you to be outside when that happens."

Gert looked back up the stairs at his terrified wife and son. Both were dressed. "We need to leave."

"What?" Lil said. "What are they going to do?"

Before he could answer, Rostow grabbed Gert's shoulder, and he and another man dragged him out onto the street. He shouted for Lil and Joel as the mob ran inside. Gert was hurled onto the pavement. His wife and son fled the house as one rioter punched Joel in the face, and Lil was kicked as she ran. They were thrown down beside him. Half of the crowd was inside their house now, the other half standing guard around the prostrate Bernheims. The sounds of plates and glass being smashed exploded from the house.

"Stop! Please!" Lil tried to get up and was pushed to the

ground again. Gert stood up to defend his wife and received a punch in the mouth from a boy who used to mow his lawn for money years ago.

"Don't," he said to his son as Joel threatened to square up to him. "What's the point?" Several stormtroopers in brown uniforms were among the crowd, but the vast majority were his neighbors. The mob cheered as the windows on the top floor were shattered from the inside.

The horizon was lit with fires, glowing against the cold night sky. Drowning in his powerlessness, Gert crouched again and pulled his family tight around him. He watched as his car was wrecked, the tires slashed, and windows crashed in.

"We've got to get out of here," he whispered, "while they're more focused on the house than on us."

"They might kill us if we run," Lil gasped.

"They might kill us if we stay here," Gert answered.

"I say run," whispered Joel.

Rostow returned to where the Bernheims were cowering. Many of their guards had left to join the fun, leaving only one teenage boy to watch them. Rostow directed the boy to stay where he was. "Make sure they don't run off, the cowards. The SA will have some questions for them once we're done."

The boy nodded and stood glaring at the Bernheims, as Rostow disappeared into the house. Once he was gone, the boy spoke in a whisper. "Hi Joel, remember me?"

"Dirk Ortlieb?" Joel said. "We used to play football together. I don't suppose that counts for anything now."

"Yeah, that's me. If you have somewhere you can go, now is the time."

Joel stared up at him, confused, his father's arm around him.

"What are you talking about?" Joel said.

"Knock me out, you fool," said Dirk. "Pretend to hit me!"

Gert's son stood up and punched his old friend on the side

of the head. Dirk fell to the ground, his eyes closed, but held a thumb up before continuing to play dead.

Shaking with shock, the Bernheims crept away on hands and knees. The rest of the throng seemed too busy ransacking the house to notice. Gert stood up and motioned for his wife and son to do the same. The home they'd raised their sons in was ablaze as they slipped around the corner and started walking fast.

"Where can we go?" Lil panted, with tears running down her face.

"Seamus Ritter's house is less than fifteen minutes away."

Several other groups of rioters were on the half-lit streets, their faces illuminated as ghoulish masks by the torches they carried, screaming, "Death to the Jews!" A dozen or so were approaching, shoving two Jewish men along at the front of the group.

The Bernheims stood afraid. Gert looked around. They were outside the house of Erwin Flach, a lawyer he'd spoken to a few times. The lights inside were off. "Here," he whispered.

They ducked inside the gate and hid in the dark foliage just before the mob swept past with the unfortunate Jews they'd collared.

"What are they going to do with them?" groaned Lil.

"I don't want to be around to find out."

The streets were overflowing now with a seething mob. Hundreds where dozens had been just minutes before. They were destroying the Jewish houses on the block, dragging the inhabitants onto the street, and making them watch as the rabid Nazi crowd destroyed everything they owned. The anti-Jewish chants filled the night. Many shouted Ernst vom Rath's name. Others just went with the classic, "Heil Hitler."

"Where did these people come from?" Joel said. "The Nazis must have emptied every nuthouse in Germany to form these crowds."

But these people weren't from an asylum. An orgy of insanity had taken hold of the entire city. Years of conditioning had turned those most susceptible in German society into raving lunatics.

"We have to move," Gert said. "We can cut through Herr Flach's backyard."

They were edging along the wall and around the side of the house when the lamp in the kitchen flicked on. Herr Flach appeared in a dressing gown.

"Who's there?" he called out. He was holding a shotgun.

Gert stepped out of the shadows, shrugging off his wife's desperate clinging hands, praying he could appeal to his neighbor's better nature. "It's Gert Bernheim. I'm here with my wife and son. We had to flee our house when the Nazis came to burn it down."

Flach squinted and dropped the shotgun. "I'm so sorry. This is unbelievable. I can't credit what's happened to this country."

Lil and Joel stepped out.

"I can't take you in," Flach said. "My son's out with the crazies, burning and looting. He could come back anytime."

"We'll be on our way, then," Gert said.

"Wait, do you have somewhere to go?"

"A friend's house, about two miles away."

"A difficult journey on a night like this. Wait here," Flach said and disappeared inside. Two tense minutes passed before the lawyer returned wearing a coat and hat. "Come on," he said. "I'll give you a ride."

His black Mercedes was sitting on the gravel driveway. He held the back door open for Lil and Joel before covering them with dark blankets. "Herr Bernheim, you'll have to ride in front with me. If anyone stops us, say you're my brother from out of town."

Gert nodded and got in the front seat. Flach started the car, and they pulled out onto the street. The throng of rioters had dissipated somewhat, but several dozen people were still wandering around with Nazi flags, tossing stones through the windows of burning Jewish houses. Most disturbing of all were the Hitler Youth and League of German Girls cadets. They were now among the crowd, dressed in neat uniforms, spewing vitriol in perfect synchronicity. It was as if this was the moment they'd been training for all these years.

10

Thursday, November 10

Fiona was asleep when she heard the stone strike her window. Bleary-eyed, she raised herself to the curtain and drew it back. It was after two in the morning. It seemed much had changed in the five hours she'd been in bed. Harald, his best friend, Georg, and her best friends Amalia and Inge were in her front yard by her father's car. They waved as she came to the window, gesturing for her to come down. All were dressed in uniform save for Harald. Fiona opened the window.

"What's going on?" she called down in a shrill whisper. Whatever was happening, it wouldn't pay to wake her father at this time of night.

"The people are rising up," Harald said. "They're sick and tired of the Jewish menace and it's time to make them pay."

"Everyone's out," Inge said. "Come down and join us."

"What are they doing—?"

"This is history," Harald said. "Don't be the only one to miss out on it."

Fiona hesitated a few seconds. Her experience at the border flickered through her mind. Both tattered and well-dressed Jewish children playing in the mud. Below, her friends stood waiting. Somehow her decision felt important. It was as if this one moment would make her who she was meant to be. She picked her League uniform off the hanger in her closet and touched the portrait of Adolf Hitler on her wall. Used to sneaking downstairs, she barely made a sound. Her friends greeted her with excited hugs.

Amalia jumped up and down as she hugged her.

Harald took her aside once they were on the street. "Are we okay? I'm still so sorry for what I did the other night. Do you forgive me?"

"You need to be good from now on," she said with half a smile.

"I swear on my allegiance to the Führer, I'll never disrespect you like that again."

"You'd better not."

He reached down and pecked her on the lips.

"There'll be plenty of time for that later, lovebirds," Georg said. "We have important business to take care of."

"Where are we going?" Fiona said. The excitement racing through her was undeniable. Whatever this was, she was part of it.

"To the synagogue on Franklin Strasse," Georg said. "The whole troop is there."

"What are they doing at a synagogue?"

"You really don't have any idea what's going on, do you?" Amalia said, laughing. "Such a sleepyhead!"

Harald put his finger to his lips. "Let her figure it out for herself. It'll be a surprise."

The mansion behind her was dark. Her father and brother were still asleep, but the night was alive on the street. The skyline was glowing, and she could hear the faint chant of a thousand Nazi voices.

"Time to run," Georg said.

They were all supremely fit—the products of countless hours of physical conditioning to transform them into the ideal Aryans. None of them stopped for two miles.

The first sign of what was happening that Fiona saw was a house being ransacked by a mob of Hitler Youth. The Jewish occupants were on their knees outside as their house was torn to pieces by the angry throng.

"This is revenge for vom Rath, for losing the war, and for everything the Jewish scum did to the people of this country," Harald said and smiled at her without breaking stride.

The further they made it toward the center of the city, the thicker the mob became, and soon they were zig-zagging between hundreds, if not thousands, of furious rioters. Every Jewish store was destroyed. The windows were smashed, and the people flooded through to pillage and loot. She saw dozens of Jews dragged onto the street, kicked, and beaten. Were the Bernheims involved in this? With little time to think, she pushed her treacherous worried thoughts aside.

The five of them only stopped running as they reached the synagogue. A multitude of perhaps four or five hundred Hitler Youth and League of German Girls had gathered there along with the same number of ordinary citizens. It was difficult to hear with all the shouting and chanting, but no one needed to tell Fiona what was about to happen. The synagogue, which Fiona had passed by thousands of times on her way to school, was an elegant old building that had stood for three hundred years. Tonight, that history would end.

At least 20 Hitler Youth were bashing on the locked doors with bricks. The boys joined a group watching a burly SA man chopping down a wooden lamppost with an ax. Several other Hitler Youth helped pull the thick wooden pole down, and the crowd cheered as they held it aloft. Then the boys used it as a battering ram against the wide wooden doors and, within a few seconds, had smashed them in, to the bloodthirsty screams of the mob.

Howling youngsters from the Hitler Youth and League of German Girls streamed through the smashed doors like water through a broken hull. Fiona and her friends surged forward with them to witness the orgy of destruction that ensued. Dozens of young Nazis descended upon the interior like locusts, ripping up seats and pulling woodwork down. The synagogue was destroyed in minutes.

Fiona saw Harald at the head of the sacred building urinating on torn scrolls before another laughing Hitler Youth set those still dry alight. A bonfire of broken wood and scrolls was raised in the middle of the synagogue. It was soon aflame, and the throng ebbed backward out of the building, away from the heat. Amalia and Inge found Fiona, grasping her arms as they watched the place of worship burn. Several Jews were led in front of the mob and, bloodied and beaten, were made to kneel down with their hands on their heads and watch the scene.

The sound of fire engines cut through the cacophony of shouting and anti-Jewish song. Some of the crowd booed as the firefighters jumped off the trucks, but they needn't have worried. The firemen merely stood with the crowd watching the flames build. Curious about what was going on, Fiona pushed through the mass of people until she reached a firefighter.

"What are you doing?" she shouted so he could hear.

"We're here to make sure the fire doesn't spread to German buildings." The firefighter, a young man of about 21, shook his head. "We tried putting out a blaze at a Jewish store a few blocks away. A few of the men were beaten up for their trouble. That's when the orders to let the fires burn came through."

"Your superiors told you to let the flames go?"

The man looked at her but didn't answer, instead turning his eyes back toward the blaze.

Bewildered, Fiona returned to her friends, who were cheering and singing with the rest of the crowd.

"What's wrong?" Harald asked. His face, illuminated by the flickering flames of the synagogue, seemed robbed of all its inherent handsomeness. For the first time, he appeared ugly.

"Nothing. It was a fine old building—that's all. I knew it so well."

"It was a symbol of the oppression the Jews have been subjecting us to for generations. And without their synagogues they won't have anywhere to practice that pig Latin religion of theirs."

They watched the synagogue burn for another thirty minutes, but the Hitler Youth soon began thirsting for other Jewish targets. Their latent rage had been unleashed and had to be spent somewhere.

Much of Harald's old Hitler Youth troop was here; they were jogging toward some of the Jewish stores which had escaped the carnage.

"Come on!" Harald cried, beckoning the girls and Georg to follow him.

The boys and girls ahead of them picked up cinder blocks and tossed them through the store windows. Harald and Georg ran inside one store and dragged out a Jewish man with a long beard. He must have been forty years older than the two boys who punched and kicked him as the rest of the mob looted his store. Amalia and Inge were among those who ran inside. Fiona followed them as they filled their pockets with candy from the counter and then ran out, delighted with themselves.

The Jewish owner of the store was lying face down on the ground outside. Fiona stopped and peered down at him. His eyes were open, but he was still.

Amalia pulled at her arm. "More to do. So much more," she shouted.

Fiona was in a daze. She thought of everything her instructors had told her. The Jews were Germany's misfortune. They were to blame for all of Europe's wars and were the reason Germany was defeated in 1918. Somehow, they'd never fully explained why.

Fiona thought of her sister. Would Maureen ever speak to her again if she saw her subsumed by the madness of this crowd? Fiona felt like she was being swept away in a great tsunami of hate. And, perhaps unlike her friends, she was drowning.

She thought of Harald attacking the man in the park and how he said it was to protect her. Did he genuinely believe that? Did he think his actions were protecting her now from the Jews? The incident in the park...the children at the border...

Still, she followed the group. Breaking away was too difficult. How could she leave? All her friends, instructors, and future husband were there. The crowd screamed like the banshees her Irish mother had told her about when she was a child. Except this was all too real.

Harald took her by the hand, dragging her along. They ran for another mile or so with a group of several hundred. This gang was different. Most of the Hitler Youth had stayed behind at the Jewish stores. This one was dominated by young women. Harald and Georg were some of the only boys.

Fiona tugged her fingers out of Harald's grip as they arrived at their destination. Her palm was stained red from holding his hand, and there was more blood on her shirt. They had arrived at a hospital for Jewish children.

"Are we going to demonstrate here?" Fiona asked Amalia, puzzled.

"The time for demonstrating is over."

One of Fiona's League instructors took a brick and threw it

through a window. Amalia threw one next, and then Inge. All the windows were broken in two minutes, and Harald and Georg joined the older girls to bash the doors in. The rioters disappeared inside. Fiona stood on the street, a slow oozing horror transfixing her to the spot. Amalia appeared a few seconds later, pushing a child, who couldn't have been more than eight, across broken glass onto the street. The little boy was dressed only in a nightshirt and had tears streaming down his face. He collapsed on the road as Amalia ran back inside for more. A dozen girls emerged, kicking the patients or pulling them by the hair. All were sick young children.

Fiona wanted to step forward, to do something—but what? She held still.

The Jewish doctors and nurses were next. The mob descended upon them as they were brought out and kicked and punched until their faces were bruised and swollen. All were made to sit with the patients as the hospital was set alight. One of her best instructors, a 19-year-old called Hannelore Berben, kicked a crouching nurse in the face and turned to accept the crowd's adulation.

The small hospital glowed orange as the flames consumed it. Harald returned to Fiona and took her by the hand again as if this were some magnificent sight to behold. Many of the children who'd been asleep inside were in the arms of the doctors and nurses who had been beaten by the crowd. Others were lying still on the side of the road.

"At last," Harald said, trying to kiss her.

Fiona pushed him away. Something within her had broken.

"I can't stay here," she said. "These are children."

Harald shook his head as if she were an errant child. "I know what you're thinking, but it's in their blood. All Jews are equally guilty. They're all enemies of everything we hold dear. That's why Hitler says we have to be strong and steadfast."

But Fiona was done listening.

She walked away.

"Fiona, come back!" shouted Harald. "Hey, where are you going?"

Ignoring his calls, she ran past the looted Jewish stores and dead bodies. The massive crowd outside the synagogue was singing the national anthem as she ran past, but she didn't stop. She felt in danger of drowning in the horrific tidal wave of evil unleashed that night. The mobs were still surging through the streets. Their work wasn't done yet. Fiona had the feeling that it was only just beginning.

It was after three in the morning when Seamus shot up in his bed like a bolt. A distant scream had woken him, and he got out of bed and went to the window. The city was glowing in the distance. What was going on? Had the war started? He jumped out of bed and ran to Conor's room. The young boy woke as he opened the door and asked what was happening. Seamus told him to go back to sleep and continued to Fiona's bedroom.

A horrible mix of fear and anger overtook him as he saw the empty bed. He looked out her window. A handful of young people were running down the center of the street outside, waving a Nazi flag and singing a song calling for Jewish blood on the knives of the Hitler Youth. It was beginning. The pogrom to end all was underway.

Conor was at the door of the bedroom as he turned around. "What's happening? Where's Fiona?"

"I don't know. Come with me."

The two ran downstairs, and Seamus flicked on the radio. He tuned in to the official government news channel. The broadcaster was reporting from Munich, where a mob of thousands was ransacking synagogues and Jewish businesses. It seemed every major and minor city in Germany was a swirling mess of anti-Jewish rage. The newscaster mentioned uprisings in Bonn, Dusseldorf, Essen, Frankfurt, and Hamburg. He noted with pride that it wasn't the SA or the SS who'd driven this movement. It was the people. He called it the natural result of Jewish aggression.

"Some of my friends were talking about this after we played football this evening," Conor said.

"About what?"

"Vengeance for the diplomat in Paris."

"This is the natural result of years of Jewish abuse, and like the dog that's been beaten too many times, the German people have bitten back," the newscaster said.

"What do we do about Fiona?" Conor asked. "It sounds dangerous out there."

Seamus was having the same thoughts himself. His instinct told him to search for his daughter, but who knew where she was in this melee of hatred? The Hitler Youth and League of German Girls had spread across the city, infecting it like a virus. She could be anywhere, and what if he did find her? What could he say to make her come home? She was one of the mob now. Images of her throwing bricks through windows haunted his mind.

"You stay here. I'm going to look outside. Maybe she's close by."

"What about the Bernheims and the rest of the Jewish families from the factory?" Conor asked.

"I don't know, but we can't save everyone."

His heart felt like a stone in his chest. The thought of the Bernheims being dragged out and beaten was like a dagger in his heart.

"I'm coming too," Conor said.

"No, you're not. I need you to stay here in case your sister comes home." It felt like Conor was all he had left, and Seamus knew giving his son a job would keep him happy and safe. "She might not stay if the house is empty." He hugged his son, put on his coat and hat, said goodbye, and stepped out into the night. The street in his affluent neighborhood was quiet, but the pockets of flame in the city were glowing against the night sky. Some lights were on in his neighbors' houses, but it seemed most had decided to stay out of the pogrom taking place under their noses. A torn Nazi flag lay discarded on the street. Seamus stepped over it, wracking his brain as to where his daughter might be. The grisly thought that she might be at the Jewish-owned houses and businesses near where Gert Bernheim lived almost made his stomach turn, but he started in that direction.

One of the houses on the next street was ablaze. A mob of about fifty, mainly Hitler Youth, was standing outside, cheering and chanting as the fire consumed the mansion. A Jewish man, his wife, and their three small children were kneeling on the street in their nightclothes.

Seamus joined the crowd, searching for Fiona or someone who knew her. He recognized some of his neighbors among the group—the most ardent Nazis in Charlottenburg. He approached a man he'd met in the park a few times, managing to remember his name just as he reached him.

"Otto?" Seamus said and extended a hand to his neighbor.

The middle-aged man turned to him with a ghoulish smile. "Oh, yes, our American friend. I didn't expect to see you here. Come to see the Jews get their comeuppance at last?"

Seamus circumvented the question. "I'm looking for my seventeen-year-old. You know her? Fiona? Your daughter Amalia knows her, I think."

"Ah, yes, the German youth are having a field day tonight, aren't they? Who knows where our daughters are, my friend," Otto said and put a hand on Seamus's shoulder. "Wherever they are, I'm sure they're doing the Führer's good work."

"What about them?" Seamus said and pointed to the Jewish family.

"Word is that we have to keep them captive until the SA come," replied Otto.

"What then?"

"I'm not sure. Someone said they're taking the men away."

"To where?"

"I'm not privy to that information. We just have to trust in the government, don't we? They haven't steered us wrong yet."

Seamus stared at the helpless Jewish father. It was hard to imagine how the man must feel as he knelt there, powerless to defend his family.

"What's his name?"

"Greenberg," Otto sneered. "He used to swan around like he owned the city. Not so clever now, is he?"

"If you see Fiona, send her home."

"She'll come back when the night's work is done. Don't worry about our girls. They're safer tonight then they've been in years."

Unable to stomach being near this man anymore, Seamus nodded and walked away. The crowd started singing, "arise Hitler's men. Close ranks, for we are ready for the racial struggle!"

He jogged away; his breath ragged in his throat. It had been easy to pretend these last six years, but the notion that the Nazis didn't mean what they said was entirely dispelled now. Their methods were just as brutal as their words. Hitler had never tried to hide it. It was all there in what he said and what he wrote. This was the natural progression in their plan, and things would likely only get worse. The cancer of National Socialism wasn't going to stop here. The Nazis wouldn't be satisfied with burning down Jewish houses and places of business. They wouldn't stop until every Jew was eradicated, one way or the other. Seamus could see everything clearly now. No mansion or fat bank account was worth being here. Better they were poor and back living with his sister in Newark than rich in Germany.

The façade of Nazi civility had been broken. No one could deny their savagery now. Anyone who supported the National Socialist cause supported these actions also. Living here would be impossible now, no matter what Bill Hayden said. Someone else could report back to the State Department with munitions reports. What use were they, anyway? Everyone knew the Nazi army was armed to the teeth now. Arms manufacturing here dwarfed that of the United States and all their allies. What were they waiting for? Perhaps this night would open their eyes to the very real threat the Nazis posed not just to their own population, but to the rest of the world.

The local Jewish grocery store was gutted, and the plate glass window shattered. The mob had departed, looking for new targets. Seamus began running. The trail of selective carnage continued as he came to several Jewish-owned businesses next to one another. Several were ablaze. A fire engine was parked opposite, the firefighters standing in silence, watching the flames.

Seamus heard the mob before he saw it. It was about two hundred strong, evenly divided between regular citizens and Hitler Youth. He searched once more for the League uniform Fiona was sure to be wearing. He found a dozen or more girls wearing it, but none were his daughter. Seamus stood back to watch the crowd looting a Jewish department store. Rioters emerged through shattered windows like raccoons, with fur coats draped over their shoulders and carrying new suits and shirts by the boxload.

A Jewish woman lay face down outside the store.

Realizing he'd never find Fiona, Seamus decided to check on Gert Bernheim. A sudden fear overcame him, and he had to see Gert and his family just to know they were safe. Their home was only a few blocks away, and he quickened his pace to a sprint.

~

Flach slowed the car as they approached the rioters gathered at the end of the street. Gert looked around, but the other way was even worse. The crowd behind them must have numbered hundreds. The one in front was sparse, just a few stone-throwing Hitler Youth. What remained of their old house came into view. The group of Nazi thugs who'd ransacked it had dispersed. Only a few stragglers watched the flames licking at the stone structure. A tear rolled down Gert's face as he saw what they'd done to the home he'd lived in for half his life. His neighbors' latent hatred had been unleashed.

"Keep quiet in the back," Flach said, even though neither Lil nor Joel had made a sound.

Gert turned his head to stare at his burning house, bright against the dark of the night. He was glad his wife and son couldn't see it.

Flach drove on in silence but cursed out loud as they turned the next corner. A small crowd of Hitler Youth had set up what seemed to be a roadblock from furniture looted from Jewish houses. Flach stopped the car fifty paces short.

"What do we do now?" Gert said.

"What's going on?" Lil said from the back seat.

"Roadblock. Stay down," Flach said. "Let's try the other way," he said and reversed the car. But the Hitler Youth manning the checkpoint had noticed and swarmed toward the vehicle.

Flach swore and pressed down on the accelerator. The back of the car collided with a lamppost. Several Hitler Youth boys were at the windows as he tried to drive away.

"Father?" one of the boys shouted.

Another jumped on the bonnet. "I can't go any further. I'm sorry." The car came to a halt.

One of the boys opened the passenger door and hauled Gert onto the street.

"Look, boys, it seems like this Jewish rat was trying to jump ship."

Someone punched Gert in the face and his legs buckled beneath him. The boys were questioning Flach as two men in their twenties dragged Lil and Joel out of the back. The Nazi thugs punched and kicked them before throwing them to the ground.

Flach's son was shouting at his father and finished the lecture by slapping him across the face. The lawyer responded by punching his son in the eye. Two Hitler Youth grabbed Flach. One of the older boys, a curly-haired thug who looked about twenty, went to Flach's son, who was holding his face, before approaching Gert, kneeling on the road.

"Don't hurt my wife and son," Gert said. "Do what you will with me."

Joel rose to his feet and hit the Nazi closest to him, but three of them were on him in seconds, punching and kicking him until he collapsed back onto the asphalt. Lil screamed, but the Hitler Youth seemed amused all the more.

"I think we need to make an example of these filthy rats. What's the only thing to be done with vermin?" the curly-haired boy asked.

"Exterminate them," came the response from Flach's son.

The curly-haired thug drew a pistol from his waistband and held it to Joel's head.

"No!" Gert roared. "Me! Kill me!"

"The father-rat wants to save the baby-rat!" the young Nazi joked. "Have it your way, then," he said and stepped over to Gert. He held the pistol in front of his face. Gert stared up at him. The Nazi opened his mouth to say something, but the sound of footsteps distracted him. He turned as a running man tackled him, knocking him over. The gun spilled from his hand as his head hit the pavement, and Gert took his chance and lunged for the weapon. He reached it just before one of the other thugs. He backed up, pointing it at the rioters.

"Let that man go, and don't move!" Gert yelled and cocked the hammer. "Get behind me," he said to Lil and Joel.

"What took you so long?" he said to Seamus, who was climbing off the unconscious youth he had knocked to the ground.

"I'm not as young as I used to be," Seamus said and came to stand by his friend.

"Are you all right?" Gert shouted over to Flach, who had been released.

The lawyer nodded, his face red. He didn't glance at his son on the ground. "Let's get back in the car."

"Where are you going to run?" the curly-haired rioter shouted at them. "We're all over this city."

Gert sat in the passenger seat, pointing the weapon out the window as Flach reversed away. Lil, Joel, and Seamus sat in the back. A few of the boys threw bricks as the car accelerated down the street, but they fell short.

"Thanks," Gert said and put the gun in his pocket. He looked at Seamus over his shoulder. "Where did you come from?"

"I was looking for Fiona."

Another mob was marauding through the neighborhood ahead. Hundreds poured toward them, blocking the street.

"Let's get out of here. We can reach my street through that alley," Seamus suggested.

The lawyer parked beside the passage.

Gert turned to him, 'I can't thank you enough."

"What, for raising a Nazi son?" Flach's face was tense with anger. "Now, go! Go!"

"What about you?" Seamus asked.

"I'll be fine. If worse comes to worst, I'll lock myself in the basement, but they won't bother with me. They have other things on their minds tonight."

"Thank you," Gert said. The four jumped out of the car and ran up the alleyway between the houses. They saw no one and reached the other end in about thirty seconds.

"What now?" Lil said.

"Through there," Seamus said, pointing to the mansion across the street. "The back garden's massive. We can cut through it to my street."

Gert had a moment to think as he ran after Seamus with his wife and son. He'd committed no crime and had served Germany in the last war, yet he was a fugitive, fighting for his life in the only city he'd ever called home. None of it made any sense. Berlin had become a terrifying, alien place.

Joel leaped over the wooden gate and opened it for Seamus and his parents. The house was dark. It had a manicured Japanese-style backyard with a stone fountain in the center. Who knew how the owners would react if they caught Jews escaping through their backyard? Perhaps they'd help them. Maybe they'd run out to call the nearest horde of Nazis.

They helped each other over the back wall and crept through another, smaller backyard before slipping around the house to the front. With no Nazi mobs in sight, they ran head-long to the end of the street. They were all panting as the Ritter mansion appeared like an oasis in the desert.

Seamus ran up with his key, and a moment later, they were inside with the door closed against the night. The relief brought tears to Gert's eyes. He took his wife and son in his arms and held them. "Thank you," Lil whispered to Seamus.

He answered with a nod before hugging Conor, who had come to the foyer to greet them. The radio was on in the room behind him, blaring out news of other riots around the country.

"It's everywhere in Germany," Lil said as they entered the living room. "There's nowhere to run."

"We have to run," Gert said. "Our house is gone. Burned to the ground by our neighbors. I don't see any other option."

"But how?" Lil said. "Even if we could get the exit visa, every Jew in Germany has applied to the US embassy. They're not budging. The Americans don't want us any more than the Nazis do. At least Hitler and his lot are honest in their intentions."

"I don't know, but this can't go on," Gert said. "I have to tender my resignation, Seamus."

"I'll be sorry to see you go, but I don't see how you can stay in Berlin any longer after tonight."

"The entire country's been overrun by Nazi beasts," Lil said. "Maybe some people don't agree with them, but what does that matter when no one speaks up?"

"They know they'd end up in KZ if they did," Joel said.

Conor listened in silence, his eyes wide.

They collapsed into armchairs, talking for another hour, always ending up with the same conundrum. They had to get out of the country, but how? They couldn't get permission to leave, and nowhere would accept them. Entering Switzerland or France illegally meant they could be deported to the Reich. Surviving in hiding in a foreign country would be difficult. But so would staying here, and they all dreaded to think what would happen if the mob found them.

Seamus thought about Herr Greenberg and his family. His brain was tired, and his heart was sick. He had to come up with something.

Later, after he had sent his guests off to bed in Maureen and Michael's old rooms, he sat at the table with a cup of the weak, mud-flavored coffee that was the norm in Germany now, waiting for his daughter to come home.

He had little idea of what he'd say once she did, but he just wanted to hold her one last time. She'd never agree to leave

Germany. He looked around the darkened mansion he'd lived in since his uncle died. He missed his wife desperately, and this was no place to live and raise children. Not anymore.

"Better to live free in a hovel than in a gilded cage," he said out loud.

The sound of the front door opening roused him from his seat. Fiona was crying, and his first instinct was to run to her. He stopped a few feet short. His daughter looked up at him, red-faced, her cheeks glistening. Her League of German Girls uniform was blackened and torn.

"They dragged the children out onto the street," she said between gasping sobs. "Sick children. They cut their feet on the broken glass."

Seamus stepped forward and held her against him as her tears wet his shirt.

11

Thursday, November 10

Fiona woke from a troubled sleep. She climbed out of bed and went to her bedroom window. The sun was high in the sky. A few puffs of smoke were still visible over the roofs of her expensive neighborhood, rising from the ruins of what, until yesterday, had been a vibrant, wonderful city. It was a Thursday, but she doubted many businesses were open. The decent citizens of Germany were likely in deep shock from last night's events. What must the Jews have been feeling?

Her uniform was still on the floor where she'd thrown it. The portrait of the Führer stared at her with beady eyes from the wall. The previous night flashed before her eyes as if she were in a waking dream. The broken glass, the burning synagogues, the dead bodies on the street, and the sick Jewish children ripped from their hospital beds. The memories seemed to infect her like a disease, and a feeling of nausea settled in her stomach. How could she face Harald and the others again? His eyes. She saw the blood lust in his eyes as if he were standing in front of her. His soul was gone—surrendered to the Nazis.

"Is that what you wanted all this time?" she asked the picture of Hitler on her wall, speaking in English. "Was all your talk of elevating the Aryan race just so we could subjugate others? What is it about those people that terrifies you so much?"

She tore the portrait off the wall—an offense that could land her in jail.

Second thoughts poured into her mind. Maybe the previous night was the work of a few over-excited zealots. Things would settle down again. The Jews would be given safe passage from Germany, and the National Socialist Party could continue the work of rebuilding Germany after the shame of the last 20 years.

But then she remembered the firemen as they stood idly watching the synagogue burn. They'd received official orders not to extinguish the fires. And what about the police? Where had they been? The destruction of everything Jewish had been a deliberate policy. What had those dead shopkeepers, with their blood staining the sidewalk, done to deserve their fate? No League of German Girls troop leader could explain that. What crime had they committed aside from being born Jewish? Why them? What was the Nazi obsession with Jewish people? Herr Bernheim and his family were good people. She knew that now. She was glad they were here, safe in this house.

Fiona remembered Helga's speech when the Hitler Youth boys shouted her down because she was a successful woman. What were they so afraid of? Jews. Independent women. Why were the Nazis so petrified of people who didn't fit their mold?

Her head was spinning, and she sat in the desk chair by the window. The street outside was quiet. All seemed normal, but beneath the façade, everything had changed. Her thoughts turned to the victims. Who knew how many had died or how

many Jewish women had been violated? And the children. A
deep shame enveloped her like a cloak as she thought of the
sick boys and girls dragged onto the street and forced to watch
the doctors and nurses who cared for them being beaten black
and blue. She wondered where they were now. Who would take
care of them now that the hospital was a burnt-out shell?

Nothing about what she'd seen was justified or noble. It was
cowardly and nauseating. The image she'd harbored in her
mind these past few years of the brave German warriors
fighting for the rights of all Reich citizens had been obliterated
by the orgy of racial hatred and hysteria that seemed to infect
thousands of citizens.

She recalled hundreds of League meetings where their
instructors hammered the notion that the Jews were evil into
impressionable minds. Fiona had never reasonably believed
that the instructors were being literal with their words. She and
the other girls presumed that the emphasis on hating people
you'd never met was a cautionary tale and not meant to be
taken literally. How could a sophisticated, brilliant organization
like the National Socialist Party become so preoccupied with a
tiny percentage of German society? And how exactly did the
Jews lose the last war for Germany when so many of them
fought and died along with their Christian comrades? Perhaps
she needed to ask one of her instructors...

No.

She had trusted her leaders above everyone else but then
witnessed Hannelore Berben kick a nurse in the face before
turning to the crowd with her arms open, drinking in their
adulation.

The riot resulted from years of incitement by the leadership
of the Hitler Youth and League of German Girls. At least 20% of
the hooligans pillaging the city had been in the uniform of the
Nazi youth organizations. The average age of the rioters she
saw was likely less than 25. Although incited by white men in

their forties and fifties, this movement was driven by youth and by girls as much as boys. It had been League of German Girls members who'd destroyed the hospital. It was hard to imagine women being so callous, yet she'd seen it with her own eyes.

Her heart was broken. Harald, her troop leaders, her friends. Everyone she loved and trusted had indulged in the horror with smiles on their faces. She had washed her hands last night, over and over, and her shirt as well. She took it and held it up against the dull sunlight. The bloodstain Harald had left on it was still visible. A tear fell from her eye.

Voices rose up through the floorboards. She dressed in a smart pair of pants and a blouse. Her uniform was discarded, never to be worn again. She opened her bedroom door and descended the stairs. Herr Bernheim, Frau Bernheim, and their son, Joel, were sitting at the dining room table with doleful, lost faces.

Here they were: the Jewish vermin, in her own house. What would her instructors want of her now? To attack them? To berate them?

They looked at her as if they didn't know how to greet her.

Her father stood up. "Are you all right?"

She nodded. "Fine."

"Gert, Lil and Joel are going to be staying with us for a while."

"Did the mob come?" she asked them.

Lil nodded, lowering her eyes. Herr Bernheim turned his head away.

She so wanted them both to look at her. "I'm so sorry," she said. "I was there last night. My friends threw bricks and burned down the synagogue."

Her father came and put his arms around her, but she pushed him off. "I didn't do anything to stop what they were doing. I just stood back and watched as they...." She lost her words in a haze of sorrow.

Her father again tried to hug her, but again she didn't let him. "I saw my friends and the man I love act like the beasts they professed the Jews to be. They turned into exactly what the teachers and troop leaders were warning against all these years."

She went to stand at the table beside Lil. To her amazement, the older woman reached out and touched her hand. The surge of warmth Fiona felt from it shocked her.

"I'm so sorry for tossing that brick through your window. And for lying when you saw me. I did that, and I hope you can accept my apology."

Lil kept her hand on Fiona's, but said nothing.

"I was so wrong," Fiona continued. "I can't believe what happened. I just—"

She began to feel dizzy, and this time her father took her by the arms and led her into the kitchen.

"Are you all right?" he asked. It seemed like he'd had the same concern on his face every time he'd spoken to her these last three years or so.

"Yes, I'm fine," she said and sat at the table.

He brought her a plate of bread and cheese and sat with her, saying little as she wolfed it down.

"I'm glad the Bernheims are here," she said. "Is their house..."

"Destroyed? Yes. But it could have been so much worse. They were some of the lucky ones."

"How many do you think the hooligans murdered last night?"

"I have no idea," her father said. "But I saw several dead."

"Can you take me out? I want to see something with you."

"Of course. I think it's safe now. Where do you want to go?"

She finished the food on her plate. "I need to make sure last night wasn't some horrible dream."

Seamus left Conor instructions to say he was alone in the

house if anyone called, then Fiona and her father walked out to the car together. The streets were still a mess of litter and broken glass, and her father had to swerve to avoid broken bollards tossed out into the road.

They drove past the Greenbergs' house. Every window was smashed in, and the front door was gone.

"I met Amalia's father here last night. He was part of the mob. Herr Greenberg and his family were kneeling there," he said, pointing to an empty spot on the sidewalk.

The entire city felt like a crime scene. They drove on, past Nazi flags extended from windows that weren't flying the day before. It seemed last night had brought out a rush of patriotic fervor. Or at least the display of it.

The Jewish stores were devastated. Looted and destroyed. The glass windows on which the SA and Hitler Youth had taken such pains to paint the star of David were all smashed.

"Pull the car over," Fiona said.

Her father did as she asked.

A Jewish man was outside his store sweeping up the shards of broken glass left by the mob. Fiona stepped out of the car, but felt too ashamed to speak. He glanced at her as if expecting her to launch a tirade of insults.

"I'm sorry," she said as he turned away.

"So am I," he answered without taking his eyes off the pavement he was sweeping. "My family ran this store for fifty years. All gone now."

He picked up a large dustpan and swept in the glass. Fiona turned around and returned to the car with nothing left to say.

The Bernheims' house was a blackened wreck. Thick smoke plumed into the air from inside. As at the Greenbergs', the front door was gone, and all the windows smashed.

"Do you think we can salvage anything for them?" Fiona said.

"Let's find out."

They entered the house together. It had been systematically destroyed from within. Whatever the fire hadn't consumed had been torn apart by the rioters, who seemed to have attacked everything breakable with hammers or scissors. Every stick of furniture was smashed, and every piece of clothing was ripped. The pictures on the wall had been torn down and stamped on. It was as if the mob had tried to erase every sign the Bernheim family had ever lived here.

Nothing salvageable remained.

Fiona wanted to see more and directed him to the synagogue on Franklin Strasse. He didn't ask her why—he just agreed to her request. They drove in silence for most of the time.

She knew what they'd find. For some reason, she had to see it again. The synagogue, which had stood for hundreds of years, and which she'd passed a thousand times, was destroyed. Seamus parked, and they walked to the entrance through a small group of people standing outside with shocked faces. The doors, battered in by the rioters the night before, were gone, swallowed up by the fire which had consumed the rest of the building. The roof had collapsed, and the inside was a charred, smoking mess. A fire engine still sat outside, but no water had been pumped into this building. It had been allowed burn.

A firefighter approached Fiona as she tried to step inside, warning her of the dangers inherent in such a stupid act. Not in the mood to argue, she returned to the sidewalk with the other concerned citizens. The night's crimes were all too obvious in the light of day. Without the cloak of darkness to hide behind, the acts of the rioters were plain to see for the insane and callous deeds they were. Fiona felt like a curtain had been raised in her brain. What was all this for? What kind of a country could sanction something this cruel?

"I recently spoke to a business associate who met Herschel Grynszpan in Paris," her father said as they returned to the car.

Fiona was shocked. "They met the assassin? The man who started all this?"

"Did he start it? I'm not condoning the murder he committed, but did his act warrant this? Seems to me the rioters were waiting for an excuse."

"I still don't understand how your colleague knew him." A frightening thought struck her. "Did they help him?"

"Not to commit murder, no. The opposite. Herschel Grynszpan wanted to save his family. They're in the refugee camp in Zbaszyn. He wanted someone to help his parents and his little brother and sister, who are trapped there. I wasn't able to do more than give them money. That's probably why he did what he did. He likely thought if he murdered someone important, it would attract the world's attention, and some country would step in to save his family. If you like, Fiona, I am the cause of all this, for my failure to save his family."

"It's not your fault. And you're right—this was a long time coming." She was thinking about the last place she'd been to the previous night. It seemed like too much to take. The wails of the sick children were still ringing in her ears. But she'd closed her eyes to who the Nazis were for too long. "We have one more stop," she said.

She directed him along the streets she'd run down the night before. The road was blocked off, so he parked, and they walked the last block. Careful not to say anything out loud on the street, she didn't ask her father what he must have thought of her for going along with all this the night before. It was amazing that he was even here with her. The fact that he'd kept his anger with her in check was incredible.

The tears she'd expected upon seeing the burned-out children's hospital and the blood-stained pavement outside didn't come. She stood with gritted teeth as she beheld the scene, her fists balled by her side.

"This was a children's hospital," she said. "They brought the little kids outside and beat up the doctors and nurses taking care of them."

Her father hung his head. "I can't live in this country anymore," he said. "And I won't leave without you."

Fiona didn't respond, just walked forward to the doorway. She felt the indentations where the doors had been ripped out of their hinges. "I wonder what happened to the children," she said. Her voice was thick with grief and anger.

"I hope other hospitals took them in."

They stood at the entrance to the wrecked building for a few more silent moments before he took her by the hand and led her away.

They were in the car, driving back toward the house when she spoke again. "I can't go back to the League again. I saw what those words they spew mean. I thought I was like them, but I'm not."

Her father reached across and put his hand on hers. He had tears in his eyes. It seemed like the first time since her mother died. Or maybe it was just the first time she'd been paying attention enough to notice. "I'm here for you," he said.

They drove home.

"Are you okay with Gert, Lil, and Joel, staying with us for a while?" her father said as they arrived back at the house.

"Yes. I just hope they can forgive me."

"Forgiveness is something that has to be earned some-times," he said, and got out of the car.

Herr Bernheim was listening to the radio in the living room with his wife. They looked up with nervous eyes as Fiona and her father came in. Herr Bernheim seemed to cut off their conversation when they saw Fiona as if they were wary of speaking in front of her. It was hard to blame them. Joel walked in with a glass of water and eyed Fiona as if she were a spy among them.

"We drove around to your house," Fiona's father said.

"Was there anything left?" Lil asked.

He shook his head.

Fiona felt like a usurper among them, so she plodded upstairs to her room. Her father caught her by the arm as she mounted the stairs. "Can we talk later?"

She nodded and continued up to her room.

Fiona felt her father couldn't understand what had happened to her. He hadn't sat through hundreds of hours of speeches about the wonder and majesty of the Nazis and the danger that the Jews posed to civilized society. If only she could speak to Maureen or even Michael—someone who'd lived through what she'd seen. Her mind was tired from all the speeches and rhetoric these past six years. She'd been living with Nazi propaganda since she was eleven. She'd attended hundreds of meetings asserting that Hitler and his ideas were the only reasonable path for Germany to take. They'd always insisted that youth was paramount to the future of the Reich. Without them, the revolution would surely fail, and the Communist hordes from the east would overrun the entire country and subjugate the population. Her entire belief system had been turned upside down. Every pillar in her life had collapsed, and nothing was left to prop her up.

A knock on the door interrupted her thoughts. Conor pushed it open once she gave the word.

"Is Father angry at you for skipping out last night?"

"Much less than I thought he'd be." Fiona tried to smile, but her face was tighter than a snare drum.

"Were your friends out looting and burning?" he asked.

"Yes," she said. "They were all there."

"And you?"

"I was."

"Did you...?"

"Kill anyone?"

"No!" He looked shocked. "I mean, did you join with the looting and burning? I know you're committed to the cause."

"Sit down with me Conor." She took his hands as he flopped down beside her. "Be glad you weren't out there last night. It was the most horrific thing I've ever seen. People I've known and trusted for years turned into beasts in front of my eyes. I always thought the hatred for the Jews was all talk—a way to rally the troops to the cause. Seems like a good idea to have a common enemy, you know?"

"Father says we have to leave Germany now."

She wanted to put an arm around her brother's shoulders, but something inside didn't allow it. "I broke out of that school in Switzerland, to come back here, to this," she said and shook her head.

A stone hit her window, making her jump.

"I'll check," said Conor, getting up and going to the window. "It's your friend Amalia."

Fiona's initial instinct was to close the curtains and hide underneath her covers, but she fought it back. *Better this happens now.* She went to the window herself. Amalia was in her front yard and gestured for her to come down. Fiona held up her hand to signal that she'd be down in a few seconds.

"Are you okay?" Conor asked.

"I think so. I have to go out."

Amalia greeted her with an excited smile. They hurried out of the driveway and walked away from her father's house.

"Did you sleep last night? It was after dawn until I closed my eyes. What happened to you at the end? We saw you run off, but we thought you'd be back."

"I came home."

"Why didn't you say goodbye?"

"Did you see what Hannelore, the troop leader, did at the children's hospital?"

Amalia's smile didn't fade. "Of course I did. I was there with you and everyone else. Hannelore did what she needed to."

"Dragging sick children out of bed across shards of broken glass? Did you see their little feet? I went back yesterday. The blood stains are still on the sidewalk."

"What you witnessed was pent-up revenge for years of abuse. Hannelore has nothing to apologize for. No one does."

Fiona pressed her hand to her face. Amalia was her best friend. This felt like the last time they'd ever talk. She'd lost so much in one night.

"Come on, Fiona, don't let sentimentality about little Jewish maggots ruin what was the greatest night in the history of the Führer's reign so far." Amalia tugged Fiona's hand away from her face and squeezed it. "Someone wants to see you."

"Who?" She knew, of course.

"Harald, though he said not to tell you!"

"Amalia..."

"Oh, come on. I know he should have run after you last night, to make sure you were all right, but he thought you were going to come back." Still holding Fiona's hand, Amalia pulled her along as she started to run.

On the far side of a deserted soccer field, they came to an open café. Harald and Georg were sitting at a table by the window, drinking celebratory beers. Upon seeing the boy she'd once been sure she'd marry, Fiona felt tremendous relief. Something had broken within her the night before, but she hadn't been sure how she'd feel about Harald when she saw him. This was the boy she'd been sure she'd marry. She'd been wary of falling into his trap again, but the idea of touching him repulsed her now. He repulsed her now.

The boys stood up to toast the girls with massive grins. "Come, sit!" Harald said.

Fiona stood back. "Can we take a walk?"

Georg laughed. "Ooh, you're in trouble now, Harald. What have you done?"

"Sit down, Fiona," repeated the SS soldier, no longer smiling.

She turned and walked out.

She hadn't taken more than a few steps when Harald grabbed her by the arm.

"What's wrong? Why aren't you wearing your uniform?"

"Your hand left blood on my shirt."

He smirked. "I must have cut it on the flying glass."

She glanced at his hand on her arm, which looked bruised but not cut. "I can't see anything."

He dropped her arm, but carried on walking beside her. They passed the soccer field where a few children about Conor's age were now kicking a ball around.

Here was as good as anywhere. Nobody was listening or watching them.

She slowed down and turned to face him, one hand on the railings that formed the field's periphery. "I don't want to see you anymore. It's over."

He looked surprised and laughed. "Is this because I didn't come after you when you ran off last night? Amalia said you'd be annoyed about that."

"No, it's—"

"I knew you'd be safe. Anyone dangerous was hiding. No one was going to harm you."

His eyes betrayed his absolute conviction. He sincerely believed that he and the rest of the mob were performing their duty to secure the country's future. Her beliefs had diverged from his so much that it was as if they were speaking a different language.

But she stopped herself from saying anything about the looting. This wasn't a person she could trust. She might end up in Gestapo headquarters on Prinz-Albrecht Strasse. It was vital she control herself.

"It isn't anything to do with that. It's what happened in the park." She hoped he wouldn't see through the lie.

Again he laughed, startled. "What? Why? You're being ridiculous. I only lost control because I love you so much, and I apologized. I thought you forgave me."

He reached out to her, but she smacked his hand away.

"You disgust me. I wouldn't stay with you if Hitler himself got down on his knees and begged me."

He looked shocked. "Don't talk about the Führer like that!"

"We're finished, Harald. Find yourself another maiden to bear children for you."

She walked away.

"You're ugly, anyway. I never wanted you, just your father's money," he shouted after her.

She walked on as fast as she could, her head held high, and turned the corner out of sight before she burst into tears. It took her a few seconds to realize why she was crying. It wasn't because she'd miss him or his twisted ways. Her tears were the manifestation of the tumult coursing through her, but they weren't of sadness.

Seamus had been shocked when Conor told him about Fiona leaving with Amalia, and now he felt worried for the Bernheims, who were sitting with him at the dining room table, their faces still swollen and bruised. What if his daughter slid back into the Nazi maelstrom or came home convinced that everything that happened last night was justified?

"Is there anything left of our house?" Lil asked.

Seamus reached over and took her hand. "I'm afraid not. The hooligans who attacked it went inside with hammers and knives before they burned it down. They didn't trust the fire to do the job. Everything was devastated."

Her husband put his arm around her as she began to sob. "They were our neighbors," he said. "We never did one thing to them in all the years we lived there."

"Who we were didn't come into it," Joel said. "What we were is all that mattered."

"I was listening to the radio," said Conor out of nowhere. He was sitting at the end of the table. "And the announcer said that 30,000 Jewish men have been taken into KZ's from all over country."

"I think we're all in agreement that your situation in Berlin is untenable now. Mine too. I can't stay here anymore," Seamus said.

"With all respect, my friend," said Gert, "your situation is vastly different than ours. If you want to leave, all you have to do is book your steamer tickets back to America. We have nowhere to go."

"The American embassy is already inundated with visa applications from Jews," his wife said. "Everyone I know had already applied. But every Jew in Germany is going to now. Who would want to stay here after last night?"

"No one sane."

"The Americans have their quota system for visas. Those pieces of paper are like gold dust," Lil said.

"What about sponsorships?" Seamus asked.

"It's $5,000 per person. The sponsor has to be in a job of good standing, and put up the money."

Seamus looked around. "I could sell the house and the business. I could afford to bring you all over then.

"Helga would buy it," Joel said.

His father shook his head. "Helga's no fool. She knows she needs a male partner to come in with her. She can't operate two armaments factories as a woman in this country. Ten years ago maybe, but not now."

"Ten years ago, she wouldn't have had anyone to sell the guns and planes to," Seamus said.

"No, she wouldn't," Gert said. "I think we need to consider all the options we have at our disposal."

His wife took out a pack of cigarettes. She laid them on the table, and soon they were all smoking.

"What about France, or Poland, or Palestine?" Joel asked.

"The British have curtailed the number of visas for Palestine," Gert said. "I know a few people who went there—my brother included, but it's no easier than America now. Poland is too close, and look how they're treating the Jews at the border now. They don't want us either. We could sneak in, but to do what? I'm not a farm laborer or a taxi driver. I've only ever worked in white-collar jobs. I couldn't get one without a visa."

"Poland is probably next on Hitler's wish list—once he takes the rest of Czechoslovakia and renders that ridiculous piece of paper Chamberlain signed with our beloved Führer null and void. The Nazis have been talking about "living space" in the east since the start. That's Poland," Seamus said.

"So, that's out," Joel said. "What about Switzerland or France?"

"I'm so thankful your brother's safe down in Bern," Gert said. "He can stay there even after he graduates. We don't have to worry about him."

"Thank goodness," Seamus said.

"The visa situation is no better in Switzerland, although I heard people are sneaking into the south of France to wait for their visas for America to come through. I know some people have traveled to Brazil and Argentina from there."

"Anywhere the Nazis can't reach them, eh?" Seamus said. "I should have enough money in the bank in Basel to finance you and the rest of the Jews from the factory getting to the south of France, if that's what you choose to do."

"Thank you, my friend. I'll speak to them on Monday and discuss what's best. The problem remains of how we smuggle them across the border, however."

"I have two women in France who specialize in solving problems like this one—my wife and my daughter."

"You're talking about 24 families, Seamus," Gert said. "Getting them across the border is going to be no mean feat."

"Nothing's easy, is it? Especially when it's worthwhile. I'll travel to Paris in a few days. I'll speak to Lisa and Maureen about how we can get the families over the border. I'll write to Michael in New York and ask him how we can sponsor you and as many others as possible."

"This is going to cost so much money. Will you have enough?" Gert said.

"I hope so."

"I have a few thousand Reichsmarks put away," Gert said.

"Keep it for an apartment in New York," Seamus said. "I'd rather use all the ill-gotten gains I've received from the Nazis. It'll feel good to do something worthy with it."

Seamus prepared some bread and sliced meats for lunch. His guests ate for the first time since they'd arrived. Seamus didn't join them and just sat back in his chair, wondering what his old buddy Bill Hayden would have to say about his plans. Nothing would be straightforward from here on, but enough was enough. He wouldn't spend one more day in Nazi Germany than he had to. A great tempest had begun and would rage much harder before it died.

The front door opened, and Gert and his family went white, as if expecting the Gestapo to come barreling in.

Fiona nodded at them as she passed the open door and continued upstairs to her room. The conversation at the table died. Tension showed on the Bernheims' faces. Fiona was still someone to be feared.

"I'll speak to her," Seamus said.

He gave her a few minutes to settle before following her up. He knocked and waited for her to answer. When she did, her face was red, her eyes swollen from crying.

"Are you okay?" He immediately felt stupid for asking the question. She definitely wasn't. "Can I come in?" She stood back, and he entered her room. The portrait of Hitler she'd pinned to her closet was torn and on the floor. It had been a year or more since she'd allowed him into her room like this. He embraced her for the first time in a long time.

"Can you tell me what has happened, my love?"

"All of my friends were out with the mob last night. Every single one."

She moved away and sat on a chair at her desk. He took the bed.

"Did you meet any of them today?" he asked, knowing the answer.

"Yes. They're celebrating the great victory over Germany's deadliest foe," she said. Her voice was hollow, and she stared into space as she spoke. "I think Harald killed a man, Father." She looked up at him. Her beautiful face was contorted in grief. "He had blood on him. I didn't see him do it, but—."

"I understand."

"And nothing's going to happen to him. If the Gestapo saw that picture of Hitler on the floor, they'd haul me in for questioning, but killing a man on the street? That's fine, is it?"

"Most certainly not."

"I mean, what kind of a place is this, where thousands riot and the people taken to jail are the ones whose stores were looted? No police came to stop it, and I heard thousands of Jews were taken away to KZ's. It doesn't make any sense."

"Nothing here does anymore."

"I gave the last five years of my life to the cause. The Führer's meant to be the greatest man in the world, so why is he so afraid of Herr Bernheim and that man who ran the grocery store? Why is he terrified of the little children in that hospital last night?" She was crying again. He didn't move or speak. "I saw the way the Bernheims looked at me when I came in, they were frightened, and I don't blame them. I'm the embodiment of what happened to them last night—a rioter in their supposed safe house."

"They know differently now."

"Maybe they thought I was lying, getting ready to betray them. I made no secret of what I believed. I never questioned it. Harald was to be my husband and we'd live in the greatest nation in the world. I'd have a dozen sons and hand them all over to the Führer to do with them as he pleased. Oh, Father what was I thinking?"

"You didn't come up with these notions. They were hammered into you."

"Why me, and not Conor or Michael or Maureen?"

"It won't be easy, but you have to let it go. The only thing you can shape now is your future."

"I saw my whole life mapped out in front of me."

She picked up a piece of Hitler's face and tossed it into the trashcan.

"The path you're about to take isn't written yet. You saw what the Nazis did last night, and they won't stop there. It's time to return to the person you are in here," he said, pounding his chest. "Are you finished with Harald?"

"I don't ever want to see him again. He's a disgusting pig. I can't fathom the idea of being anywhere near him."

Seamus tried to hide his emotions, but the fireworks were bursting inside. "Does he know about our house guests, or what we did for them?"

"No. None of my friends do," she answered. "You think I could live with Maureen in Paris? What must she think of me?"

"She loves you as much as she always has. Or else, you could come live with me and the others in America."

Seamus was sure he'd pushed her too far and wished he could have taken his words back. He was pleasantly surprised when she answered. "I'll think about it."

"Come downstairs and talk to Joel and Frau and Herr Bernheim. Tell them again how you feel about what you saw last night. Trust takes time, my love."

"Maybe later," she said. "I need to be alone now."

He closed the door behind him, hardly able to contain his joy.

12

Sunday, November 13

The stated purpose of the meeting was to put new safety measures in place for the Jewish workers, but those attending must have known it would be much more than that. No one invited into work on that Sunday questioned why. What Jewish person wasn't fully aware of the emergency unfolding in the Reich? The Gestapo was still making its rounds, arresting mainly middle-class and wealthy male Jews by the truckload. His factory workers didn't seem to be under threat, however, and none refused to attend the meeting. According to the newspapers, the orders to arrest so many had come directly from the Führer himself, so the wisdom behind them was unquestionable. Heinrich Müller, the head of the secret police, a more pragmatic man than Hitler, who tended to express himself in parables and wish lists, ordered the arrest of between 25,000 and 30,000 Jews. The overworked Gestapo didn't have enough men to complete the job, so they enlisted the help of the local police, the SA, and even the SS. Most Jews were taken from their homes, but many were plucked from what still existed of their places of business or even from the train station as they tried to escape. It seemed the Nazis were trying to make an example of the more monied members of Jewish society or to extort wealth from them. Thieving from the Jews had become an essential facet of the National Socialist economy. The Nazis never passed up an opportunity to steal.

Seamus, Gert, and Lil were at the factory an hour before the employees began arriving. Seamus's office wasn't big enough for the gathering, so they set the chairs in an empty space downstairs where some calibrating machines had recently been removed. Seamus wondered what Helga would say if she found out about the gathering. He'd only spoken to her briefly since the riot between the Jews and the Nazi sympathizers in the factory, and that was only to have her concur that production should shut down for a day.

Helga's attitude toward the unrest seemed to be that it was an unfortunate expression of over-exuberance. Seamus didn't push her, just accepted her opinion with as polite a nod as he could muster.

The workers didn't know Helga well. She relied on Benz, the head of the Trustee Council, to be her go-between. She never dealt directly with the employees anymore because they didn't take orders from a mere woman. Benz and his rabble-rousers were an ever-increasing thorn in Seamus's side. Most of his non-Jewish workers were at least ambivalent toward Hitler. But those who did approve of the Nazis did so with such full-throated enthusiasm that they tended to drown out all others. Their actions were so brazen that they made it seem like no one else existed.

"I heard the Kaiser say he was ashamed to be German for the first time after the events of Kristallnacht," Gert said as they finished laying the chairs.

"His opinion isn't much more important than mine these

days," Seamus said. "His entire existence doesn't seem like much more than a rumor now."

"All that matters is what the Nazis decide to do from here. We're entirely subject to their racist whims now," Lil said. "I feel like all control I ever had over my own life has faded away like smoke in the breeze."

"It's up to us to wrest it back," her husband said.

She didn't respond and returned to Seamus's office to grab coffee mugs instead.

The workers began arriving a few minutes later. Their faces were ashen, the shock from Kristallnacht still visible in their eyes. Seamus and Gert greeted them at the door. Judith Starobin, who had already been beaten up by the same brown-shirts who killed her husband, was among the 24 employees who shuffled into the factory.

They sat in neat rows, whispering among themselves until Gert stood to address them. He thanked them for coming. He called for quiet, and Seamus began.

"I brought you here today to discuss the security situation."

Leonard Greenberg, a 26-year veteran of the factory, stood up. "I for one want to leave immediately. I've lived here all my life. I've never even been further than Wannsee, but things are getting worse. My brother was taken by the Gestapo last night. We have no idea where they've taken him. We have to leave. How many men lost their lives during that Nazi pogrom the other night? How many women were violated? The broken glass and burned-out houses can be fixed, but some things cannot."

A voice at the back said, "The government is also planning to levy a fine on the Jews of Germany for the damages caused on Kristallnacht."

Leonard stared at the speaker. "We're being fined? For what their thugs did?"

"It will amount to 1 billion Reichsmarks."

"We have to pay for the damage to the homes and the businesses destroyed?"

"All Jews will be required to pay for their own repairs. The fine is separate."

A collective groan filled the air. Some of the employees started talking amongst themselves. Their agitation was apparent.

"Are we going to be able to work here anymore after the new laws the Nazis passed yesterday?" Leonard Greenberg asked.

Seamus gestured Gert to come forward, and he began to speak. "Yes, for those of you who may not have heard, yesterday the government passed "The Decree on Eliminating Jews from Economic Life" as a follow-up to Kristallnacht. The new law targets Jews with their own businesses more than those gainfully employed." He pulled out a notepad and read from it. "It bars Jews from operating retail stores, sales agencies, or carrying on a trade. It also forbids us from selling goods and services at any establishment."

Gert threw the notepad onto a desk beside him as his words sank in with the crowd. Pamela Bernstein's husband put up his hand. He was a handsome man with tanned skin and dark eyes. "I've been working in my uncle's store since I was fifteen. We spent the last two days cleaning it out. Does this mean we won't be able to trade again?"

"That's exactly what it means," Gert answered.

"What are we meant to do?"

The factory manager didn't respond.

"All Ritter employees are expected to report to work tomorrow morning as usual," Seamus said. "We haven't had official word from any government officials, but as you're not selling any goods yourselves, I'm sure the decree won't apply. Strictly speaking, Helga and I are the ones who sell the items we make."

"I'm glad we still have jobs, but how are you going to protect us from Benz and the other Nazis?" Pamela asked. Her baby was asleep in her arms.

"We will be erecting barriers between sections. You will have alternate hours than the rest of the staff. The Jewish workers will begin an hour earlier and leave at 4 instead of 5. No one from the weapons section of the floor will be allowed into yours."

"You're isolating us from the rest of our co-workers?" complained a young man called Saul Menzinger. "Some of my best friends work across the floor. I've known them since I was a boy."

"I'm sorry," Seamus responded. "We don't see any other way of guaranteeing your safety."

"But what about the future?" Saul asked. "Things are only going to get worse. The riot in here was nothing compared to what every Jew in Germany experienced on Kristallnacht."

Seamus glanced at Gert and cleared his throat. "Many of you were at a meeting in my office just over a year ago when I raised the question of emigrating from Germany. What seemed like a good policy then seems like an absolute necessity now."

"You told us you'd arrange it for us but we're still here," someone shouted.

Seamus took a breath and began again. "I'm sorry. My primary concern when I spoke to you last year about emigrating was money. I was focused on the tax rate the Nazis were applying to any Jews leaving and all I thought about was how to hide your savings and add to them, so you could get a good start elsewhere. I appreciate now how naïve I was."

Gert interrupted. "For those of you who weren't aware, Herr Ritter came up with a scheme to smuggle money to Switzerland on our behalf, but border controls have only grown more stringent since, even for gentiles."

"And I was focused on the wrong angle," Seamus said. "I'm

sorry for that. I didn't realize the difficulty we'd have securing visas and affidavits, even to Palestine."

"Every single one of us has applied to the American embassy," complained Pamela Bernstein. "We meet each other in the line there after work, it's a regular social hour for us. But the Americans have their quotas. We're all on the waiting list. Someone told me last time it could take up to ten years to get the visa. I don't know if I'll be alive that long."

The crowd was growing more restless. At that moment, Seamus seemed to become the focus of the justified rage they felt.

"You said you'd organize what we needed!" Pamela shouted above the ruckus. "But we're no closer."

"The other European countries aren't much better," agreed Saul and stood up. He turned to the crowd of workers. "Who here has applied for a French visa? Belgian? Dutch?" All hands jutted upward. "But even if we got one, we can't leave the country without exit visas, which the government won't give us because we work here!"

Seamus heard his late uncle's voice in his mind—urging him to take care of the Jewish workers.

"I'll see what I can do to help you get the visas. Money won't be a concern. I'm traveling to see my wife and daughter in Paris in a few days to discuss this issue," Seamus said, but wasn't sure anyone could hear him. Gert stood up to calm the employees again. A few seconds passed before it was quiet enough to be heard again. "I have heard talk of Jews stealing across the border into France, and waiting there or in Portugal until their visas to the US or even Brazil or Argentina come through."

"What do we know of those places?" Pamela's husband said.

"We know Hitler isn't passing down decrees there whenever the fancy takes him. We'd be safe," Gert said.

"I'm going to ask my wife and daughter to relocate to the

border, and bring anyone who wants to travel to the south of France with them," Seamus said.

"How will we get across the border?" Pamela said.

"It won't be easy, but I'll have them look into local guides who can help smuggle people across where it's less heavily guarded."

"What about the children?" Pamela said. "They'll never make it through forests or mountain passes."

"We'll find another way," Seamus said.

"The border guards will shoot us if we're caught. Where do we settle if we do make it across? You're asking us to risk our lives for vagaries," Pamela said. "And how do we live when we get there?"

"I'll see to that," he said, trying to stem the tide of anger. "I also have some contacts in the US embassy I can speak to."

"To get almost a hundred visas?" Leonard said. "All told, there are 96 of us including children. You didn't think we'd leave without our families, did you?"

"Of course not."

Seamus knew that would be impossible. Ten sponsorship visas to the US would cost him $50,000—more than every worker in this room earned in a year combined. Perhaps he could wrangle ten or so if he put up the money himself, but the Bernheims would be first on the list. Options were available, but none that weren't excruciatingly difficult, expensive, or both.

It became clear that they weren't about to solve the problems that haunted them that day, so Seamus called a halt to the meeting.

Lil approached him after the employees left. "So, get 96 Jews out of the Reich, with money and visas, before the Gestapo comes for all of them. We're going to need some luck."

Seamus took her hand and tried to think of something clever to say. Five seconds passed before he just shook his head and continued walking back upstairs to his office. The thought of seeing his wife and daughters in Paris again soothed his aching mind as he put his feet up on the desk. Gert and Lil followed him a few minutes later.

His office manager had the ledger in which they kept the savings the Jewish workers had given him. He threw it on the desk in front of Seamus.

"Not enough in here to get twenty of them across the border into France, let alone all the way to your homeland."

"Our workers don't have that kind of money even if they were willing to share it," Seamus answered.

"It takes a lot of foresight to set aside money when you're struggling to feed your family," Lil said.

"I think it's time we set a long overdue profit-sharing scheme in motion," Seamus said.

"That's not legal these days," Gert said with a smile that told Seamus he knew what he meant.

13

Saturday, November 19

Seamus savored the feel of Lisa in his arms, the aroma of her skin, the sensation of her touch. She was an oasis in the desert of his loneliness, and he didn't know how much longer he could live apart from her. Fiona and Conor had traveled with him. Only Michael and Monika were missing, but their absence didn't mean they were excluded from his plans— quite the opposite. He stood kissing his wife for as long as etiquette would allow. He stretched it a few seconds longer than he usually would have. They were in France, after all. He embraced Hannah before turning to Maureen, who greeted him with a sheepish grin. The cuts and bruises the SS had inflicted on her had healed, and she seemed in good health. He kissed her on both cheeks before wrapping his arms around her. They left the station as a family, just as it had been in his daydreams on the long train ride here.

It was a cold evening in Paris, and Seamus threw his scarf around his neck. Hannah took his hand as they strolled toward the taxi. He was determined to enjoy this for a few hours at least. They had so much to do, but he still wanted to be a husband and a father.

"Have you heard from Michael and Monika?" Fiona asked as she, her father, and Maureen got into the car. The others took the cab in front.

"Yes, I have a letter from them here," Maureen answered and handed the envelope to her sister. "They've settled in lower Manhattan. He's running again at NYU, and she's starting to learn English."

Seamus let the two sisters talk for a while.

Maureen and Lisa were eager to hear about Fiona's awakening from Nazism since Kristallnacht from her own lips. Seamus telling them was one thing, but they remained unconvinced. Maureen loved her sister but didn't trust her. Seamus was confident that Fiona would win them over, as she wasn't that good an actress. She hadn't seen Harald since their breakup and was adamant that she'd never speak to him again. Amalia called to the house on Tuesday night, but after a brief conversation at the door, Fiona sent her home alone. The joy Seamus felt at having his daughter back was unlike anything he'd ever known, but he knew the journey back wasn't complete yet. This trip was a vital step in her rehabilitation.

It wasn't long before Maureen brought up Kristallnacht. "I read about the riots all over Germany."

"I was out with the rest of my League troop that night," Fiona answered before her father could speak. Her sister turned away as if she couldn't bear to listen. "The things I saw were unspeakable. My best friends turned into beasts in front of my eyes."

Maureen swiveled back to face her. "You didn't approve?"

"Of that? Who do you think I am?" she snapped.

"I think you're a committed member of the League of German Girls."

"I haven't worn my uniform since November 9. I never will again."

Maureen smiled, looking as if she couldn't believe what she was hearing.

"Father suggested we leave Germany, and I think I'm ready," said Fiona.

"You're ready to leave the League behind? What about Harald?"

"I wish I'd never laid eyes on that gutter rat. The thought of him makes me want to vomit."

"Could I come and stay with you for a while, perhaps, until father is ready to leave for America?" asked Fiona.

Maureen burst out laughing but regained her composure. "If that's what you truly want, we can discuss it."

"We can talk about the details of Fiona's decision another time. The important thing is she and Harald are finished and she's ready to leave Germany with the rest of the family," added Seamus.

"And when will that be?" Maureen asked.

"I don't know, but we don't have any time to waste," Seamus replied.

His eldest daughter seemed to take the hint his brevity suggested and waited until the taxi ride to the hotel was over to ask any more questions. Lisa was skeptical of her stepdaughter's political U-turn, but had promised to hear her out. Although Lisa was only half-Jewish, Kristallnacht had shocked her to the core.

She didn't say much, just expressed how happy she was that Fiona would join them in America someday.

Fiona didn't seem to know how to communicate how she felt. It was hard to imagine being as young as she was and suddenly realizing the bedrock your life was built on was a lie.

Seamus, Fiona, and Conor dropped their suitcases at the room in the hotel. The maître d' greeted each of them by name as they left and expressed how glad he was to see them back in Paris.

"Not as happy as I am," Seamus said with a smile and took his wife by the hand.

The decision to bring Conor and Fiona to Paris had been an easy one.

Conor's teachers had performed their usual role as white-washers-in-chief and had blamed Kristallnacht on the Jews. They told the children that any violence that occurred had been started by the Jews and that the Hitler Youth had only been defending themselves. Seamus sat his son down and recounted what he had seen that night. Conor was open to what he said and seemed to accept his father's assertion that his teachers were either blind to the truth or were too scared to speak out. Conor wasn't interested in politics. All he wanted to do was kick a ball with his friends, some of whom were fervent Hitler Youth, and some who were not. It was heartening to witness.

Everyone changed and readied themselves for dinner. The Ritter family strolled through the Parisian night together. St. Germain was alive, and many people sat outside the omnipresent cafés in coats and scarves, braving the chilly weather.

"I booked somewhere myself tonight," Maureen said with a smile.

She led them across the river at Pont Neuf to Rue de Rivoli, where a cozy bistro with candle-lit tables awaited.

They were in a secluded corner of the restaurant but didn't talk about politics. Maureen had asked her father not to in front of Fiona. The food was exquisite. The tuna and avocado tartar melted in Seamus's mouth, and his main course of marinated salmon was the best he'd had in months.

Dinner proceeded. Seamus managed to suppress the

thoughts raging through his mind for the duration and enjoy the time.

They'd all eaten, and no one was talking when Fiona began. She seemed to take a deep breath before she started. It was as if she'd been planning what to say and was trying to dispel the nerves raging within her.

"I feel like such a fool," she said with a shaking voice.

"No need for that," Seamus answered.

"I'm not surprised at what happened on Kristallnacht," she continued. All eyes around the table were fixed on her, waiting for what she'd say next. "Everything was building to it these past five years. We were always taught the Jews couldn't be trusted. They're the enemy of everything good and pure." Tears were forming in her eyes now. "They're parasites on the genius Aryan race. They were the ones holding Germany back, keeping us from the greatness we deserve. The newspapers, the radio, and the politicians reminded us all day, every day of how corrupt and abhorrent the Jews are. We spent hours a week in meetings talking about them. Our leaders told us we had enemies everywhere, but the Jews were the most insidious of all —a race of people dedicated to destroying everything beautiful and true. And we believed them. My friends were among those pillaging and beating on November 9. They destroyed Jewish stores and beat the owners to a bloody pulp. My friends," she said, looking at her family. "Amalia, Inge, Georg, and Harald. What would they have been if the Nazis hadn't drummed this hate into them? What was I?"

Maureen reached across and took her hand. "You're still part of this family, and this is your chance to return to the person you were."

Fiona pushed her knife and fork forward and sat back. A tear ran down her cheek. "I trusted everything they preached to me. My teachers, my troop leaders—they all said the same things, over and over. I was such an idiot."

"No, you were not," Lisa said in a firm voice. "You were an impressionable child. What the Nazis did was monstrous."

"If anyone bears responsibility, it's me," Seamus said.

"No, Father, you're wrong," Maureen said. "The Nazis are the only ones to blame for the perversion of Germany's youth."

"I'm sorry, and especially to you, Lisa. You're half-Jewish, what must you think of me?"

Her stepmother smiled. "I love you, Fiona—that's what I think of you." Lisa gripped Fiona's hand on the table between them.

Seamus felt something loosen within him. This moment felt like a new beginning. He knew he needed to say something. He was head of the household. He could sense Fiona's mother looking down on them at that moment.

"The onus is on you now, Fiona. We're here for you in every way we can be, but your life is yours to color from this moment onward. Some things are beyond our control, but the person who we are and the person we'll become tomorrow is one of the few things we can decide. It won't be easy, but I know you can leave behind the poison you were fed all these years," said her father.

"It's time to become the opposite of the person the Nazis wanted you to be," Maureen said. "Starting now."

Fiona dried the tears from her face and nodded her head. She spoke little for the rest of the time in the restaurant and seemed deep in thought as she walked back to the hotel with them, hand-in-hand with Hannah.

Seamus, Lisa, and Maureen left Fiona in charge of her younger siblings and went out for a drink. They found a suitable spot down the street and settled in a secluded corner. Maureen poured the wine as Seamus lit a cigarette. It was too cold to sit outside, but the bar had large plate windows that revealed a wondrous view of the city of lights. Seamus resisted the temptation to ask about Maureen's health. She seemed to have recovered. He peered at her fingernails as she picked up her glass of merlot, remembering the bloody mess her Nazi torturers had made of them.

"What was it like in Berlin after Kristallnacht?" Lisa asked.

"Business as usual. The street cleaners and the Jews themselves swept up the broken glass and loaded it into trucks. After that, the looting was organized in proper German fashion. Members of the city's Reich Chamber of Culture were commissioned to ransack the homes of rich Jews and carry off any valuable artworks of interest to the Aryan public. Thousands of men were rounded up by the Gestapo and carted off to KZ's. Some shot themselves or jumped out of windows to escape the camps. No one knows how many killed themselves."

"What about the Jews in the factory, and the Bernheims?" his wife asked again.

"They were all lucky. None were taken," Seamus said. "It seems the Nazis were more interested in picking up Jews who could afford to buy their way out of the camps. I heard some have arrived back home already. Gert and Lil's home was destroyed, but they've been hiding out in our house since then with Joel. The job now is to get everyone out. That's where you come in," he said, looking at his wife and daughter.

Both women sat forward. "Go on," his daughter said.

Seamus smiled. "The Nazis didn't break your spirit, did they?"

Maureen held up her hand to show her fingernails. "Growing back. Now, tell us."

"Every single Jew in the factory, and in Germany probably, recognizes they have to leave now. They can't wait for visas to come through. The government isn't issuing the workers exit visas because of the "sensitive" industry."

"Still? Nothing's changed?" Maureen said.

"The Gestapo isn't budging," answered Seamus.

"Where do we come in?" Lisa asked.

"We need to get the Jews into France. They can settle in the south and wait for whatever visas we can arrange for them to come through. If it takes ten years to get to America, so be it. At least our people will be safe from the Nazis while they wait."

"How do you suggest we get them across the border?" Maureen asked.

"In two ways. We're going to have to split the parents from their children, just until we get them somewhere safe, anyway. Here's what I propose." He pointed at his wife. "We arrange with child smugglers to get the kids across the border."

"How does that work?" Lisa asked.

"Women hire themselves out. They act as the child's mother and bring them across the border—for a fee of course."

"What about papers?" Lisa asked.

"The smugglers provide what's required but you'll need to see to that. Lisa, getting the children across will be your responsibility. The workers have 62 children between them under the age of 15."

"Sounds expensive," his wife replied.

"Money is something we do have. Time—not so much," he replied.

"You don't want me to help? What's my role?" Maureen asked.

"Lisa will take care of the children, but that still leaves 24 adults and 10 grown children too old to plausibly be taken over the border by our smugglers. We'll need to bring them across. Not past the checkpoints, but through the forests and over the hills."

"I'll do it, but I've never spent any time at the border in my life. I don't know Strasbourg from St. Petersburg," Maureen said.

"I'll need you to find a reliable guide—someone we can trust. They'll be well paid."

He put down his wine glass and peered out at the night. The room was on the sixth floor, and the view stretched all the way to the Seine.

"When do I leave?" Maureen asked. "I'll need to relocate to the area."

"First thing. We have to find somewhere to bring our people. Down south, away from the Nazi agents in Paris. Somewhere closer to the sea."

"I'll take a trip in a few days," Maureen said.

"What if the French police come for them?" Lisa asked.

"We'll deal with that unlikely event if it occurs."

He didn't want to say that the French police would likely be open to bribery should the need arise, but he was prepared for that eventuality.

"Do you have enough money for all this?"

"I hope so. I have a substantial amount put away in Switzerland." Maureen took a few seconds as if to digest what her father had said. "I swore to my uncle that I'd look after every one of his employees when I took over the factory. The Jews are proud people and would never say it, but they need help. Sometimes we all do."

"If the Gestapo finds out what we're doing, we'll be the ones who end up in a concentration camp," Lisa said.

"I'm well aware of that," Seamus said. "The stakes couldn't be higher, but I can't just walk away from these people."

They sat for another twenty minutes discussing the details. Lisa found a newsstand and bought a map of France. Once sure they were alone, she spread it out on the table.

"Let's try not to venture too far south, unless our friends are keen swimmers. The Rhine forms most of the border to here." Seamus pointed at a region east of the German city of Karlsruhe.

"Then the forest begins," Lisa said.

"I'd bet my fortune the Nazis have more border guards along here than there are bushes," Seamus said.

He remembered the last time he was in that area—during the Great War. Many of his friends were still there.

"That's the Maginot Line. 280 miles long and 16 miles deep. All the bunkers and fortress positions France needs to keep the Germans out," Maureen said

"And the Germans are staring at it across the border," Lisa said.

"That leaves two plausible ways of smuggling people in— hidden in the backs of cars or on foot through the Vosges Forest, here," Seamus said, pointing at the thick blob of green on the map.

"Not a great choice," Maureen said.

"We can't get the workers across legally."

"I'll find a guide to get across here," Maureen said, pointing to a thick clump of green by the border of France and Germany. It was marked as the North Vosges Nature Reserve. "The woods should provide us some cover from the thousands of troops staring at each other across the border."

They stopped talking as the young waitress came to the table. Lisa put her bag on the table to cover the map. Seamus ordered some more wine, and they were alone again.

"So, the kids cross the border through the checkpoints and everyone else comes through the woods? Difficult in winter," Lisa said.

"I don't know if we can wait until spring," Seamus said. "The Jews are understandably keen to get out as soon as possible."

"But we'll need somewhere to house them when they come across. Somewhere away from prying eyes," Maureen said.

"And a safehouse in Germany to come across from,"

Seamus said. "It'll take time to procure those places, no matter how much money we have."

"Months," Lisa said. "Perhaps winter will be over by then."

"Our friends won't be able to work in France either. They can survive on their own money for a while, but it all depends on how long it takes for all those visas to come through," Maureen added. "How long will that take?"

"Weeks. Months. Maybe years," Seamus said.

"I know the workers have their own savings, but still— keeping that many people for that long will be expensive."

"I'm well aware," Seamus said. "We'll keep in touch about this, but there's only so much I can do from Berlin. I'm relying on you both to organize all this."

"We'll get it done," Lisa said without hesitation.

"I wouldn't have asked you if I didn't believe you could," Seamus said. "One complication remains—Fiona."

Maureen agreed. "Can we trust her? I'm happy she's seen the light at last, but two weeks ago she was a dedicated Nazi."

"I think we should get her out of Germany while we still can. People who change their minds are just as liable to flip back, especially at her age," Seamus said.

"Do you think she'll stay in France?" Lisa asked. "Sending her to boarding school in Switzerland didn't work out so well."

"There's a better chance if Maureen asks her," Seamus responded. "I don't know. I thought she was lost, but she still had a hold of just enough of her soul to see Kristallnacht for what it was."

"Why didn't the others?" his daughter asked.

"The other rioters? Maybe because they weren't privy to the other cultures that Fiona was. She's seen other ways of life that the rank-and-file Nazis never have. All they know is what the Ministry for Propaganda has been feeding them for the past five years. They probably don't remember anything before that except for strife and misery."

"She's my sister, and I hate saying this, but one word from her to the wrong person and we'd all end up in concentration camps," Maureen said. "If she's not fully rehabilitated—"

"I'll speak to her tomorrow morning about staying with Lisa," Seamus said.

"I don't think it's safe that she come with me. I'm going to have to move to the border. I can't lie to her every day. What do I tell her, that I'm off for a ramble in the country, and when I get back, I might have several exhausted Jews with me?"

They spoke for another hour, savoring the taste of the wine, the ambiance of the bar, and being with each other. If he didn't before, Seamus certainly knew now why Maureen hadn't taken the steamer to New York with her brother. Life in America wasn't for her. Not yet at least. Not while so many people needed her here.

Maureen decided it was too late to return to the empty apartment, so her father and stepmother invited her back to the hotel. They said goodnight at the door to the children's room before Maureen went inside. Fiona woke up as she closed the door behind her.

"All right if I get into bed beside you?" Maureen said.

Her sister sat up and pulled back the blanket for her. Conor and Hannah didn't stir. Maureen curled up in bed beside her sister.

"How was the wine bar?" Fiona whispered.

"It was great spending time with Lisa and Father." Maureen held back. She wished she could share what they'd talked about. "Are you serious about leaving?"

Fiona hesitated a few seconds. "I don't know. I thought I'd live the rest of my life in the Reich."

"But you see what kind of a country it's become," her sister replied. "Father told me how you came back crying after Kristallnacht. I can't imagine the horror you witnessed."

"It was terrible."

"Are you finished with Harald?"

"That disgusting pig? Yes, you could safely say that."

Maureen couldn't keep the smile from her face.

"I can't imagine ever speaking to him again, let alone marrying him," her sister continued. "I know you all want to leave Germany. I don't want to stay alone. What would I do? I had a plan for the rest of my life until 10 days ago. I was to marry a handsome SS man and have his babies, but what do I have there now? Without my family, I have nothing."

"I built a life in Berlin too. I thought I'd marry Thomas and become a doctor. My whole future was mapped out for me—just like yours, but our plans and our fate are two very different things. I started over, and so can you. Leave the Nazis behind. The world existed before Adolf Hitler, and it'll keep turning after he's gone." Fiona was silent for a few seconds. She seemed unable to find the words, so Maureen spoke again. "I felt a huge sense of relief when I left Germany. The pressure faded—the Nazi flags, the SS soldiers marching on the street, the portraits of Hitler in every classroom. Everything that dominates life in Germany ebbed to almost nothing here. I was able to breathe again. This country isn't perfect—far from it, but it's free. People have freedom to be what they want, to say what's in their hearts. I think you'll find that's extraordinary."

"Maybe I will. I was too young when we left America. I couldn't compare it to Germany."

"I understand. Don't approach your time here with prejudice. Just open your eyes and observe the way people live their lives outside Germany, and the fulfillment freedom provides."

"Can I move in with you in Paris?"

Maureen spluttered, her face suddenly tight. "I have some work to do outside of the city. You might have to stay with Lisa for a while. Father will be here soon too. He'll bring you to America."

"What kind of work do you need to do? Why do you have to leave Paris?"

"I'm not sure right now. It's for Father. He has some contacts—"

"I can help, Maureen. If you're doing something to help the Bernheims and the other Jews—"

"What? I don't know what you're talking about." Fiona looked at her as if she knew she was lying. "We can talk about this another time. You're just moving here. Let's take this step by step, okay?" added Maureen.

"I was wrong," said Fiona. "I see that now. Let me make amends somehow."

"Go to sleep," Maureen said and rolled over. As much as she wanted to believe her sister's redemption was complete, trust was something that had to be earned.

~

Sunday, November 20

After a sumptuous lunch, Seamus took his family on a river cruise along the Seine. It was a fine day, and the winter sun shone down on the grey surface of the water. The glory of Paris passed them on either side, but Seamus found it hard to concentrate. He walked up on deck alone and lit a cigarette. They passed Notre Dame Cathedral. He paused to behold its gothic beauty before taking a drag. The full weight of what he was planning to do descended on him like an anvil. He had money, but was it enough to do all of this? And sponsoring Gert and his family and whoever else for $5000 each? He hadn't mentioned his intention to sell to Helga yet, but knew she'd offer less than his share in the factory was worth. He'd signed a contract back in '32 when he'd taken over the factory that he wouldn't be able to sell it for ten years, or it would revert to Helga. Uncle Helmut had tried to guard against him selling it and immediately moving back to America with the profits. He was trying to keep the business in the family, but Seamus was beholden to Helga. His only hope was that she'd agree to sell the factory, giving him an advance on the payment, which would have to be finalized in '42. She had him over a barrel—unless he stayed three more years. She wasn't going to let him out of his contract and would squeeze him for what she could extract. He didn't hold that against her—any decent businessperson would do the same. The Nazis wouldn't let him out of the country without taking their own bite. It wouldn't be comparable to what the Jews had to pay, but it would hurt.

The question of Bill Hayden, his old friend, masquerading as a diplomat in the US embassy in Berlin, bobbed up in his mind. The spy wouldn't be pleased when he heard his prize asset was leaving Berlin. Hayden's reports went directly to Roosevelt, or so he said anyway. Seamus wondered what barriers his old war buddy might erect to his leaving or what carrots he might dangle in front of him to stay. Either way, Seamus needed to see his friend.

Fiona emerged from the boat in her coat and hat. "It's cold out here," she said with a smile.

"I just wanted a few minutes to gather my thoughts," Seamus replied.

"I've been doing a lot of thinking myself."

"About what?"

"Who I want to be."

"And what have you decided?"

"Maureen told me that she was leaving Paris. She said she had some work to do, but wouldn't tell me what it was."

"You can stay with Lisa. Maureen will be back sooner or later."

"I want to help. Whatever your plans are, I want to be part of them." Seamus opened his mouth to speak, but Fiona held her hand up to stop him. He kept quiet, respecting her wishes. "I understand that you don't trust me. I was a committed Nazi supporter until Kristallnacht, but that part of me has fallen away. I want to change. I know Maureen's up to something. I recognize that look in her eyes."

"Fiona—"

"Can you talk to her for me? I can be useful. I know it's something to do with the Bernheims and getting them out of Germany. Please let me help. I owe them that. Who would I tell? It's not like I can go to the Gestapo here."

Seamus finished his cigarette and stubbed it out before placing the butt in the trash can. He desperately wanted to believe she was genuine. "It's too much."

"Let me stay in France and oversee things from afar. Please, Father. I need this."

Seamus stared into his daughter's eyes. The longing was there to see. He believed her; it was the most beautiful feeling he could remember. He tried to evaluate the risk. Fiona wasn't a Nazi agent—just a young woman swayed by years of propaganda. Perhaps this was her way back to the person she'd been before he'd taken her to live in Berlin.

"I'll speak to Maureen and Lisa. I'm not promising anything."

A huge grin spread across her face. He reveled in her embrace.

He went to Maureen and Lisa a few hours later and managed to convince them of what he now believed in his heart—that Fiona was a changed person and could be an asset to them in their mission. Maureen was more skeptical, but his wife agreed to let Fiona help her procure and keep the house in the south of France. They wouldn't tell her much at first, but could reveal each piece of the plan to her in time if she proved trustworthy. It was as much as Seamus could ask for. He went to bed confident in what they needed to do and in the parts both of his daughters could play.

Seamus woke from an otherwise peaceful sleep at four in the morning. Lisa was dead to the world beside him. The curtain was open a chink more than he wanted, and he got up to close it. Soon, it would be just him and Conor in that mansion in Charlottenburg. What he wanted most was to be with his family, but saying that the trappings of wealth meant nothing to him was a lie. He'd lived in abject poverty only six years before and had stolen to get back to his children, who were mired in a single room in his sister's house in Newark. It felt good to provide for them and be an important man that others looked up to. Before he came to Germany, he was unemployed and sleeping on his sister's couch. In Berlin, he was a member of the new class of armament kings, getting rich off the Reich's feverish obsession with building the world's greatest military. In America, he'd be a nobody again, without the status he currently enjoyed or the means to gain it.

The last six years seemed like a dream. He looked around the lavish hotel room until his eyes settled on his wife in the massive bed that was its centerpiece. Seamus shut the curtains, climbed into bed beside his wife, and spiraled into a deep sleep.

14

Berlin, Monday, December 5

With little other choice, the Jews returned to work. The Gestapo had stopped the relentless pursuit of Jewish males they'd begun after Kristallnacht. Apparently, the Nazi authorities were happy with the 30,000 taken and were starting to release them in greater numbers now. The ones who returned told of horrific abuses such as standing for hours in freezing cold and driving rain for roll call. The middle-class values of those taken meant nothing in the horror of the concentration camps. Men who'd worked all their lives to exert control over their destinies were suddenly as vulnerable as children. Anyone who spoke up was beaten, many to within an inch of their lives. Some Jewish families received letters that their husbands or fathers had suffered an unfortunate accident while in detention and were charged the price of shipping back the bodies of their loved ones. With no one to appeal to, the families had to accept what they were told and plan for their eventual escape from Germany.

Seamus had returned from Paris the day before and

already felt the lack of Lisa and the children. Only Conor returned with him to Germany. He had thought of leaving the boy in France with the rest of his family, but the business Maureen and Lisa had to attend to was not for 13-year-olds. Besides, Seamus needed someone here. His son returned to school without grumbling. Fiona remained steadfast in her new belief that the Nazis had lost their way. She still found it difficult to declare everything she'd been taught in school and countless League of German Girls' meetings wrong, but the manifestation of Nazism was Harald and her friends. They disgusted her now, particularly the boy she once professed would be her husband. Seamus suspected something else had happened that Fiona wasn't letting on but didn't press her about it. Lisa and Maureen were on the way to the south of France, searching for somewhere to purchase a house for the people they intended to smuggle across the border from Germany. Fiona was still in Paris, under the guise of looking after Hannah.

The morning passed with no incidents between the Jewish workers and the rest of the staff. Several Jews were late because the government had banned them from driving, revoking their licenses that very day. The Jews in Germany were forced to sell their cars at giveaway prices dictated by the local Nazi officials. Anyone who refused would suffer the same consequence as the 30,000 taken after the riots.

Helga was prowling the balcony outside her office. Seamus had only seen his cousin briefly that morning but knew from her demeanor that she disapproved of the lengthy time he'd taken to visit his family in Paris. He climbed the stairs to where she was still standing as he arrived.

"Can we talk?"

She looked at him for a second longer than she usually

would have before agreeing. She offered him water as he took a seat opposite her.

"I know you're more used to whiskey or schnapps in your meetings, but I have no use for alcohol on a Monday morning."

"Water is fine," he said, taking the glass from her.

"Is Fiona coming back?"

"From France? I don't think so."

"I'm surprised as well as saddened. I never got to say goodbye."

Seamus hadn't considered his cousin's feelings when Fiona left and regretted that now. His children were the only family she had. The only other thing she had in her life was the Nazi Party. A massive portrait of Hitler stared at him from the wall behind her desk.

"I'm sorry about that. It all happened so quickly in the end. Maureen convinced her to stay in Paris. It wasn't something I could have predicted. I should have had her say goodbye though. I can only apologize for that. I'll make sure they both write soon."

"What happened to her? She seemed so dedicated to the cause, and to Harald. I'm shocked."

"We all were."

Seamus had weighed whether to tell Helga some portion of the truth about why Fiona left, but knew that even if he were to do so, now wasn't the time.

"I wouldn't have thought you'd be so surprised. Most of my family are gone. It's just Conor and I left."

"And you're planning on joining them soon?" Helga inquired.

"I am. I wanted to offer you the chance to buy me out."

"When are you leaving? Have you put the house up for sale?"

Seamus almost smiled. His cousin knew that the Gestapo would take note of a foreigner putting up a mansion in Charlottenburg for sale. The Reich would want their chunk of the proceedings, just as they would with the monies he'd gain from the sale of the business.

"Not yet," he said. "I wanted to speak to you first."

"When were you looking to get this done?"

"In the next few months."

"You're required to stay in the Reich until 1942. The legal documents you signed upon taking over the factory stated as much."

"I can't stay here any longer. My family is almost all gone. There's nothing here for me now."

"Except the business you promised to take on."

Her face was unyielding. His next words had to be carefully chosen.

"I can sell you my half of the business at a deep discount. When the sale goes through in '42 you'll reap a fortune."

"I can see what you'd have to gain from that," she replied. Her eyes were granite.

Seamus smiled and shook his head, wishing the water in his glass would transform into something more substantial. It was difficult to deny that she had him exactly where she wanted him. She knew he was up to something with the workers and that they wanted to leave. Her own spies on the floor had told her as much.

"Your behavior these past months has been unacceptable," she said. "I've been carrying the factories. You're more concerned with a certain band of workers than the business itself."

"You're right," Seamus admitted. "I'm sorry, but soon you'll be full owner and at an excellent price."

Seamus felt like he was back in school, but this was much more serious than a slap with the paddle. Each word his cousin uttered was a threat. Her plain, lined face was contorted in anger.

"You've been busy," she said. "Your family takes up so much of your time, but perhaps now that it's just you and Conor here in Berlin you could dedicate yourself to the business a little more."

"I can only apologize if other things took precedence over the factories, but you knew when I came here back in '32 that it might not be forever. My mind's been occupied with other things."

"I was aware, just as you are, that this is my father's business and I intend to do everything I can to prolong his legacy. Your obsession with certain elements of the workforce has detracted from the most important thing—producing the goods. It doesn't matter if those things are bullets or pot and pans. We are under contract with the government. Our word is our bond, and I've found myself covering for you too much lately."

"My focus was elsewhere. I admit that. My time in Germany is almost at an end. With my share of the business, you can do with Ritter Metalworks as you please."

"I already have been. Did you even know about the order for the new Messerschmitt BF 110's I negotiated while you were away?"

"I didn't, because you didn't tell me." Seamus stood up. "It seems I have a lot of work to catch up on. Please consider my offer. I'd like to keep this as casual a transaction as possible."

"I'm sure you would," his cousin replied. "Who says I have that kind of capital?"

He returned to his seat remembering the new house Helga bought a few months before.

It was time to try his story. She wasn't the only person he could sell to. "I'm sure the banks would lend you the money you'd require, or else I could put the word on the street that Ritter was for sale. I'm sure some big fish would come in and gobble up the place."

"I wouldn't do that if I were you," replied Helga. "A man in your position would do well to keep this quiet. If one of our competitors were to denounce you, who knows what would happen?" Seamus's blood ran cold as she called his bluff. She knew it had to be her that bought his share. Anything else would bring too much scrutiny. She was well aware of his hurry. All she had to do was delay. His cousin continued, "If the Gestapo were to begin investigating you, they might find something which could jeopardize your plans to move back to America and anyone else who might be intending to leave Germany with you. I'd hate to see that happen."

The blood drained from Seamus's face, and his legs suddenly weakened. The threat was understated but clear. The realization that she'd been waiting for this moment for years grabbed him like a steel vise. He searched for words to fix this situation, to convince her to let him leave with what her father had left him, but he knew they didn't exist. A faint smile appeared across her lips. Seamus was little more than a fish swimming in a barrel, waiting for the inevitable.

He regained his composure with a cough. "Please consider my offer, if not for me, for my children."

"Whatever happens will be part of a slow, considered process. I'm sure you understand that I can't rush the most important financial decision of my life."

"Of course," he said and returned to his office.

He went straight to the decanter of whiskey he kept on the side table for meetings and poured himself a glass. The burn soothed his nerves, and he walked to his desk and sat down. Shockwaves were still reverberating through his system. Helga knew precisely what she was doing and had played him like a grand piano. Everything she was saying was true. It was convenient to have a man heading up the firm to shake other men's hands and to have a tumbler of booze with the suppliers and Nazi officials who came to his office. But Helga was the heart and soul of the operation. She was the one who stayed here nights poring over sales figures and logistics. She knew the longer she delayed the process of purchasing the company from him, the more pressure would be heaped on him to leave without completing the transaction. His wife and three daughters were in France.

Seamus downed the remainder of his drink.

It didn't matter to Helga if the sale took two years, but he wanted to conclude the whole matter in two months. In two years, his wife and daughters would be back in America, and the way things were going, Germany would more than likely be at war. The thought of being stuck here while Hitler's armies marauded across Europe with the weaponry he provided them drove him back to the decanter of whiskey.

The amber liquid swirled in his glass as he stood at the window, staring down at the factory floor. It felt like a moment he'd already lived, as if this were a memory he was looking back on instead of living in the moment. The Jewish workers were safe behind the barriers, but it was only a matter of time before some other decree passed down by the government barred them from earning a living anywhere. Helga was counting on the fact that he wouldn't declare the factory for sale on the broader market because of the scrutiny it would bring. Any competent Gestapo investigation would imperil the plan to smuggle his Jewish employees to France and possibly condemn them to life in a concentration camp. But he knew anyone with the money would be delighted to buy him out. He envisaged the apartment in New York he could buy and the good he could do for his family with the money. He could return to America as a rich man.

The choice was clear—sell the house and the business and move back to America richer than he'd ever imagined, or rescue the Jews on the factory floor. Gert Bernheim was his best friend. Perhaps he could get him and his family out. Their visas to America would cost $15,000.

"You can't save everyone," he said out loud.

He tried to draw his eyes away from the Jewish workers.

"96," he said. "It's not even possible. But the hell if I'm not going to try!"

Leaving without selling his share in the factory would be the perfect cover. The Gestapo would never suspect he was planning to emigrate. What sane person would leave so much money behind? He had just enough money in the accounts in Switzerland to cover the price of the houses in the south of France and the visas and the fares to America or Brazil.

"Then what?" he said to himself. "Get an honest job—one that doesn't feed the Nazi war machine."

He finished the whiskey. Being rich never suited him anyway.

15

Monday, December 5

The call from Hayden came three hours later. They went through the usual rigmarole of disguising who he was on the phone, but Seamus knew what to listen for. Hayden mentioned the region of Berlin called Wedding and the number 310. Seamus wrote down the details and told him he'd speak to his suppliers at 5:30 that evening. Hayden agreed and hung up the phone. He sat at his desk, staring into space for the remainder of the day.

He was in a daze as he left the empty factory at 5 o'clock. Helga was still in her office, beavering away. He felt no guilt at leaving early and never would again. "You've gotten your last pound of flesh out of me," he said, and carried on out the door. It was dark and cold, and his breath formed plumes of white in front of him. The car's interior wasn't any warmer than the air outside, and he wrapped his scarf around his neck before starting the vehicle. As he drove to the city, his mind was numb, almost devoid of thought. His meeting with Helga earlier had felt like ten rounds with Joe Louis. He wondered how many jabs he'd have to take from Hayden in whatever dingy hotel room the diplomat had rented for the night.

The arrangement was as smooth as ever, and Seamus was positive no one followed him. The hotel was one step above mandatory demolition status, and in the lobby, he passed by several sketchy characters with women who frequented places such as these.

Hayden greeted him with a firm handshake and offered him a seat and a vodka soda. Seamus accepted the drink and sat opposite his old comrade. It was hard to say if the spy was his friend or not. His reaction to what Seamus was about to share with him would be telling.

"What do you have for me?" the man who masqueraded as a diplomat asked.

"Some orders for the new Messerschmitt BF 110. It's a state-of-the-art fighter bomber. Göring loves them. He thinks it's the future of the fighter-bomber for the Luftwaffe."

"And how would you know such a thing?"

"He told me on the telephone this afternoon."

"You speak to the President of the Reichstag often? Or do you refer to him as the minister for aviation or forestry even?"

"The man does like to adopt titles. I don't speak to him often—just when he's excited about one of the new warplanes. He tends to get worked up over them. These are aggressive weapons. Not for defense as much as bombing and strafing enemy positions on the ground."

"Anyone would think Hitler didn't mean what he said when he declared he had no more interest in upsetting the equilibrium in Europe. Interesting that he'd invest in planes designed to attack," Hayden said. "I tried to contact you last week."

"I was in Paris with Lisa and the family."

"Were you here for that debacle on November 9?"

"Unfortunately."

Hayden looked upset and shook his head. "It's unbelievable

when you think about it. The country that produced Bach, Brahms and Beethoven, Thomas Mann and Goethe has sunk to this level. Because the lunatics we saw that night are the same as those running the government. FDR might have waffled on condemning the riots in public at first, but word is they sickened him to his stomach."

"I read the statement he made a few days later. He seemed to communicate as much. It was a little late, but he was unequivocal in his criticism."

"He's walking a constant tightrope, especially since the losses in the midterms. He's more reliant than ever on those conservative southern Democrats. Who'd be a politician, eh?" Hayden reached into his pocket for a pack of cigarettes and offered one to Seamus, who accepted with thanks. "We were the only country to withdraw our ambassador. The embassy is a strange place without anyone calling the shots."

"I didn't think you answered to him."

"And you were right. I don't think Hitler's going to lose much sleep over the US ambassador being recalled, but they had to do something, or at least be seen to try."

Seamus's hands were sweaty, and he rubbed a handkerchief between them.

"Everything okay?" Hayden asked.

Seamus ignored his question and pressed on. "The only hope for Germany's Jews is to leave. Things are only going to get worse here. Kristallnacht was only the beginning."

"I've been parroting that point to the powers that be in the State Department for the last two years, but I may as well be talking to myself."

"They're not interested in helping the Jews?"

"The story of Kristallnacht was splashed all over the American newspapers. America was up in arms. No one could believe what a civilized country had come to. How could the German people treat their own citizens like that? But I read some opinion polls the other day that tell the real story. 94% of the American people disapproved of the events of 9-10 November, but 70% stated that the quota system should remain and no additional Jews should be allowed into the country because of it."

"The people don't see the danger the Jews are in here?"

"They do and they wish the Jews the best. They just don't want them coming to the USA. I heard a congressman say the other day that it would 'exacerbate the Jewish problem in America' if they took more in."

"What Jewish problem is that, exactly?"

"The problem the antisemites have with them, and believe me, Seamus, the State Department, and the halls of congress are rife with people who'd like to shut the borders tomorrow."

"What were those words written on the Statue of Liberty? 'Give me your huddled masses yearning to breathe free.'"

"That sentiment isn't as popular as it once might have been. I don't know if it ever was. FDR does want to help the Jews, but his hands are tied. The quotas can only be changed by an act of congress and the political will just isn't there. Quite the opposite, in fact. Dozens of bills to reduce the quotas of immigrants have been introduced in congress. Some of which even suggest closing the borders altogether."

"Who backs these bills?"

"The American Legion. The Daughters of the American Revolution, and the American Coalition of Patriotic Societies and other powerful civil organizations lobby congress almost daily to reduce the numbers of immigrants coming in."

Seamus stood up to stretch his legs. Thoughts of Gert Bernheim and the rest of the 96 swelled in his mind. "Where do they expect the Jews to go?"

"Elsewhere."

"What about the Jewish organizations in the US? What are they doing?"

"They're in some turmoil, but most of the leaders agree that they keep quiet. They don't want to poke the Nazi bear."

"You're joking."

"The Jews in America have staged some demonstrations but their leaders are cautious. They think the Nazis will punish the Jews in Germany more if the organizations in America show them up. It's a mess. Hitler holds all the cards. The British started their Kindertransport system for Jewish children to escape, but how desperate do you have to be to separate from your children? These people don't know if they'll ever see their sons and daughters again. It's so sad."

Seamus had never seen his confident, almost cocky, friend affected by events of the day so much before. The time was right to tell him.

"I've been evaluating my situation in Germany since the riots too. I can't stay here."

"How did I know you were going to say that?" Hayden said with a wry grin. He leaned forward, only a few inches from his face. "Our work here isn't over. We're on the front line. The details you provide me go straight to the president."

"My wife is in Paris, and Fiona just moved to France too. It's just Conor and me left. I don't want to stay in this horrendous place, especially not without them. I have money, but for what purpose?"

"I need you, Seamus. Just give me another year or two. You're so much more than the reports you deliver. We don't have anyone else who mixes with the chattering classes like you do. Other than the Nazis, these are the people who make the decisions in this country. They're the ones who'll help decide when this war will start. We can be right there with Hitler if we know what they're thinking."

The pressure in Seamus's mind was building. He took a gulp of vodka, seeking temporary relief.

"I need to get the Jews in my factory out of Germany."

"To America? Good luck!"

"Can you help me get the visas we need?"

"How many?"

"96."

Hayden erupted in a terrible mirthless laugh. "Seamus, I hate to disappoint you, but I'm not the President. Have you been listening to what I've been saying? I don't want you to go. I need you here. Do you think I'm about to facilitate you leaving?"

"These are people's lives we're talking about."

"And you don't think we can save more lives here in Berlin by reporting back to Washington?"

"I've given you information for more than two years, risking my life every time. If the Gestapo catches us, I'll be on the end of a rope before the sun comes up."

"They're not going to catch us as long as we stay smart."

"I spoke to Helga about selling the factory."

"The Gestapo will be on you night and day once you do that."

"I know. That's why I'm walking away."

"From your business? Are you crazy? You'll lose a fortune."

"I'm aware. All I want to do is keep my family safe and get the Jews out of Germany. I need your help. I understand 96 visas are too many to ask for. How many could you get me?"

Hayden smiled again. "You're determined to do this, aren't you? You're about to leave everything behind."

"How many?" Seamus said.

"I don't know. I could pull some strings at the embassy. Ten, maybe 15. Twenty at most."

"So, you could get me 20 American visas for my employees?"

Hayden paused a few seconds as if evaluating something in his mind.

"I'll tell you what, Seamus. You stay here, and remain as

head of Ritter Metalworks, and I'll get you all 96. I'll send a personal letter to FDR. He'll pull the strings. That's your deal—you stay here and our arrangement goes on, and I'll make sure all your friends are safe in America in a few months' time."

"You're asking me to abandon my family."

"Many have sacrificed more, my friend. I don't have a family. My service to the state is my life. I'm not saying it'll be forever—just a few years."

"Once the war begins, I won't be able to get out."

"Where the will exists, so does the way. I won't leave you."

"Comforting," Seamus said in a tone thick with sarcasm.

Hayden held out his hand.

"I'm not agreeing yet," Seamus said.

"I'm offering your friends safety," Hayden countered. "I know the kind of man you are. You want to be the hero? This is your chance."

"I want to be a father to my children."

"Then sell the business when you legally can in '42, and give them the proceeds. Set them up with homes in New York or New Jersey, or wherever they want to live. Your time in Germany can mean something. This is your chance to make a difference. The Nazis are hellbent on destroying the world order and replacing it with their disgusting racist system."

"I think you're confusing me with someone else."

"Who?"

"Someone more important."

"Not a chance. I see you for exactly what you are—my most significant asset in the midst of the lion's den. I'll do what it takes to keep you. And this way you keep your money too."

Seamus went to the door. "I'll be in touch," he said, and walked through it.

16

New York, Tuesday, December 6

The city was everything Michael had hoped it would be. It was lively and endlessly fascinating. The hundreds of neighborhoods, all tacked together, that constituted Manhattan offered a glimpse into every part of the world. He could be anyone he wanted here, and the paranoia of living in the Reich was a memory. New York had the same hustle and bustle of Berlin, but without the ubiquitous Nazi flags that infected Germany's capital like a virus. Hitler's paradise seemed a world away from here, and that was reflected in the attitudes of the people he met. The newspapers splashed headlines about the riots against the Jews in Germany. Americans read them with furrowed brows before tucking the broadsheets under their arms and getting on with their day.

East 34th Street was awash with people in hats and coats, sheltering against the scythe of the wind. Michael arched his neck to view the Empire State Building extending into the sky. What a marvel of modern engineering it was. Nothing like it existed in Berlin. Several months had passed since he and his new wife had moved back to America. His father had bought them an apartment on the Upper West Side as a wedding gift, though Michael was determined to pay him back. They were comfortable, and Monika was learning English at night. Michael stopped outside the language school on 6th Avenue and waited for a few minutes until she bounded down the stairs.

"Hello, husband," she said in English and kissed him.

"How was class tonight?" he replied in the same language.

"Good," she said and burst out laughing. She switched to German to introduce a young woman with curly brown hair whom he hadn't noticed was standing beside her. "This is Marlene. She's from Bremen."

He shook the stranger's hand. "Please to meet you."

"Shall we go for a drink?" Monika said.

Michael was pleased that his wife was making friends and agreed. They found an Irish pub within walking distance and proceeded inside. It was clean, and the clientele seemed respectable enough, so they found seats. Michael brought beers to the table. Monika was the first to drink.

"I miss the beer back home," she said, but took a gulp regardless.

"Maybe not too much else," Michael said.

Marlene squirmed in her seat and began talking about the lessons they were taking—speaking all the time in German.

"Where do you work?" she asked Michael after a few minutes.

"At a property firm downtown, but only part time. I'm in college at night."

"And training for the next Olympics," Monika said.

Marlene seemed intrigued. "What event?"

"I'm a sprinter. The 100 meters." It didn't seem right to mention that he'd represented Germany in the last games. It wasn't something he advertised in America.

"Where are the next games?" Marlene asked.

"In Helsinki. They were originally meant to be in Tokyo, but—"

"They were cancelled because of the war between Japan and China. I read about it."

"How long have you been here?" Michael asked.

"Six months."

"Do you miss more than the beer?" Monika asked.

"I do, but I keep in touch with a lot of Germans in New York. You'd be amazed how many of us are here."

"It seems like there are more foreigners than Americans here."

Marlene nodded. "I wanted to ask. Do you want to come to a meeting of the German society I'm a member of tonight? They're holding a rally in Madison Square Garden. It's sold out, but I have some spare tickets. My parents aren't able to make it."

Michael sat back in his seat. He hadn't heard a meeting described as a "rally" since they'd fled Germany in '36.

"When is this meeting?" Monika asked.

"In twenty minutes," Marlene said with a smile. "We'll have to leave now. It'd be a great way to meet other Germans."

"What do you think?" Michael asked his wife. "We don't have any plans."

Monika shrugged approval, and they stood up from the table. Marlene led them out of the pub and back into the cold night. Both women wore hats and mittens to keep warm.

"The organization is called the German American Bund. You have to be an American citizen of German descent to get in."

"That's us," Monika said. "What do they stand for?"

"Modern German values."

The first word she used set off alarm bells in Michael's mind. Anything modern in Germany referred to the Nazis. He and Monika dropped far enough behind to whisper a few words. He turned to his wife, who seemed to be thinking the same thing.

"Are you sure about this? Who is this person?" he said.

"I have no idea. I only met her tonight," Monika replied.

"You think we should go?"

"How can we counter these people if we don't know who they are or what they're thinking?"

They caught up to Marlene once more as the massive building came into view. The last of the crowd was filtering inside. Some were wearing grey uniforms Michael wasn't familiar with, but the similarity to those he'd seen in Berlin countless times was apparent. The style of the posters outside was identical to what the Nazis used, except these declared what was happening inside to be a "pro-American rally" and a "mass demonstration for true Americanism."

A thick layer of police was gathered outside, many in riot gear. Their presence provided Michael a sense of safety he might not otherwise have enjoyed.

A morbid sense of curiosity overtook Michael. Monika was silent, and the disgusted look on her face as she pulled down the scarf from her cheeks betrayed her feelings. Marlene seemed oblivious and smiled just as they proceeded inside.

"My parents will be so angry they missed this," she said like a giddy schoolchild.

Twenty thousand people were packed into the venue. The stage at the front was adorned with revolutionary American flags, with a full-length representation of George Washington draped thirty feet from the awnings to the floor. The Nazi flags were more subtle than they would have been had this rally been in Germany. They were on the walls and the end of poles the men in the gray uniforms carried. This was a very American version of Nazism.

Marlene led them to their seats. They shuffled past well-dressed German Americans, young and old. As they sat down, dozens of American Nazi stormtroopers entered the venue from the back and filled up the aisles. Each carried a banner with the swastika on it or an American flag. They seemed evenly split. Marlene was on her feet with the rest of the crowd offering Hitler salutes.

"I thought we'd left this behind," Monika whispered.

Michael didn't answer. The first speaker took to the stage at the lectern set up underneath the portrait of Washington. The portrait would have been Hitler in Germany, but Michael figured the Americanisms on show were merely lip service. This was a tribute to one man, and it wasn't the first President of the United States.

"Are you an active member of the Bund?" Michael asked Marlene.

"I give money and march when they ask me to. Are you interested in joining?"

"Let's see how tonight goes."

The speaker pulled down the microphone and began with a Hitler salute, but instead of the familiar "Sieg heil," he called out "free America." The crowd responded in kind. The banners in the aisles bounced up and down, and the American flags swayed back and forth. A little piece of Nazi Germany had made it to New York City. The Nazi at the lectern welcomed the crowd and began. He introduced himself as Fritz Kuhn, a veteran who'd fought for Germany in the Great War before moving to the US.

"We are not so different than our German ancestors who have lived here a century or more, or any God-fearing white American. We demand the same things— a socially just, white gentile-ruled United States and gentile-controlled labor unions free from Jewish Bolshevist domination." The crowd roared approval. "The bond we share with our fellow Americans is one of race, and it is something that we will lay down our lives for if necessary. The struggle the dear Führer has taken upon himself to lead is one that will determine not just the future of Germany, but of this country, and the entire white race!"

Michael's body was cold. He thought not of Willi and his family in the camp for Roma set up in Berlin, but of the hundreds still imprisoned there—those they couldn't rescue.

"Jews all over this city are firing Christian employees to make room for the invasion of refugees they've planned. The Jew is the most dangerous of all the peoples of the world due to his parasitic nature, and mark my words, the values we hold so dear as Americans are under threat. If we allow this mass migration to consume the wonderful country we call home, it will be no more. I urge you to make your voice heard. Despite the attempts of the Jews, we still possess some power in this land, and it's imperative that we let our political representatives know that we do not approve of any Jewish immigration. We will not let our country be overrun by Judeo-Bolshevism!"

The crowd erupted. Every flag was held high, and thousands of hands were raised in salute again.

"George Washington would have approved of every word I've just spoken. Truly he was the first American fascist!" Kuhn continued. "The federal government, led by the traitor, Roosevelt, is nothing but a mob of Jewish agents. We need to tell them where to stick their 'Jew Deal'." The crowd laughed. Michael felt like he'd vomit at any moment.

The speech was interrupted when a young man broke onto the stage and tried to tackle Kuhn. Several bodyguards grabbed him just as he reached the American Nazi leader. They made no effort to drag him off the stage before beginning to beat him up. The burly men in gray uniforms held him in front of the crowd, punching and kicking him. The young man was limp before they manhandled him off stage right.

Kuhn seemed to take it as a victory over the Jews and led a cheer, which rippled through the crowd.

"Time to leave," Monika said and stood up.

"Already?" Marlene answered.

"Don't approach me again. Not in class. Not anywhere." Michael's wife answered. They pushed through the crowd of grey-shirted Nazis, who were cheering once more as Michael and Monika reached the exits. A group of counter-protestors had gathered outside the Garden. A line of policemen separated them from the anti-Nazis. Michael took his wife by the hand and ran. They didn't stop until the chants of the protestors had faded in their ears.

He took his wife in his arms. "I'm so sorry," she said.

"We should have known," he answered. "I thought it would be a lark—to see the pathetic local Nazis, but when they beat up that man...."

"Our own version of Kristallnacht, right before our eyes. I'm so sorry, I had no idea Marlene was a Nazi. I didn't think their tentacles stretched this far."

"We were both wrong."

"Do you think I'll be able to live here, once the war begins?"

"What are you talking about?"

"When people read about events like tonight, they're going to think every German immigrant is one of them. People don't like feeling the enemy is among them."

"Don't be ridiculous," Michael answered. What else could he say? It was a subject they'd skirted around many times, but it was true. If the Nazis started a war, the people would see every German as a potential threat. The thought of it gave him so much pain that he couldn't bear to mention it out loud. This was his country. It was his job to protect her.

"Maybe coming here was a mistake," she said.

"No," he answered. "Those people at that rally tonight are the worst this country has to offer. The people in Germany aren't any different than the population here. They have the same prejudices and fears, and they're susceptible to the same propaganda and lies. The good people will distinguish you from that rabble inside Madison Square Garden. People are defined by their actions, not their nationality."

"That's a fine speech, but you have an American accent. You're one of them. I'll never be."

"Despite what those Nazi idiots preach, this is a country of immigrants. Those words on the Statue of Liberty still mean something. And this is still a far better place to be than Germany."

Monika shrugged off his hand but still walked beside him. They didn't utter more than a few words until they reached their apartment block. Michael gathered the day's mail from the box in the lobby and walked up the stairs behind his wife. They were inside the apartment when he took her by the hand.

"I don't have a compass or a map. I don't know what will happen here, or if there will or won't be a war between America and Germany. What I do know is that I only want to be with you—no matter where that might be. And New York seems better than most places."

She kissed him on the mouth. "You're a good boy," she said in English.

"Man." He corrected her in German.

Michael noticed a telegram among the mail he'd just thrown on the table as Monika took off her coat and hat. He ripped it open.

"It's from my father," he said. "Sent from Paris."

"Saying the things he couldn't in Germany, no doubt."

Michael read it aloud.

IT'S TIME TO GET OUT OF GERMANY. FIONA'S NOW IN FRANCE WITH THE OTHERS AFTER A CHANGE OF HEART REGARDING THE NAZIS. CONOR AND I WILL FOLLOW IN TIME. I NEED YOU TO ARRANGE IMMEDIATE SPONSORS FOR THREE VISAS. THE BERN-

HEIMS. ONE PERSON, ONE SPONSOR. YOU AND TWO OTHERS WILL
NEED TO PLACE A BOND OF $5000 FOR EACH MEMBER OF THE
FAMILY, GERT, LIL, AND JOEL. I WILL PAY.

"Fiona left Germany," Michael said as a smile spread across his
face. "I can't believe it."

"She had an epiphany," Monika said and kissed him again.
"It's because of what happened on Kristallnacht. I'm sure of it."

"Father wants to get the Bernheims out of Germany. I'll see
a lawyer in the morning. Where can we find sponsors?"

"Not among the members of the German American Bund,
that's for sure."

"I'm sure finding decent people willing to help won't be
difficult."

"We'll do it together."

They embraced. Michael smiled over his wife's shoulder.
This was what she needed—a way to make a difference in other
people's lives.

17

Berlin, Tuesday, January 31, 1939

The vise was closing on the Jews. Seamus was in his office, thumbing through the newspaper. The lead story was the speech the Führer had made the previous night in the Reichstag. The parliament had once been the hub of Germany's fragile democracy, but was now an echo chamber for whatever idea drifted into Hitler's mind. In his address, the Austrian referred to the coming war and declared that, although he desired nothing more than peace, any future conflict would mean the annihilation of the Jewish race in Europe. Anyone who thought that Kristallnacht would mean the slowing of Nazi aggression toward the Jews had misunderstood their intentions. The impossibility of being Jewish in Nazi Germany grew more apparent by the day. The ball that had started rolling back in 1933 with the unsuccessful Nazi boycott of Jewish businesses was now a full-fledged juggernaut.

The conundrum weighing Seamus down the last two months was never far from the front of his mind. If he did sell his half of the factory to someone other than Helga, they'd likely offer a fraction of what it was worth, and he wouldn't see a pfennig until 1942 at the earliest. How easy would it be to move money out of Nazi Germany then? And if war was raging? It wouldn't be difficult to find a Nazi judge willing to void the contract of sale, leaving Seamus and his family with nothing. Convincing Helga to give him an advance was his only hope, and a slim one at that.

On the other hand, he could stay, rake in the riches of providing for the Reich's military machine, and wallow in the bliss of knowing Bernheim and all the other Jewish workers were safe in America. But the cost of riches and loyalty to his employees would be his own family, who still thought he was planning to leave when the last of the Ritter Metalworks Jews departed. He hadn't been sleeping much these past few weeks.

None of the Jewish employees had secured an exit visa to leave Germany yet. Many of them were wondering if they ever would. The irony that Seamus had thought he was protecting them by giving them jobs was lost on no one. He had inadvertently barred them from legally escaping Germany by employing them in the factory. But they weren't the only ones experiencing problems. The sheer number of people applying to leave the Reich was staggering, but few governments had shown any additional willingness to take refugees. The first Kindertransport to the United Kingdom had left in early December, and more than 10,000 children had departed Germany so far. The first shipment to England was made up of children from an orphanage destroyed on Kristallnacht. No Ritter employees had sent their sons or daughters. Only the most desperate had. No parent wanted to be parted from their child when there was a real possibility of never seeing them again. The Ritter workers had a plan to flee Germany, albeit one that had been delayed by the coming of winter. Escaping through the forest into France was too dangerous in the icy cold, but some saw anything as a better option than staying in the Reich, awaiting any subsequent Nazi decrees to be handed down.

Lisa's role in extracting the families had also been delayed. The buildings they'd purchased in a village called Izieu, about an hour outside the city of Lyon in southeast France, had taken some time to get ready. Lisa, Maureen, Hannah, and Fiona had moved down from Paris before Christmas. Getting anything done in a sleepy village in rural France was hard at the best of times, but during the holidays had proven impossible. The decision was made to wait a few weeks.

Once everything was ready, the parents and children would travel to the border together. The adults and older children would be escorted across the border by Maureen and whatever guide she'd found. The kids would be met by women smugglers, issued with papers, and brought through the checkpoints. It was hard to know which way was more dangerous, but Lisa had assured him that the child smugglers were confident nothing would go wrong. Apparently, spiriting children out of Germany was a lucrative industry these days, and getting caught at the border was bad for business.

Gert Bernheim entered Seamus's office and shut the door behind him. "It seems like the Nazis crossed another threshold last night," he said, picking up the newspaper on the desk and throwing it down.

It was all too easy to fall into complacency and reason that the Nazis would eventually wake up and realize the evil they were spreading. The Führer was sincere in what he said. All the insane, hateful rhetoric he preached was a warning, a roadmap to where the country was headed. Whatever the Führer spouted one day became the country's highest priority the next. And now, for the first time, he was talking about annihilating the Jews, not just behind closed doors but on the highest political stage in Germany. His insane ramblings were now the laws of the land, and thousands were suffering because of them.

"It's one of the most dangerous things he's said yet," Seamus said. "It seems like he wants to fight a war against the Jews, not just the Soviets or the Poles, or whoever else gets in his way. He's threatening a group of unarmed civilians, and he has the most sophisticated military in the world at his disposal."

"We know more about his sophisticated military than most."

"We've done what we had to these past few years to support our families."

"The Jewish employees are skittish. The Nazi workers are singing an SS marching song, spouting 'Death to the Jews.'"

"Now?" Seamus said and stood up. The factory manager nodded.

Seamus ran to the door and opened it. The sound of singing was clearly discernible over the constant chattering of the machinery, and the violent words sent chills down Seamus's spine. He bounded down the stairs and ran to the section in the corner where he'd stationed the members of the Trustee Council and the other most ardent Nazis. They didn't stop singing as he arrived. Benz turned to him, tipped his cap, and belted the song out even louder.

"Stop this immediately," Seamus yelled.

No one did as the factory owner said. The Nazi smirked as Seamus squared up to him.

"You don't appreciate our song?"

"Stop this, Benz!"

"Or what? You'll fire us? Impossible. Those vermin shouldn't be here. The government is on our side, and word is you'll be gone the way of the dodo soon. So, why don't you scurry back to your office, Yankee Boy, before we teach you a lesson?"

Several other workers were standing behind Benz, but Seamus didn't draw his eyes away from their leader. Benz's ugly gray eyes were unrelenting. Realizing that the Nazi employees were beyond his control was like acid in his mouth. Benz knew Seamus was on the way out and that he and the other Nazis would soon enjoy free reign under Helga's leadership. Perhaps Benz even thought he could be the male figurehead of the company once Seamus left. Uncle Helmut would spit blood if he could see what his beloved company had become.

"Watch out," Seamus said. "I'm still the boss here."

"Are you?" the head of the Trustee Council replied. "It doesn't seem like you're leading too much from my vantage point."

Several other workers, men Seamus had known for six years, were staring at him with violence in their eyes. It was time to back off. He wanted to wipe the grin off Benz's little rat face, but knew he'd be putting the Jews in danger as much as himself.

"Sing your pathetic song," he said. "This is all going to come crashing down someday."

The men resumed bellowing the chorus to the SS marching song as Seamus turned around and retreated to his room. That's exactly what it felt like—a retreat.

Gert was standing at the door.

"I've lost them," Seamus said. "Someone got wind of the fact that I'm leaving."

"From your cousin, no doubt."

Seamus's initial instinct was to defend Helga, but who else could have told Benz and the others? His cousin now spent most of her time at the other factory, which was okay with Seamus. They hadn't spoken much since their meeting when she'd laid out her strategy for forcing him out. The company was suffering because of their hostility, but he didn't care, and she likely thought it a small price to pay for wresting complete control from him.

Gert shut the door, and they took their seats at the desk again. "The Jews on the floor want out now. Who knows what tomorrow will bring? They could start shooting us on the streets for all we know."

Seamus wished he could say his friend was being ridiculous. "The weather is against us. The snow in the forest is probably two feet deep."

"Better to suffer that than the Gestapo's bullets." Gert's voice almost broke as the words came out, and Seamus walked over to the desk and poured them both a glass of whiskey.

"For your nerves," Seamus said. "And don't tell me it's 2pm on a Tuesday afternoon."

"I'm well aware of what time it is."

Gert gulped back some of the fine liquor. "I can't live like this anymore. Every time I leave the house—your house—I feel like it could be the last time. My family is at the mercy of the Gestapo, and the SS, and whatever Stormtroopers might happen to be on the street. The depth of their hatred is hard to fathom. They could kill my wife and son on the street, could beat them to death in front of my eyes, and I wouldn't have any recourse. No court in Germany would convict a Nazi for murdering a Jew. I live every moment thinking it could be my last. I don't sleep at night. I have these horrific dreams where the SS come for me and I wake up sweating. Lil's the same. Joel's barely stepped outside since you took us in. I think he's read every book you have. I can only imagine what it's like for people with little kids."

"We love having him, and you too."

"But we deserve to live our own lives, to forge our own paths. I don't go anywhere but here, and those men on the factory floor would kill me with their bare hands if given the slightest provocation. We're a Nazi's whim away from death at all times, and I can't take it anymore." He took another gulp of his drink. Seamus pushed a pack of cigarettes across to him, and he lit one up. "It's like living in a pressure cooker. We're not citizens, even though my entire family was born here. We're not

Germans, even though this is the only country I've ever known. And you say the snow is two feet deep at the border? Coming to work is more dangerous for us."

Seamus reached into his desk, drew out a telegram, and pushed it across to his friend. "I got this from Maureen and Lisa yesterday. The houses in France are ready."

"What's the village called again?"

"Izieu."

"I should remember that. I could be living there for quite a while." Gert said, trying to force a smile.

"They're old boarding houses, far from finished, but the ladies have been working on them for weeks. According to this, they're ready for the first people." He pushed the telegram across to his friend. "Even Fiona's been helping."

"Fiona knows the plan?" Gert said with the telegram in his hand. He wasn't as amazed as he once would have been at the news.

"Not every part, but she's rebuilt the trust we had in her before.... everything that happened," he said with a wave of his hand.

"When were you planning on telling me and the other employees that the houses were ready?"

"We thought it would be best to wait until the weather cleared to cross. It'll be a hard route through the forest in winter, but if the workers are determined to leave now...." Seamus trailed off and reached for a cigarette of his own. "Do you want to leave first?"

"No. Lil and I agreed we'd be last. The workers look up to me. It wouldn't be right to run away before they were all safe. What about you?"

"The captain's always last to leave the sinking ship."

"I thought the captain's duty was to go down with the ship."

"Just as well I never joined the navy. I'll speak to Lisa, and we'll get the train running. How do we decide who goes first?"

"Give me a moment," Gert said. He left and reappeared two minutes later with Pamela Bernstein, one of the youngest employees in the factory. She was thin, with black hair and light brown eyes. She was also a mother to two young boys, one still in diapers.

"Just like at sea again," Gert said as they sat down. "Women and children first."

"Are you ready for this?" Seamus asked.

"To get out of Germany with my children? Yes, I am. My sister sent her girls to England. They're on a farm in Surrey. I'm just grateful we'll be together. I couldn't live without my boys."

"You think they'll be okay without you for a day or two while my wife brings them across the border?"

"They will if they need to be."

"Even the baby? How old is he?"

"He's two in July, but he's a good boy. Will the smugglers be able to handle him?

"They'll take him across when he's napping."

"Wonderful," she said and smiled. "When can we leave?"

"I'll need to speak to my wife. She's a few hours away from the border, in the village you're bound for."

"Izieu," Pamela said. "Just saying the name brings tears to my eyes. I never knew one place I'd never heard of could sound so much like paradise."

"Let's concentrate on getting there in one piece."

"Pamela has 900 Reichsmarks in the fund," Gert said.

"Okay," Seamus said. The workers had started funneling every spare pfennig into the escape fund after Kristallnacht but couldn't afford to spare much from their paltry, government-controlled wages. "Money won't be a problem. The boarding houses are paid for, and we have an expense fund."

Pamela didn't ask any questions about where the cash came from, but surely she knew.

"What about my sister and my parents?" the young woman asked. "I can't just leave them here."

"And your sister is married, I presume?"

Pamela nodded. "Her children are in England. Perhaps she could travel to join them?"

"I can't get everyone out."

"It's only a few more people. Just four more adults walking through the forest with the guide," Gert said. "Six isn't many more than two."

"If we do this for her, the 96 is going to swell to hundreds." Gert looked back at him but didn't respond. "We can't traffic all those people across. If the border guards catch them without exit papers, they'll end up in a concentration camp."

"And what fate do you think awaits them if they don't try to escape?" Gert asked.

"They can apply for visas to other countries. Your sister already sent her kids to England."

"Even if they do get visas," Gert said. "They'll leave the country with nothing. The Nazis are stealing everything from us. Only the richest Jews in Germany are emigrating with anything. The rest of us will be dumped in Paris, or London, or New York with nothing. We'll be destitute. Stealing across the border—your way—is the only chance any of us have of getting out of Germany with enough money to start again."

Seamus pushed out a breath and reached for the pack of cigarettes again. He offered one to Pamela, but she declined with thanks.

"This plan is nuts," Seamus said. "We can't take the entire Jewish population of Berlin to France."

"No one's asking you to," Gert said.

"If we do this," Seamus said, holding up a finger, "and that's a big 'if', we have to set rules in place. Only direct family. Not second cousins, and no grandparents. They won't make it."

"That sounds fair," Gert said. "So, can I tell the employees they can bring their family members and their children?"

Seamus felt the weight of Gert and Pamela's stare. "Okay. You win!" he said. "I have no idea how we're going to manage this. 96 was close to impossible. This is just a fantasy."

"You told me once, 'where the will exists, so does the way,'" Gert said.

Seamus threw up his hands, but his reaction didn't detract from the rare smile on his friend's face.

"When do we leave?" Pamela said.

"This weekend," Seamus responded. "Pack light. Wear the warmest clothes you have, and your best boots."

"Thank you, Herr Ritter," Pamela said. "I only met your uncle a few times, but I know he'd be proud of you today."

She stood up and walked out.

"Seems like we have some work to do," Gert said.

Seamus shook his head in disbelief at what he'd just agreed to do.

18

The village of Lembach in northeastern France, Saturday, February 4

It all felt rushed to Maureen. Although she, Lisa, and Fiona had been working on the plan to extricate the Jews from Germany for over a month, the sense that they were unprepared haunted her. Her worries were countered by Fiona's awakening from Nazism. Her sister didn't ask questions or grumble and was an invaluable help in preparing the houses for the workers' arrival. The dissenting voices in Maureen's mind were fading, and though they were still audible, questions like, "is she waiting until the Jews arrive to report them?" were answerable now. Fiona would be far from the border, at the houses when the Jews came across. Who could she tell in the French countryside?

The houses, large as they were, would be a tight fit—two families to a room. But all the rooms would have mattresses, blankets, pillows, and, most importantly, food. The hardest part was not knowing how long the workers would stay, but Maureen and Lisa would adjust to that as the visas came through. The houses were a launchpad to another life in a country far from Germany, and she was confident that the Ritter Metalworks employees wouldn't grumble. The homes they'd found with the help of an agent in Lyon were Lisa and Fiona's responsibility. Maureen's mission was to get the refugees across the border. Her father had bought an old farmhouse in Schönau, just across the border in Germany, to launch the fleeing workers across the border. They'd chosen the village of Lembach, deep in the North Vosges Forest, as their base in France. It was just a matter of bringing the people from one town to the other across the low mountains and thick, freezing woods that lay in between. Finding a reliable guide was paramount.

It seemed like so many things could go wrong. She'd been down to the border a dozen times. The demarcation line was difficult to discern through the thick forests and rolling hills, but the French and German soldiers were easy to find. She'd been questioned several times by border patrols, amazed to see a girl out hunting in treacherous terrain so close to the border. Each time she fluttered her frozen eyelashes and made an excuse, but she knew a group of fleeing Jews wouldn't be treated with such compassion. The roads were passable but full of troops on maneuvers. The French were far more concerned with the Wehrmacht across the border, but would not look kindly at people sneaking in illegally. The German forces would be looking for Jews and other enemies of the state attempting to steal across. Even in this cold and desolate region, it wouldn't be easy.

Maureen pushed open the door to the tavern and walked inside. Deer and wild pigs' heads jutted from the walls. Their dead eyes stared into space, transfixed. The young American took a seat at a table in the back. She was ten minutes early and ordered some breakfast. The meat and bread were excellent, and she wolfed them down, knowing she'd need all the sustenance she could get. The hunter was 20 minutes late. She watched him kick the slush off his boots and order a beer at the bar. It was eight in the morning. He was about 40 and cut an imposing figure, towering over the barmaid who pointed out where Maureen was sitting. He put his beer on the table opposite Maureen. The stench he emitted reminded her of a farm she'd often visited in New Jersey as a child.

"Good morning, Vincent," Maureen said in French.

"You ready for this, little girl?" he said, exposing his yellowing crooked teeth. He knocked back half his beer before she had a chance to answer.

"Today's the day. You think the weather's going to hold up?"

"It's about as good a day as you could expect this time of year. Why the people you're meeting couldn't wait a month is beyond me. If the weather changes, they could die out there."

"You're being paid to do a job, which you accepted."

"I know, girlie, just offering my opinion. I've been hunting in these hills my whole life. I know how dangerous they can be. The weather can turn bad in minutes at this time of year, and if it does, I'm not hanging around."

"Just do the job I paid for."

"And what is that job, exactly? I don't even know where we're going. All this secrecy isn't productive."

"We're meeting some people in a farmhouse, just across the border in Schönau. Do you know the place?"

"Know it? My first wife was from there. My father-in-law still lives outside the town. If you notice me cowering for cover when we arrive, you'll know why."

Maureen almost smiled but instead excused herself and went to the bathroom. Her hands were shaking as she washed them in the icy water from the faucet. They needed a guide. The roads at the border were crawling with guards. She'd met Vincent in the tavern the week before, and he'd accepted the job. He'd initially been reluctant, but when she offered him what must have been several years' income for a few weeks' work, he changed his tune. He was astute enough not to ask too many questions about who they were meeting and where they were going afterward. Pamela, her husband, Isaac, her sister Allison, Allison's husband, Nathan, and her parents, Avi and Abigail, were waiting in the farmhouse her father had purchased in Germany. That many strangers, particularly those recognizable as Jews, had to be hidden away. The Gestapo's tentacles reached everywhere in Germany, even to the tiniest hamlet like Schönau.

Maureen reached for the towel and dried off her hands. She took a few seconds to stare into the mirror. How had she ended up in the forest along the French border in wintertime, about to hike through the snow? A tiny voice in the back of her mind urged her to turn back, to return to her comfortable apartment in Paris, or take the next steamer back to the safety of America. She ignored it and returned to the table where Vincent was now standing.

"We'd better get moving," he growled. "We don't have more than ten hours of daylight left."

"But that will be more than enough, won't it?"

"If nothing goes wrong. Are these people of yours in good shape?"

"So I'm told."

They emerged onto the street. "It's a few miles to the border. We'll ride as far as we can. We'll have to walk the last mile or two, and then all the way to Schönau."

The sky above was clear, with only a few rogue clouds interrupting the winter blue above their heads. But it was cold. She put her mittens on and pulled her scarf around her face as they mounted Vincent's horse and cart. The back consisted of two benches facing one another. How many refugees would sit on those seats in the coming weeks? She thought of Lisa. Her job was more straightforward and hopefully easier. She was in the

German border town of Saarbrücken, an hour north of the forested region they'd chosen to sneak the adults through. The smugglers weren't cheap, but the eight women they hired were helping Lisa move thirty children into France that day. Once they were across the border, Lisa and Fiona would travel to the city of Lyon with the fleeing children and, from there, would take a bus to Izieu.

Some would be reunited with their parents in a week or two. For some, it would be several weeks, but the plan was that every child would be back with their parents by the end of March when the battle to secure the refugees' visas to America and other safe countries could begin. Maureen had last seen Lisa the day before. They'd parted with a casual wave, downplaying the danger they knew they were facing. Hannah and Fiona were down at the massive boarding house they'd bought in Izieu, cleaning night and day to prepare it for the avalanche of humanity about to descend.

Maureen and the hunter spoke little for the duration of the journey toward the border. She was more concerned about staving off the cold than conversing. The forest on either side of the road was thick and foreboding. Snow hung on every drooping tree branch, and she noticed few signs of life from within the thicket. The only other people they saw on the road were a platoon of French soldiers on patrol, who waved to her as they passed, even though she was barely discernable as a female behind her thick scarf.

Twenty minutes passed before Vincent spoke. "We'll leave the cart here." He jumped down and tied the horse to a tree. "Good girl, Amelie. Don't worry, we'll be back soon."

The trail he took her along was just wide enough to walk down without having to turn her body. Her snow boots submerged in the snow, and she had to pluck her feet out with every step. Vincent broke a branch and stripped the twigs from it. "Here," he said. "A walking stick." The thick forest protected them from the biting wind, though her face was still numb in minutes. It wasn't long before her legs began aching, but she strode on regardless. Vincent seemed unaffected by the conditions and remained quiet as she followed him.

Almost an hour passed before he turned to her. "You want a break?" She wanted nothing more in the world, but shook her head. "Okay," he said. "The border is just ahead. I don't expect any Boche in the middle of this, but you never know. Keep quiet, and don't do anything I don't do. Got it?"

He turned around and continued through the brush before she could answer. A few more minutes of picking through the snow passed before he turned to her again.

"Welcome to Germany."

She wondered how he had any idea that this clump of forest was in Germany and the clump behind them was in France, but once again, he didn't give her a chance to ask questions. Her limbs begged for rest, but she kept plucking one foot out of the snow and driving the other in. The forest thinned, and the incline reversed, so they were now walking downhill.

"How far to Schönau?" she asked.

"Not far. Perhaps thirty minutes or so. You want to stop for a rest? Some food?"

"I'll eat when we reach the farmhouse."

A force within her wouldn't let her take a break until she knew the Bernsteins were at the farmhouse. Vincent had explained in detail how difficult this trip would be even in good conditions, but it was only now that she fully appreciated what he was trying to warn her about. What age were Pamela's parents? In their mid-fifties? She was 22 and struggling. And the night was coming. Out here in the dark, you were dead. Vincent was carrying a pack on his back, and she saw a tent peeking out, but what use would that be for eight people? It was vital that it wouldn't come to that.

Vincent raised a snow-encrusted glove to signal her to halt

and turned to face her. "The village is just through these trees." Maureen squinted to make out anything but was unable. "Do you want to walk through the village or go around?"

"What do you suggest?"

"Walking through would be easier than the trees, but the road would be easiest of all, and that's crawling with Nazis."

"Let's go around."

"Good choice."

After trudging through the trees for another twenty minutes, they emerged into a field. The village was behind them, surrounded by rolling hills covered in snow-tipped trees. It was beautiful. She took a few seconds to admire the view before turning to him. He pointed across the field at a small wooden house in the corner.

"That's it," he said. "It's 12:10. We rest here for half an hour and then start back. They're older than you. What took us three hours could take them five, and that brings us dangerously close to sundown. At 5:30 you won't be able to see your hand in front of your face."

"Got it," Maureen said and followed him through the field. The road was only a few hundred yards away, and although they saw no traffic as they crossed, they kept low for the duration. Being back in Germany, somewhere she thought she'd never return to, felt not like a homecoming but as if she were trespassing. Vincent waited for her at the door to the small wooden farmhouse. She knocked three times, and a woman in her late twenties answered.

"Maureen Ritter?" the woman said.

"You must be Pamela."

Pamela held the door open and brought them inside. Her husband and the others stood up. All were dressed in hiking gear. Herr and Frau Bernstein looked fit for their age, but she noticed Vincent's face.

"Are you ready for this?" he asked Pamela's parents.

"Yes," Herr Bernstein replied. "Our bags are packed."

Maureen walked into the bare kitchen with Vincent, where they sat down to share a lunch of bread and cheese. Vincent didn't say much as they ate, but Maureen knew what he was thinking—Pamela's parents would slow them down. A few minutes passed before he pulled her outside.

"Is there no other way for the parents to cross? You've experienced how tough the journey is. Is it worth escaping if one of them dies in the snow?"

Vincent's face was unyielding, and she returned to the refugees.

"I just hiked here from Lembach. It's a tough journey, through the woods and deep snow. Frau and Herr Bernstein, can you make it? Pamela and her husband can't get exit visas because of her affiliation with the factory, but that shouldn't stop you."

"We didn't want to separate," Pamela said. "My parents are strong and fit."

"We don't trust the Nazis," Pamela's mother said. "I heard stories about border guards sending Jews to concentration camps instead of letting them through. Besides, getting any exit visa is hard."

"I didn't fully realize how dangerous the journey was before I traveled here. I thought it would only be an hour or two over some trails. But there is no trail," Maureen said.

Vincent nodded. "If one of them falls or needs to be carried, we'll never make it."

Maureen walked over to the large backpacks sitting in the corner by the fireplace with Vincent. "Open them up," he growled. Pamela's father did as he was told, revealing books, photos, cash, and spare clothes for a week. "I thought you were serious about this," he said to Maureen. "If they take these bags, they'll never make it to France."

"Dump your personal items," Maureen said.

"This is the absolute minimum we could take," Pamela said.

"Take enough food and water for the trip, and all the cash you can carry. Everything else goes in there." Maureen gestured toward the fire.

"You can't be serious," Pamela's mother said. "The photos of my mother? The bible she gave me on her deathbed?"

"Or else you can carry them to France. If you come with us, you have to burn them. You have cash?" Maureen asked.

"Only a little," Isaac said. "We did as your father advised. We sold everything and bought diamonds." He held up a small velvet bag—almost their entire worldly wealth.

"And you went to different pawn shops?"

"We visited about ten altogether."

Maureen nodded, content that they were following her father's rules.

Maureen and Vincent stood at the door waiting as the Jewish refugees talked among themselves.

"We're all traveling together. My parents might not be able to secure exit visas. We're not taking that chance, particularly when we've come all this way," Pamela said.

Maureen nodded and looked at Vincent for his approval.

"Just keep up," he growled.

They set off a few minutes later. Vincent set the same blistering pace as earlier, and it wasn't long before Pamela and the others started falling behind. They had to stop several times before they reached the French border. The guide was correct about the time it took them to get to the wagon. With all the rests and stoppages, it was closer to five hours rather than the three he'd suggested. They saw no German soldiers in the middle of the forest or on top of the hills they crested, but were exhausted to a standstill as they mounted the cart. Maureen could hardly sit upright. Pamela and the others didn't even try. Her mother looked as if she was asleep on her feet, and her father groaned in pain, rocking his head back and forth as they sat in the cart. It was a strange triumph.

Vincent rode them back into town, where a warm bed awaited in a boarding house. The journey south was saved for the following day. The refugees exhibited little elation as they rode in the horse and cart. They were too filthy and drained to realize what they'd achieved, but they were free and still had the means to make a fresh start. Few of the hundreds of thousands of Jews who'd fled Germany could say the same.

"Anyone coming across needs to be in excellent physical shape, at least until spring comes," Vincent said. "And even then, it's not going to be easy. Can your people wait a couple of months?"

"They have no idea if the Gestapo is going to come for them tomorrow. Everyone wants to get out as soon as they can. Who knows when the next law is coming to throw them all into concentration camps? Would you trust your life to the Nazis' whims?

"Not even a little."

They passed a platoon of French soldiers on maneuvers, but none seemed concerned at the people riding in the back of the cart.

"When do we meet again?" the hunter asked.

"In a few days probably. This is just the first of them," Maureen answered.

"I think we have our model to get them across," Maureen added.

"Bring fifteen next time," Vincent said. "As long as they're fit and stay quiet, I'll get them across the border."

"I'll let my father know."

Maureen watched as the hunter disappeared around the corner. The trial run had been a success. Now it was time to ramp up the process.

19

Berlin, Thursday, February 23

All the Jews were gone from the factory. The section they'd once worked in was manned by new employees, interviewed by Helga, and vetted for their loyalty to the party. The Nazi flags and portraits of Hitler were on every wall now. Only Bernheim remained, and his days were numbered. Soon Seamus would be alone in a sea of Nazi sympathizers and fanatics. It seemed like the walls were closing in on him.

He hadn't seen Hayden in a few weeks, but knew a call would be coming soon. The American spy didn't know about the mission to move the Jews across the border to France. It was hard to know how he'd react. Hayden had sympathy for the Jews and often spoke of the hardships they endured, but he also knew they were the anchor that had held Seamus in Berlin for the past year, and now they were gone. The offer to provide the visas for the workers haunted him like some Dickensian spirit. The proposal to stay here and spy for the U.S. government was hard to refuse—every Jewish worker would find safety in America, and he'd be performing his duty to his country in helping keep Nazism in check. But what of his family? Would they ever forgive him? Lisa was a young, beautiful woman and was eager for him to join her in Paris or New York or wherever Hitler's tentacles couldn't reach. His marriage might not survive staying in Berlin. And he'd let his children down before when he left to find work during the depression in 1930. Two lost years with them had taken a long time to recover from.

Who was he without his family? It was hard to envisage remaining here alone. The thought that Bernheim and the rest of the Jews would be safe would comfort him, but how much longer could he feed the Nazi war machine?

Michael and Monika were working on sponsorships for the Bernheims in New York and had the money they needed now —from him. His once bountiful fortune was dwindling, but it felt good to use his ill-gotten gains for a good purpose.

Seamus was behind his desk when Gert came in with a piece of paper in his hand. Seamus knew what was about to happen, but that didn't make the moment any less surreal. The factory manager's face was lined with sadness as he sat down opposite his old friend.

"This is it," he said and pushed the paper across the table. "My official letter of resignation."

Seamus didn't have to look at it and kept his eyes on the man he'd worked with since 1932. "I've thought about this day so many times and what I'd say, but now that it's here, I can't think of anything other than thank you." He stood up and shook his hand. "One last drink in my office?" Seamus said and walked over to the whiskey decanter.

"Of course," his friend replied. "It could be a while before I drink out of a crystal tumbler at 11 on a Thursday morning again."

"Let's make the best of it, then," Seamus said as he handed

over the glass. "Maureen sent another letter. Everyone's across. One way or the other. It seems the guide we hired was a good one. With all the trekking she said she's as fit as Michael now."

"She still needs the guide after all the trips she's made?" Gert asked.

"We thought about her going alone, but it's too dangerous. Better to have a local with her, just in case. The weather can change in an instant."

"Will it be passable by the weekend, when I leave with my family?"

"Maureen thinks it will, but it won't be easy." Seamus saw Gert's face. "You'll make it. Everyone has so far, despite a few mishaps."

"I know we'll be okay, and I'm glad Maureen will be with us." Gert looked around the room.

Seamus let him have a few seconds with his thoughts before he broke the silence.

"It's almost over."

"It's hard to believe." Gert turned around. "It's a noble thing you've done here, Seamus—looking out for so many others."

"It's nothing my uncle wouldn't have done."

"He was a good man too. Everything still going well in Izieu? I haven't heard from anyone in a while."

"It's a tight squeeze. The kids are packed in, six or nine to a room, but so far so good. The locals are more welcoming than we could have hoped for."

"That's heartening. I've never been to France before. Soon I'll be living there." Gert's voice was faint and distant.

"Only until your U.S. visas come through which, according to Michael, should be soon."

"I hope so. It's almost hard to imagine not being under constant threat. We've lived under an ever-increasing yoke these past six years. It took a few months to believe it, and even longer to come to terms with it. But every time I got used to their laws, they passed more. Lil and I used to talk about it all the time—all Jews did. We kept thinking each Jewish law was the last. The Nuremberg Laws back in '35 seemed like the worst they could possibly come up with. I mean, what more could a government take from a person than their citizenship? Little did we know."

"But we do now. The Nazis won't stop until every Jew is gone. They'll stop at nothing to achieve that."

"How can life change so much in such a short time? I always knew the hatred existed, but it was below the surface. You'd meet people who looked down on you and move on. But now those people are the ones who make the laws which govern our lives."

"Do you have much more to do before you leave?"

"No. I've monetized everything I could. It didn't take long considering what happened on Kristallnacht."

"You don't have to worry about cash, my friend."

Gert walked back to the desk and sat down again. "I don't want to be a charity case. None of us do."

"I know when I need help someday, you'll be there for me too."

Gert reached forward and clinked glasses with Seamus.

"If it ever comes to that, I'll be at your side."

"You can start repaying me by bringing Conor to Saarbrücken this weekend. He won't need to be smuggled across the border. Fiona will meet him."

"I'd be delighted to. You're not taking him yourself? You're going to be all alone in that mansion."

"Yes," Seamus said, staring into his drink. "It's not worth the risk, and he's well able to travel without me. I can comfortably conclude my business here if I know he's safe."

"And you? When can I expect the pleasure of your company in France?"

"I wish I knew. But one day we'll be drinking a beer together in the sun. I just don't know when or where yet."

His friend smiled and raised his glass, and the words spilled out of Seamus's mouth.

"Gert, there's something I didn't tell you. I had an offer from a contact of mine at the U.S. embassy, someone I've worked with for a few years."

"I won't ask what kind of work you've been doing with this 'contact,'" he answered.

Seamus laughed, but he was tired. "Just...something to help." His friend didn't respond, so he continued. "This man I've known for more than 20 years, offered 96 American visas—one for every worker in Ritter and their wives, husbands, and children."

Gert's face didn't change. "What's the catch? They don't give away visas for nothing."

"That I stay here and continue my work."

"What about your family?"

"I'd have to send Conor to Paris or New York with Lisa."

The now ex-factory manager took a sip of his whiskey and stared out the window for a few seconds. The sounds of the machines below filled the silence.

"You could sell the factory in '42 for full price and you'd be a rich man."

"Yes."

"Would your marriage survive that?"

"I don't think so, and I don't know how my children could forgive me for doing that again."

"But the workers would be safe, and Maureen, Michael, Fiona, Conor and Hannah would never have to worry about money again for the rest of their lives."

"No, they wouldn't."

"You have money put away?"

"I had plenty before I bought those houses and filled the

escape fund. I own the mansion in Charlottenburg and half a thriving business."

"But that's not a lot of use to you if you flee the country to escape the madness here."

"But I'd be with my family."

Gert took a few seconds, rolling the amber liquid around in his glass. "I can't make that decision for you, my friend. Getting those visas would be the most precious gift you could ever pass along, but you've already done so much. No one expects this, and the workers don't know."

"I know," Seamus replied. "I have the power to see them all the way to America. They could live in safety, and not have to look over their shoulders, waiting for the next decree to come down."

"We have a plan in place, Seamus. All the Jews who lived in fear on that factory floor are gone. They aren't subject to the paranoid insanity of the Nazis any longer, thanks to you."

"It's only three years."

"It's your life, my friend," Gert said in a firm voice. "You've done more than anyone could ever have expected, and I know the money doesn't matter to you that much."

"Maybe a little," Seamus answered, and they both laughed.

"Stick to the plan. You've already prioritized your Jewish workers, now prioritize your family, and yourself. We'll all get away. We just have to be patient."

Hearing his friends say those words was like icy water on the fire raging within his soul. He thought of his children. His wife. The workers would be all right. They didn't need Bill Hayden, and the guilt from turning his back on his work for the State Department would fade in time, just as everything does.

Seamus stood up and took his friend's hand once more. This moment felt important. "Do you want me to take you for a drive? One last look around Berlin?" he said.

His former factory manager shook his head. "At the Nazi

flags and posters? No, I'd rather remember the city the way it was before all this."

His friend walked to the door and out of the factory.

Several hours passed. Unable to move, Seamus stared into space. The Jews were gone and would all be safe in France soon, but for how long? No one trusted the French military to hold out against a Nazi invasion. He doubted even Hitler knew when the troops would rumble across the border. It seemed the Jews had little time to lose.

The sounds of the machinery and shouts of the workers on the floor downstairs continued unabated. He swam through an ocean of memories, alone in his office. The phone buzzing beside him roused him from his thoughts.

He picked up the receiver and recognized the voice straight away.

"Hello," Hayden said.

"What can I do for you today, sir?" Seamus asked though he knew what was coming. Hayden told him the name of the hotel —one they hadn't visited in a year or so. It was the kind of place one didn't forget easily. Seamus agreed to meet him that evening and hung up.

He locked the door before going to the large safe beneath the long window. It opened with a clunk, and Seamus reached in for the documents he'd been hoarding for Hayden. They sat beside a pile of cash and jewelry he'd accumulated. It wasn't much compared with what he was leaving behind, but it would be enough for a new home in America and to give them a start.

The Swiss bank account was almost empty, save for a few hundred dollars and the diamond necklace he'd stowed there years ago. But that was for Maureen on her wedding day. His uncle had made him promise as much when he'd given it to him. The Nazis had put new, harsh restrictions on moving money out of the Reich. Not just for Jews but for German citizens and businessmen alike. Smuggling assets across the border to the bank in Basel was too risky now. Most of the wealth he'd put aside was in this safe.

Even without selling the factory, the sum he'd saved would support his family for years. If he stayed for another year or two, he could return with a sum that would resonate for generations.

A knock on the door interrupted his thoughts.

He shut the safe and walked to the door. He recognized the man standing behind it. One of the metal polishers from Benz's sections, Klaus Becker, held a hand up to him behind the glass.

"Can I see you for a moment, Herr Ritter?"

"Yes, of course," Seamus said, and unlocked the door.

Becker was in his mid-forties and had been working in the factory since he returned from the western front in 1918. He wasn't an ardent Nazi but worked with many who were. Seamus remembered seeing him standing at the back of the crowd during the melee after Kristallnacht. He was one of the silent majority of workers who supported the Nazis because of the pride they'd brought back to Germany. They all had work, and that was something that wasn't guaranteed before Hitler came to power.

"Come in, take a seat," Seamus said, leading him to the desk. He thought of offering him a glass of whiskey or schnapps but decided against it.

"What can I do for you, Klaus? Everything is well in ammunition supplies, I trust?"

"Yes, everything is fine with the machines. No problems." The man took off his flat cap and sat forward. "It's about you, Herr Ritter."

"What about me?"

"The workers are talking. There are some rumors flying around the factory floor."

"What kind of rumors?"

The man didn't answer his question. "I respect you, Herr Ritter,"

"Thank you."

"Some of the things the men say aren't fair. You've been good to us over the years." Klaus's face tightened as if he wasn't sure he should say what was on the tip of his tongue.

Seamus walked over to the decanter of whiskey and poured two glasses. Klaus accepted his with thanks.

"What did you come in here to tell me? It wasn't about the rumors swirling around. The workers have been chattering about them for years."

"This is different. Benz has been talking about the Jews, asking where they've gone."

"I would have thought he'd be delighted."

"He's saying you're in cahoots with them, that you helped them escape."

"In front of all the workers?"

"Whoever was around."

Klaus knocked back half his drink and grimaced.

"What else?" Seamus asked.

"I overheard him talking to Borst earlier today. They were outside on a break; they didn't see me around the corner." Klaus shut his eyes before continuing. "Benz said Helga told him if he denounced you for smuggling Jews, he could take over as factory manager. "

"That's ridiculous!"

"Perhaps, but he also mentioned something about you pulling a gun on some of his son's friends on Kristallnacht. It's all so ridiculous."

Seamus felt the blood drain from his face, and his legs

suddenly weakened. His mind returned to the night of the riots and the boys who'd threatened Gert and his family.

The realization that Helga had been waiting for a moment like this for years squeezed the breath from his lungs. His desperate attempt to hide his genuine emotions was causing his entire body to tighten like a steel cable. "That's ridiculous," he answered. "You're sure?"

Klaus nodded.

"Have you any idea when he plans to denounce me?"

"No. That's all I heard. Someone walked over and they stopped talking. But I got the impression it was soon."

Seamus balled his fingers into a fist and thought about the money in the safe. He downed the whiskey in his glass. "Thank you for coming to me with this. It's insane, but in today's climate, it's good to know what people are thinking."

"You should speak to Benz tomorrow and calm him down."

"Definitely," Seamus said, though he knew the futility of talking to Benz or any other hardcore Nazi.

"I should get home," Klaus said.

Seamus shook his hand again, knowing it was the last time he'd see him.

"Thanks for coming to me, my friend," he said and saw the worker to the door.

Seamus locked the door and picked up the phone as soon as he left.

His palm was wet on the handset as he dialed the number for his house. Gert picked up on the third ring. "Herr Ritter's house, this is his butler...."

"What's wrong?"

"Get out now."

"What are you talking about?"

"The plan for the weekend has to happen tonight. You know what to do."

"Are you certain?"

"Someone came to me with some information about our friend, Benz. The head of the Trustee Council is planning on visiting Prinz-Albrecht-Strasse." Seamus knew his friend would recognize the address. Gestapo headquarters was the most dreaded place in Berlin.

"What about you?"

"I have some things I need to attend to. Pack up. I'm trusting you with my son. Go now."

Seamus hung up and opened the safe again.

He set the documents for Hayden to one side and picked up a briefcase beside his desk. His hands were shaking as he placed the cash and jewelry inside. The briefcase was heavy. His family's future lay inside it. An envelope on his desk served to hold the documents Hayden wanted. Seamus gathered his coat and hat and stood at his desk one last time. He looked around the office, remembering the hours he'd spent here.

This shouldn't have been his last time in here. He cursed Benz and the fact that the Nazi would likely forever be one up on him.

"My revenge will be the life I lead," he said. "You can drown in your Nazi obsession, and one day all of this will come crashing down.

With no time for nostalgia or tearful recollections, he shut the door to his office and ran down the stairs, the briefcase in one hand, the reports for Hayden in the other. He jogged across the factory floor and out the front entrance. He started his car and didn't look back as he drove away.

The sun was fading as Helga's new mansion came into view. A huge Nazi flag fluttered in the breeze outside. Helga had the flagpole erected as soon as she moved in to show her neighbors where her loyalty lay. Seamus jumped out of the car and jogged up to the front door. He slammed on the thick wood with his fist, and seconds later, Helga's butler answered. Seamus calmed himself and asked for his cousin. The butler gave him a knowing look and led him inside to a massive drawing room. Seamus refused the drink he was offered and took a seat on a red leather couch.

It was a space fit for one of the new masters of the Reich that the booming armaments industry had created. The ceiling was paneled, with a dozen heavy beams in one direction and another dozen crossing them, forming squares. They were made of beautifully carved dark brown wood, and from them hung chandeliers, each a ring of thirty or so slim white candles with electric bulbs in the tops. A great open fireplace with high-backed lounges in front of it was lit at the end of the room. The walls of the room were wainscoted three or four feet high, and above were paintings, several of which depicted the harsh right-angled lines of Nazi art.

"Impressive," Seamus said as Helga entered the room. "All those weekends and late nights paid off."

Helga sat down opposite him, still wearing the Nazi armband across her bicep. The flickering light from the fire illuminated her pale skin, and her dark eyes flitted everywhere in the room but rarely met his.

"What are you doing here, Seamus? It's been a while since you made a social call."

The butler followed her with a tea tray and poured each of them a cup. Seamus waited until he left to begin again.

"Yes, and look what I've been missing out on." He gestured to the grandeur of the room. She didn't respond, so he continued. "I heard something disturbing today."

She didn't respond.

"Why did you do it, Helga?"

"What are you talking about?"

"Is Benz to be the new male figurehead for Ritter Metalworks? It makes sense—he's a committed Nazi, and someone you can control."

"Benz?" she spluttered. "I don't know what you heard, but—"

"You made a plan with him to denounce me. But why?"

She stirred her tea but spoke before she brought the cup to her lips. "I've been carrying you for years. I've watched you grow rich from my efforts, only because of your gender. I'm the more capable businessperson. It was my idea to go into armaments." The vitriol in her voice intensified with every word. "You fought me at every turn. If you had your way the company would have folded years ago."

"Why have me thrown in a concentration camp? We're family."

"If you choose to commit illegal acts, then you should be prepared to suffer the consequences of your actions. Your ridiculous affection for the Jews has driven you to do things no sane person would. I don't blame you. Really, I don't. You're to be pitied more than despised. But that's what the Jews do. They hypnotize you with those beady rat eyes. You've been under their power for years. I know it seems like harsh medicine, but perhaps some time in captivity will help you recover your senses."

Seamus laughed. "So, this is all for the good of my health? And what's to happen to my share of the company if I take a trip to a concentration camp?"

"Nothing will change so long as you stay in Germany. Of course, the chance to sell to any outside parties has passed now. I could make you an offer, an advance on the sale that would go through in '42."

"I'm listening."

"I couldn't possibly draw up anything tonight."

"100,000 Reichsmarks. In cash. Now. And you get everything."

His share was worth at least five times that amount.

A tiny smile crossed her thin lips. "I would never take advantage of you like that, cousin. Let's figure this out over the coming months. We'll sit down with our legal team and hammer out something more equitable."

He searched for words to fix this situation, to convince her to let him leave with a tiny piece of what her father had left him, but he knew they didn't exist. "Please consider my offer, if not for me, for my children."

A faint smile appeared across her lips. He was little more than a fish swimming in a barrel, waiting for the inevitable.

Seamus picked up the cup, threw it on the Persian rug, and stood up. She drank her tea and looked down at the stain he'd created as he walked away.

He stopped at the door and turned back. "You'll die alone," he said. "This Nazi madness is all going to come crashing down. The weapons orders will stop, and you'll be sitting on your craven perch, fumbling in your greasy till. My family will never speak to you again. Goodbye, Helga."

She looked at him with the tiniest tinge of regret before bringing her eyes to the floor again.

Seamus hustled past the butler, unable to hear the question he asked him. The cold air outside hit him like a bucket of water. The briefcase was still sitting on the passenger's seat of the car. It would be enough. Helga could drown in her ill-gotten gains.

He got into his car and started the engine, thinking of his children. The scheme Helga and Benz had hatched mattered little. He was always going to leave. If Kristallnacht hadn't revealed to him the true nature of what Germany had become, nothing would. And if that hadn't forced him out, then the longing for Lisa and the children would have. Helga had merely solidified his decision and quickened his actions. And damned whatever remained of her soul by doing so.

"You and Benz can choke on that place."

Seamus lit a cigarette as he drove into the city. This hotel was further east, in the working-class area of Kreuzberg. Seamus almost smiled as he noticed the hotel's address—on Ritter Strasse. The street was dark as he pulled up. Seamus took the briefcase and ignored the beggars and prostitutes as he bounded up the stairs to the reception area. It was behind fortified glass. With no bathroom, Hayden had left the key at the desk, and the Turkish man working behind it handed it to him with a pleasant smile that seemed out of place here.

Hayden was sitting by the bed, drinking as always. Seamus threw him the envelope he'd taken from the factory.

"The Nazis are turning everyone into devils, Hayden."

Seamus stood facing him, his arms folded. "I'm leaving tonight. Helga has arranged a plan to denounce me. I'm heading back to the house to pick up my passport and getting out."

Hayden picked the envelope off the bed and opened it up. "I'm sorry to hear that. What about your Jewish friends and the visas I was working on?"

"They're all gone. In France."

"How did you—?"

"Smuggled them across. The government wasn't issuing them exit visas."

"So, everything's changed," Hayden said in a calm tone.

He took a few seconds to survey the documents in the envelope, but didn't hit Seamus with the usual barrage of questions about the new planes.

"You're sure you have to run?"

"Positive. I have no intention of spending the next five years in a concentration camp."

"Of course. You're a loss, but who knows when this will all blow up? The war's coming. A blind man can see that. The weapons you produced these past few years will be used on the battlefield soon."

The briefcase in his hand felt heavier. It was full of blood money. But he could put blood money to good use. He already was. The house in France for the refugees and the endowment for their escape were funded with armaments money. The apartments in New York and Paris he bought for his children were both paid for with the wealth he'd accumulated pedaling instruments of death.

"Are your Jewish friends still in your house?"

"Gone by now, I hope."

"A liberal-minded foreign businessman like you is a big fish to the Gestapo. I'd bet dollars to donuts two agents in cheap brown suits are smoking cigarettes and drinking bad coffee in a car across the street from your house right now."

"I need my passport."

"Is there a back way in?"

"Over the wall."

"I'd take it. And don't turn on any lights in the house. You don't want them rushing in. Make sure your car is gassed up beforehand in case you need hit the road in a hurry."

"It is already."

"Then stop wasting time talking to me. Where are you going to cross?" Hayden stood up before Seamus could answer. "Actually, don't tell me. The less anyone knows the better." The diplomat shook his hand. "At least I won't have to come to these awful hotels anymore."

"Thanks, Bill."

"Good luck, my friend. I'll see you stateside sometime."

"I look forward to it."

Seamus shut the door behind him and paced down the stairs to the street, where two boys about Conor's age were standing by his car.

"Hey mister, how about a few pfennigs for looking after your car while you were inside cheating on your missus?" one of the boys said with a sly smile. It seemed like a line he'd used many times.

Seamus shook his head and reached into his pocket. The boys' eyes almost popped out as he handed them a 10 Reichsmarks note. "It's your lucky day."

They were still staring in shock as he got into the car and drove away.

Driving west, Seamus tried to clear his mind of the dread infesting it. He tried to absorb the sights of Berlin—a city he had grown to love despite the stranglehold the Nazis had on it. He'd miss the hustle bustle, the beautiful buildings, and the way of life. Somehow the people here retained a relaxed air despite the fast pace. But nothing remained for him here. His time was at an end.

Memories came like moths to a flame, and he had to fight them off. He drove past the street where Lisa killed Ernst Milch in self-defense and where he helped her dispose of the body. His life had taken a turn in Berlin he never could have imagined, and it was somewhere that would always occupy part of his soul. He just hoped he might see it again someday.

He stopped at a hotel just off Kurfürstendamm, close to where he and Lisa had their first date, to make a phone call. The call to his house went unanswered. He breathed a sigh of relief until the horrible thought that the Gestapo had taken them all burrowed into his head. Only a trip back would tell, and he ran to the car.

Fifteen minutes later, Seamus pulled up on a street parallel to the one he'd lived on since Uncle Helmut left him the house.

Old Frau Weiss's garden backed onto his, and the wall was climbable—at least it was the last time one of the kids had gotten over it about three years before.

He stowed the briefcase under the seat. Even in an affluent area like this, it paid to be careful. The kitchen light was on in Frau Weiss's house, and Seamus could see the old lady by the window. She was half-blind, and he knew he could make something up on the off chance she did spot him. Even with that, he kept low as he got out of the car. It was almost eight o'clock, and the clouds had cleared above his head to reveal a blanket of stars. His breath was a cloud of white condensation as he crept toward the side of his neighbor's house. The gate was locked, but he climbed it with ease. The manicured back garden, a sea of color during spring and summer, was about fifteen yards long. The back wall it extended to was about eight feet high.

He listened for a few seconds to make sure the coast was clear. Confident that it was, he jogged toward the old rock wall. With several foot and hand holds, it proved easy to traverse, and he was over in ten seconds. He jumped into the darkness of his backyard and stayed still for a moment, listening once more. The house was dark, and he stood up with a degree of comfort.

The spare key to the back door was on the second shelf in the shed, and Seamus plucked it from the darkness without needing to see. The door opened with the barest of sounds, and he stepped inside.

The house, which had been full of life hours before, was like a gilded mausoleum. It was bizarre to think that this was likely the last time he'd set foot in here. He wondered what Uncle Helmut would have made of his situation but dismissed the thought. Helmut never knew the Nazis as anything other than annoying rabble-rousers. He never knew them in power, so trying to comprehend what he might have thought about the gargantuan changes in German society since then was an exercise in futility. The country would have been unrecognizable to him or anyone else who had known it before the National Socialist revolution.

A note on the dining room table drew his attention. Seamus read it by starlight at the window.

WE ARE GETTING THE 7.30 TRAIN. I CONTACTED M, AND SHE WILL MEET US AT THE HOUSE FIRST THING IN THE MORNING.

BON VOYAGE, MY FRIEND, AND SEE YOU SOON.

It was unsigned, but he recognized Gert's neat handwriting.

Resisting the temptation to cook himself some food in the kitchen, Seamus went to the staircase. He kept to the sides to minimize the noise of walking up the wooden steps. Who knew how close the Gestapo was? Perhaps they were just outside the door. His passport was in the safe behind the picture in his bedroom. His eyes now used to the dark, he went into Maureen's old room to look out the window. Hayden was right. Two men were sitting in a car parked just down the street. One of them was smoking a cigarette through the open window. A prickly fear ran through his body, but he shook it off. They'd never know he was here, and the Bernheims were safe.

He took a breath and walked into the bedroom he had shared with Lisa before her exile to France. Thoughts of her dominated his mind as he took the painting down from the wall, but then he heard a voice from the corner of the room.

"Herr Ritter, I presume."

A man was sitting in the darkness, pointing a pistol at him. Seamus was drenched in terror.

"Who are—?"

"Agent Hilzer of the Gestapo. Why did you come creeping into your own house like this?"

"I could ask you the same thing."

"I think you'll find I'm the one asking the questions here."

He stood up with the gun still trained on Seamus's torso. He was a small, wiry man with beady brown eyes and a receding hairline—hardly the picture of Aryan dominance.

"I need something from the safe," Seamus whispered. His voice was weak. Standing wasn't easy.

"Let's take a trip to Prinz-Albrecht Strasse," Hilzer said with a wicked smile. "You've been a person of interest to us for quite a while. I'm looking forward to making your acquaintance."

Seamus let his hands fall from the safe and turned to face the Gestapo agent walking toward him.

"Move," Hilzer said and gestured toward the door with his handgun.

Seamus knew that if the man brought him downtown, he wouldn't see his family for years, if ever again. Everything he'd worked for and dreamed of since he arrived in Germany was slipping away like water through his fingers. He put one foot in front of the other, walking toward the door. But he knew he was moving too slowly for Hilzer and felt the barrel of the agent's pistol in his back. He quickened his pace and darted through the doorway, and as Hilzer followed him through, Seamus grabbed for the gun.

The two men wrestled over the pistol, their faces almost touching. Seamus shoved the Gestapo man backward, and the weapon went flying. It landed by the bed, and Seamus threw a punch at the German that landed just below his eye. Hilzer jumped to the floor in a desperate lunge for his pistol, but Seamus was on top of him in a millisecond and wrapped his hands around his face, wrenching him back. Hilzer was inches short of the gun and elbowed Seamus in the ribs, knocking the wind out of him. The American responded with several punches to the other man's midsection but was powerless to stop him from reaching the pistol. Hilzer elbowed him again and turned his body to whip Seamus across the scalp with the weapon's barrel. Seamus fell off the stricken man and, dazed, raised himself to his feet. Hilzer let out a fiendish laugh as he pointed the gun. Seamus met his eyes as he pulled the trigger. *Click.*

The Gestapo man pulled back the hammer in frustration, but Seamus was on him again and threw him toward the doorway. The German stood up just as Seamus launched his body at him, and the two men toppled over the railing outside the bedroom door, plummeting to the floor twenty feet below. Seamus landed on the Gestapo agent's torso with a sickening thump. He rolled off, his body aching, ready to fight on, but Hilzer didn't move. His eyes were open, staring into the darkness.

Seamus raised himself to his feet, breath rushing in and out of his lungs. The man was dead, and so would he be if he didn't get out in seconds. His side ached, and he could only limp up the stairs to the bedroom. He opened the safe and placed the precious passport in his pocket before shuffling to the window. The other Gestapo men were still sitting in the car, oblivious that their colleague was dead inside the house. But it wouldn't be long before they missed him and unleashed the hounds of the secret police. The gun was on the floor where Hilzer had dropped it. Seamus picked it up and checked the action. The jam was cleared. The next shot would have killed him. He placed the weapon in his pocket and turned for the door.

Progress was slow and painful. He rubbed his hand along his left side where he'd landed. Some ribs were probably broken. He longed to sit down and catch his breath, but he knew every second counted. The possibility of taking the train to the border was gone now. His only chance was to drive through the night.

Seamus edged past the dead Gestapo agent's body in the middle of his house, trying not to look into the man's eyes. The door was still unlocked, and he pushed through it into the cold night. The wall at the end of the garden looked much more daunting now. He went to the shed and picked up a ladder. An old pair of heavy boots sat beside it, tied together at the laces. Seamus hefted them over his shoulder. Knowing that the other Gestapo men might come looking for Hilzer at any moment, Seamus climbed the wall as quickly as he could. He sat on top and pulled the ladder up to place it on the other side, praying that the secret police didn't follow him.

Frau Weiss was still in the kitchen. Seamus stayed as low to the ground as he could all the way to his car. He threw the boots in the back before opening the driver's side door. Getting in was like someone stabbing him in the side, and he almost yelped in pain. The agony subsided as he got into a comfortable position behind the wheel. He took a few seconds to evaluate his situation. Schönau, and the relative safety of the farmhouse, was 8 hours away. But once he arrived, he'd have to struggle through the snow into France with broken ribs. *Don't worry about that now. You probably won't even get there.*

He started the Mercedes and drove away from his neighborhood for what he knew would be the last time. Grisly visions of what the Gestapo men would do if they caught him dominated his mind as he went.

"How long do I have?" he asked himself. The other men might wait outside for two or three more hours before they started to miss Hilzer. Then they'd need to report it. Every agent in the city, as well as the regular police, would be looking for him. That would take a few hours, and it'd be the middle of the night then. They'd alert every regional and border office to hunt him down by morning. But if he could make it to the farmhouse by first light, he might just get out of Germany alive. But Maureen didn't know he was coming, and he'd never make it across the border alone.

The suburb of Charlottenburg where he and his family had lived all these years behind him, Seamus entered the

Grunewald Forest, where he and Lisa had buried Ernst Milch's body back in '32. The darkness of the trees on either side of the road infected him with horrific memories of that night. The picture of his wife, and the thought of seeing her again, was the only antidote to the horror, just as it always had been.

He drove past Wannsee, where they'd vacationed at Dr. Walz's house by the lake, and then past Babelsberg, where Maureen witnessed the doctor's experiments to kill human beings more efficiently.

Berlin and the life Seamus had led there these past six and half years faded behind him. The open road and all its mysteries stretched out ahead. Seamus kept driving. He fended off the almost irresistible urge to sleep by singing to himself or thinking about the children when they were young. He so longed to see their children someday. What would Fiona be now? The change in her had to be reinforced by moving back to America. He had to get to her.

Expecting to be pulled over by police at any moment, he drove on through Leipzig and Frankfurt. The roads Hitler had constructed to move his armies to the border were largely empty, and Seamus pushed the car as fast as it could go.

The first rays of morning came like some ancient god over the horizon. He pulled over to check the map on the passenger's seat.

Schönau was still more than two hours away. The Bernheims' train would have arrived in Kaiserslautern about one AM, and it was an hour to the farmhouse from the station. A few hours of sleep would be more than enough, and then they would set out just after first light. If he missed them, he would be on his own and in no shape to catch up. He pushed his foot down on the accelerator, hoping they'd delay leaving, but not able to see a reason why they would.

20

Lembach, France, Friday, February 24

Maureen was awake before dawn and slipped into her trekking gear for what was to be to the last time. The rough pants and thick coat fit her like a second skin, and her boots were scuffed and worn. The light of the morning sun broke through over the horizon, casting gold on the snowy ground below. The guesthouse she was in was as silent as it always was at this time. She opened the window. Frigid air flooded through the gap she created, but unperturbed, she closed it and finished dressing. She had grown used to trudging through the snow, and the subzero temperatures didn't bother her anymore.

After a dozen trips through the frozen forest, her legs were as strong as granite. Today Herr Bernheim was crossing the border with Frau Bernheim and their son Joel. But there was some kind of emergency, and Conor was with them too. Soon, only her father would remain in Germany. Gert had assured her in succinct language on the long-distance call that her father was fine, but she'd sensed something behind his words and had slept little afterward.

Focusing on the job at hand, she finished getting dressed. She took her compass and some leftover food, shoved them in her pockets, and walked downstairs, where the landlady was preparing breakfast. She greeted Maureen as the young woman took a seat at the table.

"I see you're dressed for the outdoors again this morning," she said.

"I have to check on the traps."

"A woman hunting in wintertime? All the way out here? I've never heard of such a thing," the landlady said.

Maureen didn't answer, just drank some warm coffee.

"I think this will be the last time I stay here," she said. "My time's almost at an end in Lembach. I'm moving south."

"To warmer places?"

"Something like that."

After breakfast, the young American strolled across the small town. The light from the sun was just beginning to penetrate the blanket of night. The people had stopped staring at her a few weeks ago, but that only made her warier. She'd be glad to leave the border region and the final residue of paranoia from Germany behind. One informant or Nazi sympathizer among them would be enough to have her and Herr Bernheim dragged to a concentration camp once they crossed the border.

Maureen waited on the corner of the local tavern, though it was still closed at this early hour. She and Vincent had perfected the system of spiriting the refugees across since the first time they'd crossed three weeks before. The first thing they'd changed was leaving earlier. It was colder, but the German troops were still snoozing in their barracks at this time. They began their maneuvers in mid-morning and continued through the afternoon. They'd almost run into patrolling German soldiers on several occasions and once had to hide in a cave while the patrol passed by just a few yards away. She was under no illusion of how dangerous this task was, even if they'd sneaked all the Jews from Ritter Metalworks across thus far. It was only a matter of time before the Wehrmacht troops spotted them and hauled them in. *Just one more trip,* she said to herself as a man appeared around the corner. He was dressed in winter gear and seemed ready to trek into the woods. He was tall, with massive shoulders and a thick black beard that covered a weather-beaten face.

"Are you Maureen?" he said.

She had never seen him before and spluttered her reply. "Who are you?"

"I'm Serge. Vincent sent me. He couldn't make it."

"What happened to—?"

"He's sick. I saw him last night. He asked if I could guide you over to Schönau."

"What's wrong with him? I never—"

"Do I look like a doctor? He can't bring you today. If you need to travel, I can take you."

Maureen took a moment to try to evaluate the man's character by the look in his eyes, but it was useless. The thought that she could do it alone dawned on her again, but reality set in before those ideas crystalized. The forest was a mess of trees, hills, and paths that led nowhere. Perhaps she could do it, but it wasn't worth the risk. Herr Bernheim was waiting for her in Schönau, and it was too risky for him to stay there any longer than he needed to. The fact that he'd called her the night before to rush the operation meant something was going on, and they didn't have time to waste. She had to make a decision.

"You know the way?"

"I've been trekking these hills since before you were born, girlie," he said with a crooked-toothed smile. "You got the money for me?"

"I paid Vincent in advance. Can I see him? I'd like him to vouch for you."

"I've known that degenerate my whole life. He's half the tracker I am on my worst day. We need to leave." He gestured at a group of gray clouds on the horizon. "The weather's fine now, but in a few hours, it'll be a different story. There's a storm coming in." Maureen hesitated, trying to look through the man's black eyes. "You can take your chances alone, girlie, but I know the fastest route over, a way Vincent's never dreamed about. We'll get to Schönau and back in three hours. Guaranteed. And we're going to need to be that fast today."

The man's confidence was hard to resist, and as much as she hated to admit it, she needed help. Vincent wasn't the only man around here who could have taken her—just the only one she'd asked. This man was probably as reliable as he was.

"Okay," she said. "We leave right away. You can see Vincent about the money."

"Fair enough. Follow me."

Serge led her around the corner to where a brown flea-bitten horse that looked like it hadn't eaten in days stood tied to a cart. Maureen almost asked if the old nag was up to it but kept her mouth shut. She climbed onto the cart, and they set off.

The new guide was even less chatty than Vincent, and Maureen found herself missing him. Serge stopped off at a different spot on the road to the border. She didn't ask questions as she was sure he'd shrug them off. They entered the forest and began along a path together. It was even narrower than the ones Vincent led her on, but her legs were stronger now, and she kept up with his speedy pace.

Serge didn't stop or ask if she wanted to until they reached the border. He turned to her, put a gloved finger over his mouth, then pointed down to a log cabin on the other side of the hill they had just crested. "*Boche*," he said. Maureen's blood froze as she saw a bored-looking German soldier patrolling the exterior of the building with a rifle slung over his shoulder. She was boiling inside. *Why did he take us so close to the Wehrmacht positions?* Before she could whisper her thoughts, the guide was gone again. Maureen shuffled after him, wary of the noise of her footsteps in the snow.

Several minutes passed before Maureen felt confident enough to speak out loud.

"Why did we walk right past the German positions?" she hissed.

"Because look where we are now," he said, directing her toward the end of the woods a few steps away. The sleepy village of Schönau, which was comprised of a church and a few stores clumped together in the middle of hundreds of acres of farmland, lay just in front of them. "I told you I'd get you here faster. And look at the sky," he said, pointing upward. It was darkening by the moment, and a few snowflakes were already drifting down. "We're going to have to hurry. Skirting the German troops is our only chance to beat the weather."

Maureen directed him around the town. The snow was even deeper on the way to the farmhouse, and it took them fifteen exhausting minutes to reach it. The smoke billowing from the chimney was the signal, and Maureen pushed through the door without knocking. Herr Bernheim was sitting by the fireplace with his wife and son.

"Where's my brother?" she said as she kicked the snow off her boots.

Conor appeared before Gert could answer, and Maureen embraced him.

"What's going on with Father? Is he in trouble?"

"He'll follow us later. He's having some problems with Helga and the factory," Gert said.

"What kind of problems?"

"I don't know. He couldn't say much over the phone," Herr Bernheim replied.

It had been more than two years since they'd seen each other, and he greeted her with a hug. Serge stood at the door behind them, watching.

"We need to leave," the guide said, but no one responded.

"There's something else. I heard from your father last night. Benz denounced him."

"What? When?"

"I don't know. We spoke on the telephone. He couldn't say too much."

"Is he okay? Did the Gestapo come for him?"

"I don't know any details. He told us to take Conor and get out. I asked him if we should wait for him, but he told me to go ahead, that he had things to do."

Maureen threw her gloves down in frustration. The tiredness that had been coursing through her body moments before was gone. Herr Bernheim took her by the shoulders. "He implied to me he was leaving soon too. But he won't have to cross the border through the forest and the snow. He can just drive across the border like he always does. He's not subject to the same laws as the Jews."

"But what if he's on the run from the Gestapo? They won't just let him waltz across the border!"

"What does this mean?" Serge said. "Are we leaving?"

"Yes," Maureen answered. "Let's get my brother and the Bernheims across the border as soon as we can. I need to come straight back."

Serge laughed. "Are you sure? You did great on the way here, little girl, but traveling to France and then back again today? You won't make it."

"Why don't you just stay here and wait for your father?" Lil asked.

"Because I don't know the fastest way, and the snow's coming. I need to walk back to the French border and double back for him."

She didn't mention her concern for her brother and the Bernheims. She didn't know Serge and wasn't positive she could trust him.

"Are you almost ready, Frau Bernheim?" she said.

"I just need to put on my hat and boots."

"You're crazy," Serge said. "I'll be out looking for your body with the rest of the search party tomorrow."

"That's a chance I'm going to have to take."

It was just after 8:55 when Maureen stood up and announced they were leaving. Serge grumbled under his breath, but they stepped out into the icy air once the fire was extinguished. The local guide took the lead, with Maureen taking up the slack at the back of the line.

She looked back at the farmhouse before they entered the trees. She had a sudden odd feeling that they should wait a little longer, that her father would appear through the falling snow.

Or was he in a windowless room staring at a light bulb hanging from a ceiling? If he was, there was nothing to be done but hope the Gestapo showed some mercy—something they weren't known for. His wealth would do him no good with those fanatics. Nothing mattered to them other than their devotion to Hitler and the bloodless revolution he'd inspired in Germany. Maureen laughed at the phrase "bloodless revolution." What about those men she'd seen murdered at the back of the hospital in Babelsberg? Or the hundreds killed on Kristallnacht, or the thousands who'd died in concentration camps like Monika's father? The myth of the bloodless revolution was just one more falsehood the Nazis pedaled to the German people.

But surely her father was one step ahead of the secret police. Surely he'd gotten out of Berlin while he still had the chance.

9:15 AM

Seamus had only visited the farmhouse in Schönau once before—when he'd bought it from a local farmer whose eyes had almost popped out of his head when he saw the offer. Seamus nearly experienced the same feeling as the tiny house came into view.

A faint wisp of smoke wafted from the chimney into the morning air, but the snowflakes were falling in earnest now and getting thicker.

He pushed down on the gas pedal, almost skidding on the slushy dirt track leading to the house. The car skidded as he pulled up outside, and the stabbing pain came again as he did his best to jump out of the driver's seat. The cold hit him. He was still dressed in the same suit he'd worn to work the day before. He had no hat and cursed himself for not bringing one from his house, although he hadn't been thinking clearly in the moments after killing the Gestapo agent. The heavy boots he'd stowed in the back of the car and his wool coat would have to be enough.

Wary of slipping on the uneven surface leading up to the house, Seamus slowed down. No sound. Nothing. He was utterly alone. Not even a cow or bird in the air above his head. He pushed the door open and called out. Running through the house as best he could with the slight limp he still had from falling on the Gestapo man back in Berlin, he searched each room. It took him less than a minute, and he returned to the living room, having found nothing. The sticks in the fire were still smoldering. *They were here a few minutes ago. I have no idea of the way, but if I follow their footprints in the snow, I'll find them.* His other choice was to sit and wait, but who knew when the Gestapo would begin the search for him? *Someone* saw his car leaving the city last night, and if the police checked his financial records in the safe in his office, they'd find the purchase record for the farmhouse—even if it was in Conor's name. The only chance to catch Maureen and Gert was to leave right now. The urge to escape the Reich and the horrific paranoia that had consumed everyone here was too much. The time had come. A vision of Lisa appeared in front of his eyes, beckoning him. It was too much to resist. Germany had given him so much these past six and a half years—a wife, a daughter, a career, and a fortune, but his time here was done.

He rifled through the old desk in the living room, looking for something to help his journey, and pumped his fist as he came across a pair of woolen gloves. The heavy boots were in the back of the car where he'd left them in case of emergency, and he brought them into the house. His dress shoes clattered on the wood floor as he threw them down. He tied up the boots in seconds. His ribs burned like the fires of hell, but he was ready. The fresh footprints were still just about visible in the snow, but falling snow would cover them all in minutes. If his calculations were correct, they were only 20 or 30 minutes ahead of him, and even if he didn't catch them, he could follow in their wake all the way to the border. He would head back if things got too much and the journey was too strenuous. No use dying in the snow or stumbling into a German patrol, but this was worth the risk.

The suitcase with all that remained of his worldly wealth was all the luggage he carried. It was the only thing he was taking from Germany besides the clothes on his back and Hilzer's pistol in his pocket. He thought of the bank account and the safe deposit box in Basel, all but empty now save for a bit of cash and the diamond necklace Uncle Helmut left him when he died. "For Maureen on her wedding day," Seamus said aloud.

He began following the footprints in the snow, hurrying

before they faded to nothing. They led across an open field and then into the trees. The chill in the air hit him like a hammer as he entered the shade of the woods. Grateful for the gloves, he slogged on. Despite the cold and the burning pain in his side, his confidence in finding his son and daughter grew. They must be close.

"One foot in front of the other," he said. The only thing he was afraid of was pushing himself too far and not being able to return to the farmhouse if needs dictated a retreat. But he felt better than he had thought he would and kept on at the fastest pace he could manage.

∼

9:45 AM

They were struggling, and Maureen would never admit it out loud, but she was beginning to doubt her own ability to make the journey twice more that day. But what other choice did she have? She marked the trees as she went, breaking branches and scraping bark, waiting for the right time to turn around.

Serge wasn't setting quite the blistering pace of earlier as Herr and Frau Bernheim weren't capable of it. Conor and Joel seemed comfortable and strode beside Serge at the front of their little convoy. Maureen reached forward and took Lil by the shoulder.

"How are you doing?"

Gert's wife smiled back at her. "I'm glad I don't have to do this every day. How far to the horse and cart?"

"I'm not sure. I don't know this way," she answered.

Maureen jogged ahead and asked the hunter. He turned to

her with anger in his dark eyes. She almost asked him what the matter was, but he cut her off.

"We'll be in France in a few minutes. Keep your mouths shut as we move."

She wanted to fire back at him, but didn't see the point and returned to her place behind Herr and Frau Bernheim.

They climbed up the hill that led down to the German barracks. Maureen held a finger to her mouth. The Bernheims acknowledged her without words and continued on. The same German sentry was on duty. He was sitting on a bench outside the wooden building, smoking a cigarette as they passed. His gaze remained fixed in front of him, and the risk that Serge took bringing them this way seemed justified.

Herr Bernheim asked to rest a few minutes later. Serge looked incensed by the suggestion to stop, but Maureen insisted. The truth was she needed a few moments herself, and they took a seat on a fallen tree trunk. She sat beside Conor, who told her he was fine. The thick coat and boots he wore were keeping him warm. Joel also seemed fine, but his father was struggling. The weight of the satchel he was carrying seemed almost too much.

"Maybe you could let Joel carry that?" she suggested.

Her father's friend agreed and handed his life savings to his son to carry.

"Time to move," Serge called out.

"How much farther?" Maureen asked as they stood up.

"Not far now," the Frenchman said in a gruff, dismissive tone and set off.

"I need to head back to my father soon. You mind if I leave you?" Maureen asked after a minute or two but didn't receive an answer. They entered a small clearing devoid of trees. The dull winter sun shone through from above, offering minimal warmth. Serge turned to her as the gray uniform of a Wehrmacht soldier appeared through the falling snow.

"Hands up!" the soldier shouted. He was alone and pointing his rifle at them.

"We're just out for a walk," Maureen said.

"That's not what it looks like," the soldier said. "You're Jews! We were told to watch out for vermin like you. What's in the bag?" he said to Joel.

"My belongings," the young man said

"I personally think we have more than enough Zionists in France already," the trooper said and pointed his rifle at Joel. "Give me the bag."

Gert's son stood frozen.

"Can we talk about this?" Maureen said. He trained the weapon on Maureen. "Take another step and I'll put a bullet in that pretty face of yours."

"Okay, take the money, just don't hurt her," Herr Bernheim said.

"Seems like it's my lucky day," the man said and reached out to take the bag, smiling as he felt its weight. "Now, back down the hill, all of you. The Gestapo will be eager to make your acquaintance."

"No way you're taking me in," Serge said, reaching into his pocket for a pistol.

"Don't do—!" Maureen shouted.

Her shout was interrupted by gunfire, and blood spurted from Serge's chest. The German soldier swung his weapon toward her and braced to fire. She saw his terrified eyes and his finger curl around the trigger when another shot rang out, striking him in the shoulder. Maureen's father stood behind a tree twenty feet away. The German soldier whirled around and fired as her father shot back at him. The sentry was hit in the chest and fell on his back. His first bullet hit a briefcase her father was holding, ripping it open and spinning him around. The second hit Seamus in the left hip, and he collapsed on the snow. Maureen and Conor both screamed and ran to him with

Herr Bernheim. Crimson stained the snow where he'd fallen. A hole in his trousers at the top of his left leg oozed garish blood. The ground was littered with cash and jewelry from the briefcase.

"What are you doing here?" Maureen said.

"I followed you. Figured you could use some help—turns out I was right. Are they both dead?"

The soldier wasn't moving—but neither was Serge. Herr Bernheim ran back to check on him, returning a few seconds later. "As Julius Caesar," he replied.

"And we will be too, if we don't get out of here right now," Seamus said. Conor hugged him with tears in his eyes as Joel began gathering the banknotes strewn in the snow.

"Those German troops at the bottom of the last hill will have heard those shots," Maureen said. "Can you move?"

Her father tried to stand but grimaced in agony as he put weight on his left leg. He collapsed onto the snowy ground, resting against a tree, panting in pain.

"You need to get up now," Maureen said with tears bulging in her eyes.

"I don't think I can. The soldiers will be coming in a few seconds. You two go. I'll tell them I had a dispute with our friends over there. They'll never know you were here. You'll be free."

"But they'll take you in," Herr Bernheim said.

Maureen dried the tears running down her face and bent down. "Get up, Father. I'm not leaving you."

"Neither am I," Herr Bernheim said.

"We'll never outrun the soldiers. This is suicide for us all. You have to leave me."

Conor bent down so that he was inches from his father's face. "We're not leaving without you, and we don't have much time. So, get up, Father!"

They helped him to his feet, and he put his arms over Joel's and Gert's shoulders. He hopped along with them. Conor picked up his briefcase, and they set off. Maureen heard something from behind them. "The soldiers are coming! We have to hurry."

"I haven't finished picking up Herr Ritter's money," Joel said.

"Leave it," Seamus said.

Joel hurried after them, stuffing wads of bills and jewelry into his pockets as they shuffled past the two lifeless bodies. The trees beyond the clearing offered some cover. Maureen prayed that the bodies and the thickening storm would provide enough distraction to escape. The noises behind them grew louder, and someone shouted out in German. Maureen turned to see soldiers in Wehrmacht uniform fifty yards behind them in the clearing. Two others arrived beside him.

Maureen, her father, and Herr Bernheim watched from behind a tree for a few seconds.

"The French border can't be far," Maureen said. She didn't say out loud that she didn't know where. The snow was pummeling them from above now, and visibility wasn't more than a few feet.

They struggled another hundred yards before they dared to look back. The Wehrmacht soldiers didn't seem to be following them. "Seems like the storm is too much for them," Maureen said between deep, heaving breaths.

"Or maybe they think Serge and the German shot each other," Joel said.

Her father hadn't spoken in a few minutes. His blood-stained side was wet and sticky.

"Get some snow on the wound," Seamus said. "Wrap it in something."

Herr Bernheim took off his scarf and filled it with snow. They lay her father down and tied the scarf around his hip, pressing the snow against the outside of the wound. It held, though they'd have to stop to refill it within minutes.

"I can make it," her father said, but his voice was weaker than it had been even two minutes before.

Gert looked at Maureen with wordless concern.

It was at least another hour to the horse and cart.

They needed to get to the road as soon as possible. But where was the border in this mess of hills and trees? They could take their chances with French patrols on the road—better that than her father dying up here, but if they came out of the forest too soon, they could run into Nazi soldiers. The money to distract them was gone. Maureen knew all their lives were in her hands. But she'd never traveled this route before today.

"How is your hip?" she asked.

"Better," he answered. "The cold is numbing the pain."

"We have to go," Herr Bernheim said.

"The French border is close, and when we cross, we're making for the road."

"Won't the French border guards stop us if we get too close?" Lil asked.

"That's a chance we're going to have to take," Maureen answered.

"How will we know when we're in France?" Conor said.

"I'll tell you that when we get there."

They picked up her father again. "I'm proud of you, Maureen," he said as she put his arm over her shoulder.

"Save the goodbyes," Gert said. "You'll be between clean white sheets in a hospital bed in a few hours. It's just up to us to get you there."

The German soldiers were no longer a concern. The elements were the enemy now. They battled along, every footstep a minor miracle. Her father seemed to be getting heavier with each passing moment.

Gert kept her father talking as they trudged along. They spoke about the business and clients they knew. Gert told funny stories that her father reacted to less and less as time passed.

Maureen took a map out of her pocket, but it was impossible to know where they were. She'd never traveled this way before.

"We have to make for the road," she said. "I'm sure we're in France now."

"Where is it?" Gert asked.

Maureen looked around, not wanting to admit she didn't know. They were on a hill, surrounded by trees. She reckoned the course Serge took her was north of their usual path, but was she willing to bet her father's life on it?

"I have no choice," she said out loud. "I have to make a decision."

"What?" Gert asked.

They were still on the same route Serge had taken her. The footprints she and he had made that morning were the only ones visible.

"We should hit the road if we veer south."

"How do we know which way?"

She already had the compass out, and the arrow pointed down the hill toward the road and freedom.

"Do you need to rest?" she asked her father.

"Not until I get between those crisp white sheets," he whispered.

The incline was steep, and they had to take it one step at a time. She knew a fall might kill her father if he didn't bleed out first. Gert still spoke to him as they descended, although Seamus's replies were little more than grunts now. The trees never seemed to end, and when they reached the bottom of the hill, even more stood between them and where she hoped the road was. With no time to rest, they kept walking. Maureen tried to ignore her own screaming limbs and the biting cold. Her body begged her to sit and relax, close her eyes, and lie down. Nevertheless, she persisted.

"We're almost through, Father," she said. "Stay with us."

His body was limp, but somehow, he was still moving his feet as they went, helping in whatever small way he could. Giving up was impossible. She'd never stop. Would die before she'd admit defeat.

Ten more minutes of slogging through untouched snow passed before the sound of cars broke through the woods. The trees parted, and the sky opened up above their heads. The weak winter sun shone down on the road. The border was perhaps two hundred yards away, and the French guards looked over in disbelief.

"What about them?" Joel said as two French soldiers advanced toward them up the road.

"Use the money in your pockets, Joel," Seamus whispered. The young man went white. Maureen took Joel by the hand and ran down to the approaching soldiers. They were both young men, not much older than she. It was a tiny, desolate road and they likely weren't used to dealing with more than a few cars a day.

"What's going on here?" a guard with a thick mustache asked.

"We're refugees from Nazi Germany," Maureen answered.

The guards looked at each other and then back at her. "We'll have to take you to the station."

"And deport us?" she asked. "My father is shot. We need to get him to a doctor."

"He'll receive the help he needs," the Frenchman said.

"But if you send us back, we'll all die. Or else," she said reaching into Joel's pocket for a fistful of cash and jewels. "You could forget you ever saw us, and no one will ever be the wiser." The men looked at each other again. "Help us!"

"Okay," the guard said. The other man ran to a truck parked a few yards away and drove back a few seconds later. Maureen handed over a small fortune as they lifted her father onto the back seat.

The soldier motioned for the rest to get in and seconds later, they were speeding into town. Maureen cradled her father's head in her lap as they went, running her numb, frozen fingers through his hair as they drove.

His words came as a whisper, and she had to bend down to hear his voice.

"You saved me," he said.

She didn't answer, just kept stroking his filthy mop of hair.

"I'm broke, Gert," her father said. "I wonder if they're hiring in town."

His friend smiled through the tears. "You keep your strength, Seamus. You have everything you need."

"Yes, I do," he answered.

21

Strasbourg, France, Thursday, March 16

It was almost all gone. Everything he'd worked for since 1932. And he was back to where he began. The apartments in Paris and New York were all he had to show for his time as one of the Reich's new armament kings, but it seemed apt that he'd left his wealth behind in Germany. He'd been a different man there, and now he was back to being the person he'd always been before his uncle's offer to come work in Berlin. The doctor in Lembach was no stranger to gunshot wounds, having been a medic during the Great War. Seamus was confident the physician had saved his life. He remembered little of the first day or two before he was transferred to the hospital in Strasbourg. What he did remember were the faces by his bed. Lisa, Maureen, Fiona, Conor, and Hannah were with him the entire time. He drew strength from their obstinate refusal to let him die and knew he'd never have made it without them. His best friend, Gert Bernheim, also stayed with him for a few days before leaving to join his family at the boarding house in Izieu.

The newspapers were plastered with headlines about the Nazi occupation of the remainder of Czechoslovakia. The Nazi juggernaut was picking up steam. He wondered how many of his planes and bullets had been used and would be in the coming war. The reckoning was coming for Hitler and the Allies, though perhaps his had already come and gone. He looked around the hospital room he shared with two other men. No Nazi flags adorned the walls, and no portraits of Hitler stared down with beady eyes. But although Seamus had escaped Berlin, he had little doubt that the Nazis would soon follow him into France. The Rhineland, Austria, and now all of Czechoslovakia would never be enough to quench the Führer's thirst for conquest. France and Britain still stood as obstacles to his ultimate goal of conquering the east and achieving the lebensraum he'd spoken of since the '20s. The only unanswered question was what would happen to the people already living in those countries. The Allied powers could be in no doubt as to who Hitler was now. The agreement Chamberlain had brought home from Munich the previous year had proven to be worth little more than the paper it was written on. War seemed as certain as the sun rising in the east or the spring rain. He just hoped Hayden was wrong about the unprepared Allied military forces. He had witnessed the Nazis' obsession with building the world's finest military machine firsthand. It would take some beating.

Lisa entered the room. It was a fine day, and the sun streaming in the window turned every speck of dust floating in the air to spun gold. Her smile lit a radiant flame inside him.

"You're the most beautiful thing I've ever seen," he said.

"Thank you for telling me that every time I sit down," she said, handing him a piece of paper. "A telegram from Michael. It arrived this morning."

Seamus accepted it with thanks.

. . .

FATHER,

SO HAPPY TO HEAR YOUR RECOVERY IS ALMOST COMPLETE. WE ARE BOTH WELL AND ARE LOOKING FORWARD TO SEEING YOU. MAKING PROGRESS ON VISAS FOR OUR MANY FRIENDS.

MICHAEL

"I wonder how happy he'll be when he finds out we're all moving into that apartment he's living in in New York. He mentioned being able to get more visas?" Seamus asked. "I thought the American ones were going to take another year."

"From a place we didn't expect," Lisa said.

"What's going on?"

His wife smiled at him. "The Cuban government is accepting Jewish refugees."

"What? How did you hear about this?"

"Maureen just told me," she said. "She's booked many of our friends on steamers leaving in May. Bought the tickets on Monday."

"With the last of the escape fund?" Seamus asked.

"We still have a little in the coffers. Not everyone's going to Cuba. Some are sailing to Argentina. A few secured landing visas in Brazil, and the rest are off to Bolivia while they wait for their visas."

"Bolivia?" Seamus said with a smile.

"One of the most powerful men in Bolivia is a German Jew. He persuaded the President to let in some refugees and we took advantage. Almost everyone wants to end up in America. Especially those traveling to Cuba. They're going to stay in Havana for as long as it takes for their US visas to come through. Securing all the landing permits isn't an easy task, but Maureen assures me that paying off the right people is a learned skill."

"My daughter has been corrupted!" Seamus said with faux

histrionics. "How long's it going to take once they arrive to secure their US visas?"

"For some it'll take months. Others might have to wait a year or two. Maybe some will like Argentina or Bolivia and decide to stay. Who knows?"

What about the Bernheims?"

"Booked to sail to Cuba on the Orduña on May 27."

"And their American visas?"

"Michael has secured sponsorships for the Bernheims through Jewish organizations in New York," Lisa said. "They won't have to wait long."

"Sounds like you've all been working hard these past few weeks."

"Just greasing the right wheels," Lisa said. Then, after a moment's hesitation, she said, "Fiona's been an invaluable help."

"I'm proud of her," he said.

"Our steamer tickets are booked for Friday of next week."

"America will love you just as much as I do."

"What about Maureen? Is she coming with us?"

"You'll need to ask her yourself."

"Are you nervous about moving?" asked Seamus.

Lisa's face tightened, and she sat forward. "A little," she said in English before returning to her native German tongue. "But I understand. I just hope I'll see Berlin again someday. I know it's not the same city I grew up in anymore, but it's all I've ever known."

"The Nazis won't last forever. We'll return once that evil troll and his minions are deposed."

"It looks like it's going to take a war to rid Germany of him." She pointed to the newspaper.

"It was always going to be so. Despots don't relinquish power without a fight. It's the only thing that matters to them."

They looked up as his attending physician entered.

"You ready to leave, Seamus?" the doctor asked him in German. "That hip's going to need some rehabilitation, but I'm satisfied to sign you out. You're out of the woods, if you'll excuse the pun."

"I'm never venturing into the woods again as long as I live. I've had enough of trees and snow. Not to mention getting shot."

The doctor performed a few cursory tests before signing him out. Seamus was issued with a cane and dressed in the new suit Lisa bought him with some of the last of their dwindling savings.

The taxi was waiting for them, and they climbed in together. He had no baggage, just the passport he'd risked his life for in Berlin.

"I need to take a trip to Basel before I travel to Izieu tomorrow," Seamus said. He turned to his wife. "It's only a two-hour train ride from here. I'll be there and back the same day."

"Of course," Lisa said and kissed him.

"I'd like to take Maureen with me. Just the two of us. I have the feeling it'll be the last time we spend alone together for a while."

The taxi brought them to a hotel in the city. It was less luxurious than he was used to, but all he wanted was to sleep beside his wife. To his joy, Hannah, Conor, Maureen, and Fiona came to meet him. Seamus smiled like a child as his daughters helped him through the lobby. The evening sun felt like new life, and he kissed each of his children.

The night brought glorious dreams of a sparking future surrounded by his family.

22

Friday, March 17

The following day the Ritters went to a local café for breakfast and gathered around the table together. Fiona sat on his left. Maureen's influence on her showed in the makeup she now wore and the care she took with her hair. The Nazis' disapproval of such things didn't matter anymore. It was like being around someone new, for the person she'd been before the League of German Girls changed her was just a little girl. She was a woman now.

Conor played with Hannah, both excited to move to America. Lisa knew the challenges ahead but prioritized her family's safety over her trepidation about moving to a strange country where she didn't speak the language.

Seamus hadn't spoken to Maureen about where her heart was leading her—that was for their trip to Basel.

Seamus hadn't experienced happiness like this in years. The waitress brought croissants so fresh they melted in his mouth and coffee and hot chocolate better than he could ever get in Germany these days. He tried to savor each second, for he knew his family would be fractured again soon. The joy of seeing Michael and Monika in New York would be tempered if his brave, magnificent daughter was left behind.

"I have to go to Basel today. You want to see Switzerland one more time?" he asked Maureen. "One last trip together before we return to the states?"

"Yes. I'd like that," she said and reached over to place her hand on his.

Seamus parted from Lisa at the train station with tender embraces and promises to meet in Lyon that night. It made little sense to try to make it out to Izieu after the six-hour train journey from Basel, so Lisa and the others would wait for them in a hotel in the city before they all headed out to the village in the countryside the following day. Seamus took a moment with his wife, holding her cheeks as he kissed her on the platform before they left.

Seamus had no luggage at all. He had no clothes or personal belongings now. But nothing he'd left behind would define him. The mansion and his fancy car had never made him a better person, but his wife and children did, and he had them. He and Maureen boarded the train to Basel and took seats by the window to wave to the rest of their family, who waited on the platform to see them off. They sat in silence until Lisa and the children disappeared, and the French countryside flooded their sight.

"Why did you ask me to come with you? I thought you'd want to spend the time with Lisa. Being apart from her all this time can't have been easy."

"It wasn't," Seamus replied. "But I know she's coming back to America with me."

"It's funny," Maureen said. "I didn't want to move to

Germany back in '32. I had a life in America and a boy I thought I was going to marry."

"I remember."

"But I think I changed when I came."

"We had no idea what we were getting into. No one did. Hitler was an irritating upstart when we arrived in Berlin. Now he's one of the most powerful men in the world. Germany's barely recognizable as the country we emigrated to."

"Growing up in that atmosphere had an effect on me. Who knows what I would have ended up becoming if I'd stayed, but I know who I am now."

"And who's that?"

"Someone who's not willing to lie down or turn their head in the face of evil. I can't maintain neutrality in the face of what's occurring every day in Europe. I have to fight. It's the only way I can live with myself."

"What about when the war starts?"

Maureen hesitated a few seconds before answering. "So many people need help. The Jews from Ritter Metalworks are proud, independent people, but they needed us. Wouldn't you want support from other people when you needed it most?"

"Of course, but they're leaving in May."

"I won't go until I know they're all safe, and then what? Do I leave?"

"You can't save everyone."

"I know, but look at what we've achieved already. We have the house in Izieu now. I know a route out to Cuba and South America through Marseille. I've spoken to people in embassies, and Michael established the connection with the Jewish organization in New York to sponsor refugees. All that goes to waste if I leave. I'm too valuable an asset to just get on the steamer to America and a comfortable life."

"What's wrong with a comfortable life? I want you to be safe and happy."

"What about fulfilled? I know how I'll feel if I leave with you. I'll be thinking of the Jews coming across the border and the house in Izieu sitting vacant when it could be full of people with nowhere else to run. Hitler created something so massive, so evil, that it's going to take an army of people to stand up to him."

"And you want to be a part of that army? I've dealt with the Nazis a thousand times. I've seen how ruthless they are, and most of all, how obsessed with the military they are. I have no idea when this war will start but I do know the Germans will crush everyone who opposes them."

"I'm not going to run to the front lines and pick up a rifle. If war does come, I'll be doing the exact same thing as I am right now—helping those who need it."

"And when does that end?"

"I can't tell the future."

"I'm worried about you, Maureen. You've witnessed first-hand how brutal the Nazis are. If they catch you again—"

"I can't leave, Father. I just can't. Not while people still need me and the knowledge and resources I've built up."

Seamus looked out the window. The German border was little more than ten miles away. Hitler's armies would be here soon. The Jews from the factory would likely be all safe by then, but his daughter would not.

"Will you come to America for a while, just to see if you even like it?"

She shook her head. "I'm sorry. I'm sure I'll go back some-day. But I have to stay at least long enough to see the workers off. I couldn't possibly leave before that."

"So, you'd consider coming to America once they were all safe?"

"Perhaps."

Seamus took this small victory. He knew it was the only one he was going to get.

Maureen changed the subject and talked about the plans to extricate the refugees. Her eyes lit up like torches as she spoke.

An hour later, they were at the bank in Basel. The manager led them through to the safe deposit box room.

"I'm sorry to lose your business. I hope you enjoy living in America again."

"I'm sure we will," Seamus said and looked at his daughter.

Seamus went to the wall and extracted the metal safe deposit box. He flipped the lid open and reached for a small wad of American dollars. The banker handed them the key and left.

"This should help us settle in New York," he said. She couldn't see into the box, and he reached in and plucked out the diamond necklace.

"Uncle Helmut left me this. Said it was a family heirloom to be given to my oldest daughter on her wedding day."

The diamonds shone in the artificial light of the enclosed room. Maureen stared at it for a few seconds before reaching out. Seamus put it in her hand.

"It's so beautiful," she said.

"It's yours."

"I hate to tell you, Father, but I'm not getting married anytime soon."

"I went to great pains to keep this in the family. I've always respected Helmut's wishes. He gave us so much. I want you to have it."

"And what am I to do with it? I'd much rather you sold it. You weren't able to sell the house, or the business, but this is the last gift Helmut left us. Sell it. Take some of the money yourself and give the rest to me to help the Jewish children in need. I've already spoken to several smugglers bringing boys and girls across in the next few weeks. They're going to need to eat and stay warm on cold nights." She handed the necklace back. "Do something good with it. I will get married one day, but I won't need any fancy jewelry. Just a husband. And my family."

"I promised."

"Uncle Helmut could never have envisaged what has happened to Germany these last seven years. He'd understand, Father. He was a good man. Just like you."

Seamus embraced his daughter with a tear in his eye. They stood together for a few seconds before he slipped the necklace into his pocket.

"We have a train to catch," he said.

~

Izieu, southeastern France, Saturday, March 18

The village was set in a valley, and the mountains rose behind it to a perfect, powder-blue sky. Lush green fields spread on either side of the road. It looked like something from a painting one would hang above a fireplace. Izieu wasn't much more than a smattering of houses, a few stores, and a church. Most of the people here were farmers, fiercely patriotic but welcoming nonetheless. None had ever grumbled about the Jewish refugees in the previously vacant houses outside town. Several locals brought flowers or bread to the homes and shook hands with the new arrivals. Nothing was hidden from them. The townspeople knew who the refugees were and were delighted to hear their stories of escape from the cruel clutches of the Nazis.

It seemed his wife and daughter had found the perfect place, set amongst breathtaking beauty.

Maureen drove the car. Seamus sat in the passenger seat with the rest of the family in the back. The feeling of giddy excitement among them was palpable as they saw the sign for the village.

"Just wait and see!" Hannah called out.

Her mother shushed her, but not before a wide smile spread across Seamus's face. He turned and put a hand on the little girl's leg. Thoughts of her real father flashed across his mind, but he extinguished them as quickly as they ignited. Lisa had told him for years that he was her real father. Her not sharing his genes didn't matter. His dedication and love for her were all she needed.

"You never were much good at keeping a secret," he said with a laugh.

Driving through the village took seconds, and they turned a corner to a country road that led up toward a rock face. The houses stood beneath it, set in a dilapidated estate that had once been a rich man's country home. The crowd standing outside cheered, holding up signs welcoming him, beaming warm smiles. The children were at the front, their parents holding them back as the car pulled up. Gert Bernheim stood at the front with his wife and son. He walked to the car as Maureen pulled up. Seamus got out and embraced his friend as the crowd of refugees applauded. Losing the money, the factories in Berlin and everything that had happened these past ten years seemed worth it for this moment. Lisa was beside him as he turned around. A dozen children ran to him, handing him flowers. He looked at the crowd. His workers. His promise to Helmut, but also to himself, was complete.

EPILOGUE

New York City, Sunday, September 3, 1939

What had once been a spacious apartment for a young married couple was now crowded with almost the entire Ritter family. It was one of three properties Seamus still owned, the others being the mansion in Berlin, which would be taken over by the Nazis soon, and the apartment in Paris, which he'd decided to leave to Maureen for her use. Seamus woke beside his wife. Hannah was asleep on a mattress on the floor, and Fiona and Conor were in bunk beds by the wall. Lisa was still asleep. Seamus slipped out of bed, grabbed his cane, and shuffled past his daughter. Monika was in the kitchen making breakfast and greeted her father-in-law with a smile.

"Good morning," she said in English.

"And to you," he responded. "Your accent is improving by the day."

"Thank you," she said. "I've been thrown in the water in the deep side," she said. "I must learn to swim."

"Yes, you must!"

Monika insisted on speaking English all the time in the apartment now. Nothing would stop her. Seamus was confident she'd be ready to recite Shakespeare's soliloquies next summer. She took off her apron and began slicing bread. She'd found work as a filing clerk at a local marketing firm. Her determination and attention to detail more than made up for her lack of fluent English, and she enjoyed the role. The mountain of bacon and eggs she cooked was soon ready, and she placed it in the middle of the kitchen table.

"I'll clean up," Seamus said.

Conor was next to arrive and rubbed his eyes as he approached the table. Seamus greeted him with a ruffle of his hair and walked to the window to stare down at Fifth Avenue. The cars and the noise never stopped here, but it was hard to deny the exhilaration the city brought. It was just past eight on a Sunday morning, and people were already out. Not one Nazi flag polluted his sight. No SS marched, and no brown-shirted bullies patrolled the streets. This place felt similar in many ways to Berlin, but while Nazism was a minuscule undercurrent in American society, it was the bedrock on which Germany was based. And now Hitler had done it. He had started his war.

The sound of the door opening drew their attention, and Michael pushed inside, sweat pouring from his brow, dressed in a running singlet with the newspaper under his arm. He threw it to his father at the window and kissed his wife. "Look at who wrote the main story. Clayton's hitting the big time."

Clayton was still in Berlin but was due to return in a few months. Perhaps the Nazis would expel him before his editor brought him back. Seamus looked forward to seeing his friend again.

"Oh no," Michael said and walked to the bathroom door. "Fiona, can you hurry up, please?! I just got back from my run."

Seamus stayed out of it, choosing to open the newspaper instead. Hitler's armies were running rampant. Some had said it would take six months to take Poland, but the might of the Nazi military had conquered the country in six weeks. France and Britain were expected to declare war today. It was beginning. The thought of Maureen in Izieu caused his heartbeat to quicken, and he was happy to feel Lisa's touch on his shoulder and her kiss on his lips. His wife noticed the newspaper.

"Maureen will be fine," she said in German. Her English wasn't as advanced as Monika's, and she spoke German whenever she had something important to say. "She's been keeping a low profile lately. When was the last time she even left the village?"

"Not for a few weeks according to her letters."

A couple dozen of the original Jews from Ritter Metalworks were still waiting on visas in Izieu, and Maureen had stayed with them. The rest, including Gert and his family, had set sail for the new world months before. Seamus had received letters from Bolivia, Brazil, Argentina, and from Gert and several others waiting in Cuba. They were all safe and settling in. Gert had signed off his last letter with an ever hopeful "see you soon." Seamus hoped so. He longed to see his friend again and shake his hand.

Fiona emerged from the bathroom and arrived at the breakfast table. Michael was last to join them. He washed himself off in a few seconds and returned to take his place.

"You're not going to shower?" Fiona said.

"I wanted to sit down for breakfast with my family."

"You're disgusting," Fiona answered.

Michael began pointing out that she'd been in the bathroom when he tried to wash before, but Seamus cut him off.

"I wonder how long this war will last," Fiona began. "Someone in school said it'd be over in a few months."

"It all depends on how far Hitler is planning to push things. His pact with Stalin makes no sense to me," Lisa said. "It runs counter to all his ambitions in the east."

"I wouldn't trust the Führer as far as I could throw him," Conor said.

Seamus looked over at Fiona, but she didn't react to her brother's jibe. She just kept eating.

"Any word from our friends in Cuba? Or Bolivia, or wherever they are?" Fiona asked.

"Not for a few days," Monika said.

"I have someone I'd like you to meet, Father. A man who might help us bring them here quicker," Michael said.

"Who?"

"Someone from the embassy. I arranged an early lunch with them."

"Is Bill Hayden in town? I spoke to him last week. He's in D.C. fulltime since he came back."

"No, it's someone else. And they're bringing their family. We should all go."

"Sounds good," Lisa said. "Where is it?"

Michael told them the address, and they all agreed to meet there before Seamus could say another word. Even Hannah and Conor seemed keen.

Michael was first to stand up as breakfast finished. He looked at the newspaper and threw it down. "The Olympics aren't going to take place next year if there's a war on." No one answered. They'd spoken about this possibility before. The bitter disappointment in his voice was difficult to disguise. "No matter," he said. "I'll keep on training. I can't stop now."

He returned to the bathroom. Seamus cleaned up, insisting the others relax while he did so. He thought about work as he washed the dishes. His bank job was a million miles from selling bullets and airplanes to Nazis in Berlin. He'd been an important man there. Here, he was just another investment manager. One among thousands. But it was enough. Lisa was happy working at a department store. Soon, they'd move into a place of their own.

Michael and Monika had insisted initially that they be the ones to move out, but Seamus wouldn't hear it. This was their home—a wedding present when he'd been able to gift things like this. With the money from the necklace and their savings, it wouldn't be long until they could buy somewhere. In the meantime, he intended to cherish every breakfast together.

The Ritter family spent the morning listening to news reports from Europe until Seamus asked to turn the wireless off. The sound of the planes and bombs he'd built was too much after a while.

When noon came, Seamus dressed in his best suit, and the family descended to the street together. It was a bright, beautiful day in the city. The stultifying heat of summer was breaking, and a cool breeze blew in their faces as they strolled to lunch. Michael didn't offer any further details about his mystery contact as they walked, and no one else seemed to have any questions.

The restaurant wasn't one he knew and was dark as he entered. The tables were set in large booths with black leather seats facing one rounded table. Michael spoke with the man at the door, and he directed them to the back. Seamus followed his son before the younger man stood back to let him take the lead. The contact was sitting at the table, facing away, and Seamus could make out the top of his head. He was about to turn to his son to ask what was going on when Gert Bernheim rose with a massive beaming smile with Lil and Joel beside him. Seamus threw down his cane and hobbled to his friend, shouting as he lifted him into the air. The entire family surrounded him. Lisa was crying. Every face was illuminated with joy and relief.

"You knew about this?" Seamus said to his wife.

"She set it up," Gert said. "The visas came through last week."

Seamus stood back, embraced Lil and Joel, and then stood with his arms around them.

"Thank you for everything you did," Seamus said.

"No, Seamus. Thank you," Gert replied and hugged him again.

They spent the afternoon eating fine food, reminiscing, laughing, and mourning. Seamus ordered wine he could no longer afford as lunch and dinner blurred together. They toasted Maureen, still fighting the good fight in France, and Seamus kissed his wife. He knew times would get worse before they got better, but this was a shining moment, a jewel to be treasured for the rest of his life. He'd never known happiness like it.

The End

But Maureen will return, with her own series! Coming soon.

A NOTE TO THE READER

I hope you enjoyed my book. Head over to www.eoindempseybooks.com to sign up for my readers' club. It's free and always will be. If you want to get in touch with me send an email to eoin@eoindempseybooks.com. I love hearing from readers so don't be a stranger!

Reviews are life-blood to authors these days. If you enjoyed the book and can spare a minute please leave a review on Amazon and/or Goodreads. My loyal and committed readers have put me where I am today. Their honest reviews have brought my books to the attention of other readers. I'd be eternally grateful if you could leave a review. It can be short as you like.

ALSO BY EOIN DEMPSEY

Standalones

Finding Rebecca

The Bogside Boys

White Rose, Black Forest

Toward the Midnight Sun

The Longest Echo

The Hidden Soldier

The Lion's Den Series

1. The Lion's Den

2. A New Dawn

3. The Golden Age

4. The Grand Illusion

5. The Coming Storm

6. The Reckoning

ABOUT THE AUTHOR

Eoin (Owen) was born and raised in Ireland. His books have been translated into fourteen languages and also optioned for film and radio broadcast. He lives in Philadelphia with his wonderful wife and three crazy sons.

You can connect with him at eoindempseybooks.com or on Facebook at https://www.facebook.com/eoindempseybooks/ or by email at eoin@eoindempseybooks.com.

PRAISE FOR EOIN DEMPSEY

Praise for *The Hidden Soldier*:

"A heartfelt trip into two entangled time periods that fans will want to read in one sitting. Engrossing and surprising at every turn, the book is yet more proof that Dempsey is a master of the historical fiction genre."

— LYDIA KANG, BESTSELLING AUTHOR OF A BEAUTIFUL POISON AND OPIUM AND ABSINTHE

"The Hidden Soldier is a poignant page-turner that will leave you breathless. Gorgeously written, Eoin Dempsey carries you back in time and inserts you into the heart of this tragic, pivotal moment in history. Part thriller, part love story, I was completely enthralled from beginning to end."

— SUZANNE REDFEARN, #1 AMAZON BESTSELLING AUTHOR OR IN AN INSTANT AND HADLEY AND GRACE.

""I didn't see that coming! Or that!" I yelled across the house as Eoin Dempsey's wonderful World War II book raced to an utterly satisfying wallop of a finale. His spare, dialogue-driven style, matched with his strong knowledge of the war and masterful ability to dance between two time periods, made for one heck of an enjoyable read."

— *BOO WALKER, BESTSELLING AUTHOR OF AN UNFINISHED STORY.*

Praise for *The Longest Echo:*

"...a chilling page turner that explores a shocking, little-known episode in history and manages to include a touching love story."

— HISTORICAL NOVEL SOCIETY

"A beautiful, heart wrenching novel that captivated me from the very beginning. This is historical fiction at its absolute best, and one of my favorite reads of the year."

— SORAYA M. LANE, AMAZON CHARTS BESTSELLING AUTHOR OF *WIVES OF WAR* AND *THE LAST CORRESPONDENT*

"Based on the true horrors of WWII Monte Sole, this story tugs at the heartstrings while delivering authentic, engaging champions and page-turning scenes that continue beyond the war."

Praise for *White Rose, Black Forest* (A Goodreads Choice Award Semifinalist, Historical Fiction):

"*White Rose, Black Forest* is partly a lyrical poem, an uncomfortable history lesson, and a page-turning thriller that will keep the reader engaged from the beginning to the end."

"There is much to praise in Eoin Dempsey's *White Rose, Black Forest*, but for me it stands out from the glut of war fiction because of its poetic simplicity. The novel does not span a massive cast of characters, various continents, and the entire duration of the conflict. It is the tale of one young man, one young woman, and the courage to change the tide of a war. Emotional, taut, and deftly drawn, *White Rose, Black Forest* is a stunning tale of bravery, compassion, and love."

"Dempsey's World War II thriller is a haunting page-turner. The settings are detailed and the characters leap off the page. I couldn't put this book down. An instant bestseller."

"A gripping story of heroism and redemption, *White Rose, Black Forest* glows with delicate yet vivid writing. I enjoyed it tremendously."

"Tense, taut, and tightly focused, *White Rose, Black Forest* is a haunting novel about courage and compassion that will keep you gripped from the very first page."

ACKNOWLEDGMENTS

Writing my first ever series has been an incredible experience, made all the easier by all the wonderful people who helped me along the way. Firstly, massive thanks to the two patron saints of this book, Carol McDuell and Cindy Bonner. I can't thank you two wonderful ladies enough. Also to Michelle Schulten, Maria Reid, Richard Schwarz, Frank Callahan, Ave Jeanne Ventresca, and Cynthia Sand.

As always, much love and gratitude to my mother, sister, Orla and by brothers Brian and Conor. And of course, my gorgeous wife, Jill and my three boys, Robbie, Sam, and Jack.

Made in the USA
Las Vegas, NV
27 June 2024

91556902R00154